THE POET & THE PRIVATE EYE

ROB GITTINS

First impression: 2014
Second impression: 2015
© Rob Gittins & Y Lolfa Cyf., 2014

Cover design: Sion Ilar

Paperback ISBN: 978 1 84771 899 0
Hardback ISBN: 978 1 84771 983 6

The publishers wish to acknowledge the support of
Cyngor Llyfrau Cymru

Published and printed in Wales
on paper from well-maintained forests by
Y Lolfa Cyf., Talybont, Ceredigion SY24 5HE
e-mail ylolfa@ylolfa.com
website www.ylolfa.com
tel 01970 832 304
fax 832 782

THE POET & THE PRIVATE EYE

For Becki and Dave

THIS BOOK EMPLOYS the form and techniques of a novel to tell a true story involving real people and real events.

All of the events depicted here actually happened. However, to shape these events into a fictional form, certain dramatic liberties have been taken; most specifically, events from four different American tours undertaken by the poet at the heart of this story have been amalgamated into just the one.

Various characters who, in actuality, feature at different times on those four tours, now feature on just this one tour also.

However, so far as the events involving those characters are concerned, nothing has been invented.

In contrast, little, if anything, is known about the other, major, real-life character in this story, the private eye. His character, background and history is, necessarily, entirely my invention.

Rob Gittins
New Year's Day, 2014

1

INVESTIGATION. DERIVING FROM the Latin *vestigare*, meaning to track or to trace. Further defined, so I'd once read, as an uncovering of facts requiring an inquisitive mind and a close attention to detail. A patient, step by step, inquiry.

Which is what I was doing outside Idlewild that unseasonably warm morning in the fall of '53. I was setting off on yet another patient, step by step, inquiry. I was about to begin uncovering yet more facts. Or at least that's what I was supposed to be doing. But the incoming flight that was carrying the subject of that step by step inquiry had been delayed.

Instead, I was a thousand miles away. I may have been outside an airport terminal with a roof shaped like a swooping wave but I wasn't seeing anything that looked like a terminal or that even remotely resembled a wave. I may have been parked directly opposite three houses of worship – Jewish, Christian and Muslim – but I wasn't seeing any houses of worship right now either.

The last time I'd been here I'd been enveloped in the chaos that had greeted the returning Christine Jorgensen – the world-renowned GI who'd become a blonde beauty and celebrity courtesy of a highly publicized sex change – but I wasn't seeing Jorgensen or any of that accompanying rat-pack chaos right now either.

It was happening more and more these days. Images from another time and place swimming before my eyes; particularly at times like these when there was nothing to do but sit and wait.

Images unbidden and unwanted.

Impossible to dispatch.

But I could make the effort at least. So I took a file from the attaché holder on the passenger seat beside me and tried concentrating instead on the case, now literally, in hand.

One week before I'd been in an office on West 42nd Street, one block away from the Port Authority Bus Terminal, two blocks up from Times Square.

Sitting opposite me, behind a desk that dwarfed him, Con, a pugnacious prize-fighter of a man, rifled through a small forest of papers and depositions at the same time as fielding roughly a thousand phone calls. Con had called the previous evening and asked if I was interested in a few days' work. Nothing too heavy, just a simple tail job.

I told him I was and we'd arranged to meet for a briefing. Con had started and abandoned that briefing around ten times in as many minutes. It was that kind of place. Once he'd sifted some more of that small forest of paper and fielded around a dozen new calls, he'd try again. After another dozen or so interruptions he'd finally do what he should have done at the start of all this and take the phone off the hook.

As I waited for Con to dispense with the latest mini – or possibly major – crisis I looked round the office. Framed front covers covered every available wall space. The magazine he represented had been going for around thirty years and came out weekly. That all added up to one hell of a lot of copies and most of them seemed to be staring down from those walls right now.

The magazine in question had been started in the Twenties by a couple of newspaper guys who'd worked together on the *Yale Daily News*. One in particular, the co-founder Briton Hadden, had set the tone from the start which was light and fun, setting out to explore the issues of the day, not through dry facts or weighty analysis as he put it, but through people and personalities; which explained why the magazine always featured just the one face on the front.

Within a year Hadden, along with the original circulation manager, Roy Larsen, had moved the fledgling enterprise into another infant medium, radio. He'd first initiated a fifteen-minute quiz called *Pop Question*, replacing that with a ten-minute program culling news summaries from current issues of the magazine which he then sold to more than thirty other stations across the US.

But the real breakthrough came in the early Thirties. A new radio show began called *The March Of Time*, offering eager listeners a dramatization of that week's news. The radio broadcasts sent circulation of the magazine into the stratosphere but there was still the same guiding principle behind everything they did.

People, people, people.

In their every weird and wonderful guise.

Exploring and laying bare every weird and wonderful thing they did.

'OK, Jimmy, this is what we've got – .'

Then Con broke off again as the phone rang once more. He barked into it, pausing as he heard the voice on the other end of the line. Then, obviously deciding he had to take just this one last call, he thrust a dog-eared copy of the magazine across the outsize desk.

'Page forty-seven.'

I leafed through the magazine, suppressing a grin, as always, at the distinctive, breathless style. Between these pages, tycoons were always beady-eyed, friends always great and good. OK, the sentences weren't always as convoluted as the *New Yorker* was wont to allege in its famous parody

– 'backwards ran sentences until reeled the mind' – but it was still pretty florid stuff. I'd just reached page forty-seven when Con slammed down the phone as if daring it to disturb him again. It did and he threw it across the room and we finally got down to business.

'The magazine's being sued.'

Which could hardly have been a novel experience, but I didn't point that out.

'By this guy from England.'

I nodded down at the magazine.

'Is this the guy who borrows with no thought of returning, seldom shows up on time, is a trial to his friends and a worry to his family?'

Con eyed me, heavily.

'Finally got to page forty-seven have you, Jimmy?'

'Just started on the first paragraph, Con.'

Across the room the telephone emitted a small squeak, then fell silent. It looked as if Con had inflicted some seriously heavyweight damage this time.

I looked back at the magazine as Con picked up the tale.

'So this guy from England gets his lawyers to slap a writ on us.'

I was reading on.

'This is the slob, the liar, the moocher, right?'

Con eyed me heavily again as I kept on reading.

'Who's also a thief, a two-fisted boozefighter, a puffy Priapus – .'

I broke off, nodded across the large desk.

'What does that mean, Con – a Priapus?'

I knew and Con knew I knew. I was shooting the breeze and Con knew that too. Priapus was a minor fertility God, protector of livestock, fruit, plants, gardens and – most famously – male genitalia. Priapus was noted for his large and permanent erection, giving rise, if you'll pardon the pun, to the medical term, priapism.

See what I mean about florid?

I scanned some more of the profile.

'Who regularly assaults the wives of his best friends while being an icy little hedonist who indifferently lives it up while his children go hungry?'

Con's voice was flat.

'Yeah. That's the guy.'

But I hadn't finished yet. Hell, the magazine hadn't, why should I?

'Who looks like a choirboy, argues like a Bolshevik, dresses like a bum, drinks like a culvert, smokes like an ad for cancer and once committed an act of gross indecency with a Member of Parliament?'

Con cut across.

'It came out a few months ago. He was back home by then, it obviously took him a little while to get round to it.'

'Maybe he was too busy stealing candy from the corner store, smoking cigars in the local cinema and spying on the nursemaid while she washed her breasts in the hand basin.'

'Jimmy, just put the magazine down a minute will you?'

I did, but it wasn't easy. This kind of stuff was seriously addictive. One of the reasons the circulation was still in that stratosphere and why movie stars and politicians the world over checked each week to see if they'd made the cover.

'You're the lawyer for this fine magazine Con, you actually let them print this stuff.'

'It's the truth.'

'So why's he slapped a writ on you?'

'And you are going to prove it.'

'Meaning you don't actually have any proof as yet?'

'Do you want this job or not, Jimmy?'

I did a quick mental calculation, offsetting the balance in my account against the various bills coming in at the end of the month which, another quick mental calculation informed me, was in just over a week or so's time.

'I want the job.'

I placed the magazine face up on the desk, cabaret over for now at least.

Con nodded, approving.

'He's coming back to the city, he's booked on the last flight out of London tonight and no, before you ask, his trip's nothing to do with us, he's not planning on storming round here and demanding satisfaction or whatever the hell those crazy Limeys do, he's leaving all that in the hands of his lawyers.'

'So what is he coming over for?'

Con ignored that for now. In the corner the smashed phone was still silent but other phones were now ringing outside, lots of phones in fact and he probably had a shrewd suspicion most of those calls would be for him. The magazine had profiled a lot of people in the course of the past thirty years and quite a few had decided they were less than happy with the result.

'I want you to shadow him, Jimmy, block out a couple of days, maybe a bit more if you need to, follow him, watch him, see where he goes, what he does, who he does it with.'

I nodded down again at the magazine.

'Basically, prove everything in this profile is gospel.'

It wasn't a question and Con didn't need to provide any sort of answer.

'Get everything down on paper. Get some nice technicolor close-ups too if you can. So if this crazy writ ever comes to court I can take the stand on behalf of my clients, all bright-eyed and bushy-tailed, and tell the judge we were just doing our duty, keeping the good old American public up to date with the truth behind the headlines, the facts behind the fiction, shining a light on all that would otherwise remain hidden from view.'

'You should get a medal, Con.'

'We'll all settle for this being laughed into next week's trash.'

Con waved the writ at me. But not too hard. It looked as if it might disintegrate at any moment.

I glanced back at the magazine again.

'So what does this guy do?'

I paused.

'Apart from sleeping with any woman who's willing – ?'

Con took it away. The profile guys really did know what they were doing. Once you started on this kind of stuff you just couldn't stop.

'The guy's called Thomas.'

'Thomas what?'

'That's his surname.'

'First name?'

'How the hell would I know, it's in the profile somewhere.'

'So what does he do?'

'Mr Thomas is a poet.'

I blinked. That had come from way out of left field.

'He's a what?'

'Something wrong with your hearing, Jimmy?'

I kept staring at him.

'A poet?'

I looked back at the magazine.

'Never met a poet.'

Then I grinned.

'Seems nice work if you can get it though.'

Con nodded.

Maybe it did to him too.

'Here's his flight details.'

He pushed a piece of paper across the table.

'And this is a mugshot, we lifted it from the back of one of his books but we've also got a guy working in Arrivals, he's going to check with the airline, let you know when he comes through.'

'Just in case the plane's racked with slobs, liars and moochers?'

'Just in case.'

I stood, pocketing the pieces of paper.

But Con was already nodding across at a large bag in the corner.

'Hey, Jimmy.'

I looked across the room, heavily. I was hoping he'd cut me a bit of slack on this one, but Conor had obviously decided not to take any chances.

Inside the bag was a state-of-the-art Nagra tape recorder. A prototype had been launched a couple of years before, but this was the first production model. Developed by one Stefan Kudelski, the name came from his mother tongue. Nagra, in Polish, meant to record and that's what I'd be doing with this little beauty which would be even more of a beauty if it was little, but it wasn't. In fact it filled that large bag to capacity and was every bit as heavy as it looked.

I risked a painful double hernia by hoisting it up from the floor, fastened the straps of the bag over my shoulder and made for the door. But as I got there, Con cut across again.

'Oh – and Jimmy.'

I looked back at him. He was staring straight at me. He knew I wouldn't like what he was about to say and in a perfect world and an ideal time he probably wouldn't have chosen to say it, but his world wasn't perfect and neither of us lived in ideal times either. If he'd been the owner – or even a major shareholder – in the magazine he currently represented, he probably wouldn't have said it at all.

But Con was, like myself, an operative, a freelance.

'Any chance you get to – you know – .'

I nodded. I did know. I also didn't need to finish it but I did.

Just for the record.

Just so we both understood each other.

'Help the guy hang himself?'

'Hey – .'

Con spread his arms wide.

'Would I say that?'

'Never in a million lifetimes, Con.'

I'd let myself out of his office, taken a right and then a left along Seventh Avenue before heading on into Times Square. Beth – my wife – was celebrating a birthday in a few days' time, although in her eyes there wasn't too much to celebrate, not with the way the years were beginning to advance on us both. I may have been hitting the big three-zero a year before she vaulted that particular hurdle, but so far as she was concerned it was still a not-so-welcome milestone that was approaching way too fast.

To sweeten the pill I'd decided to check out the roof garden at the Hotel Astor. According to an ad I'd seen it was the place for high rollers to see and be seen. Neither myself nor Beth qualified as any kind of roller, high or low, but what the hell? Maybe we couldn't run to a five-course banquet but a simple lunch might just be within our reach.

Five minutes later I was in the lobby looking at the kind of prices that turned dreams into something resembling nightmares and feeling lousy.

'Hey.'

The cop rattled on the window with his nightstick. Somewhere in his tunic he probably had his daystick too but like most cops he didn't bother with that. Both were made of wood, usually oak or mahogany and both sported a leather thong or lanyard through the handle. But the daystick was roughly eleven inches long while the nightstick came in at well over double that, measuring a mammoth twenty-six inches in length. No prizes for guessing which one of those commanded the most immediate attention.

I wound down the window and flashed what I hoped was a winning smile.

'Move on, pal.'

Which, clearly, wasn't remotely winning at all.

'Just give me a minute officer, yeah?'

'I said, move on.'

'I'm waiting for someone.'

The cop gestured across the wide avenues feeding the terminal towards a distant wasteland, currently home to acres of vehicles stretching so far as the eye could see.

'We've got this new invention. It's called a car park.'

I dropped the winning smile, nodded at his badge instead. Time for the second weapon in the arsenal, the next rabbit to be extracted from the hat. If this didn't work I was going to have to drive away from that terminal entrance and begin this tail job on foot.

The badge was that of the newly-formed City Transit Authority. Responsibility for transport in and around the city had been in the hands of various bodies for most of the last few decades, but lately it had been put in the hands of the city police.

But old habits die hard. These guys didn't do the job of the more usual officers out on the beat and they wanted to keep operating as a separate, autonomous unit. The debate as to whether they should do so had become something of a hot potato in the last few months.

'Ask me, you should hold out. So many guys out there have got a beef against NYPD. Once you're in with them, you're tarred with the same brush.'

His eyes examined me, amused. He wasn't about to fall for the all-too obvious soft-soaping as I knew he wouldn't. No-one's that naïve, right? But I was hoping he might give me credit for the attempt at least.

'NYPD goes back a long way.'

I nodded, encouraged.

'Too long, some people say. Sent some really bad shit down the line over the years too.'

I nodded again, ever more encouraged by his silence which I was taking for assent.

'Transit is new. A clean force. No history, no baggage. Keep it that way is what I say.'

'So who are you waiting for?'

I studied the mugshot Con had handed to me, read out some of the more innocuous descriptions itemized in the profile.

'Short guy, about five-three, four – curly hair – round face.'

If I hadn't had my nose buried in the paperwork I'd have seen it for myself.

'Sort of a snub nose?'

I looked up at him. What was this guy, clairvoyant or something? But he was just looking towards the terminal entrance.

'Currently assaulting a security guard with a whiskey bottle.'

'Currently what?'

I followed his look.

Framed in the doorway clasping an inhaler in one hand and that whiskey bottle in the other, he looked like a blow-up toy that had been over-inflated. It was a warm day, too warm for the time of year, but even so he should never have been sweating like that. And he shouldn't have even tried to tangle with the burly security guard deputed to escort him – so I'd discover later – from the terminal building where he'd been demanding two raw eggs in a glass of beer for his breakfast.

But I think Subject Thomas realized that himself. Just as his nose hit the Idlewild tarmac and the whiskey bottle smashed beside him a moment later. He tried to stand but didn't make it, leaving a tall, somewhat angular, brunette at his side to attempt to restore him to something approximating an upright position.

The Transit officer put his nightstick back in his pocket before heading over to help out. But before he did so he nodded back at me.

'For the record, I'm NYPD myself.'

I paused.

'Oh.'

'Three of us are down here on temporary transfer.'

I paused again, not too sure what to say.

'Right.'

'Holding their hands more like. Showing them what real cops do and how real cops behave.'

'The City's finest, I've always said so.'

Those same eyes looked at me again.

'Yeah. I bet you do.'

2

IT TOOK SOME time getting out of Idlewild that morning, although that wasn't totally due to Subject Thomas. The airport was used to troublesome drunks. What it wasn't used to were planes that suddenly dropped out of the sky and that's what had happened the previous evening which explained – again I was to later discover – the increased police presence around the terminal buildings. Just in case it turned out to be more than a simple accident.

A Lockheed L-749A Constellation operated by Eastern Air Lines and bound for San Juan in Puerto Rico had crashed moments after take-off. The plane was only four years old, so that ruled out metal fatigue and it made mechanical failure unlikely too. Some of the rust buckets up there had almost twenty years on that new entrant to the jet-set age. There were five crew on board, all of whom survived the impact, and twenty-two passengers. Two of the passengers had died at the scene and several more had been injured, some seriously.

Investigations were still ongoing to use the official expression, but the most probable cause was what they called, somewhat impenetrably, a loss of visual reference and orientation on the part of the captain. Apparently he'd encountered drifting fog shortly after becoming airborne. As an explanation it raised more questions than answers which was probably why the whole terminal seemed edgy. The presence of the additional police officers didn't exactly do much to soothe the general sense of unease either. All in all, no-one was in the mood for a short little visitor from across the water with a strange predilection for unusual breakfasts. No wonder Subject Thomas had been deposited on the unforgiving sidewalk like that.

The tall, somewhat angular, brunette poured her charge into a cab a few moments later and the driver headed for the Midtown Tunnel. I followed at what I'd always seen described in the pages of detective novels as a discreet distance.

The brunette was called Reitell. Her first name was somewhere in the papers Con had handed to me too. According to the dossier she was assistant to the director of the Poetry Center which was housed in the YM-YWHA – Young Men's and Young Women's Hebrew Association – up on 92nd. Miss Reitell was six years younger than Subject Thomas and they'd made each other's acquaintance on his previous Stateside trip that summer when she'd been deputed to work with him on a play, but their relationship soon went beyond the strictly professional.

According, once again, to the dossier – and the dossiers provided by Con were rarely inaccurate – they'd been lovers since the summer too.

Subject Thomas had a wife and children back in the UK. Reitell already had two failed marriages behind her. These two looked to be a pretty combustible mix to me but that wasn't, strictly speaking, any of my business. All that concerned me right now was that profile on page forty-seven of the magazine Con represented and how close a relationship that bore to the antics of its subject.

The cab came up out of the tunnel, then made a right, heading uptown on Second Avenue before heading down onto First and pulling past the newly-opened United Nations headquarters. Despite missing his breakfast – so far no stops had been made for those elusive raw eggs in beer – Subject Thomas seemed to be in the mood for a little sightseeing. Then the driver pulled back onto East 42nd and headed northwest crossing Park and Madison before cutting across Broadway and making a left onto Eighth.

Every detail of the journey went into the logs. It was one of the lessons first drummed into every operative back in their agency days. Partly it reassured the client. If he was proffered that amount of detail it tended to make him trust whatever else that operative came up with.

It also made it easier for the agency to check up on the activities of the operative himself. Say you were tailing a guy south on Lexington and you'd told them you'd taken a left onto 27th. If you did, then just about every cabbie in the city would be sending up a chorus of blaring horns because you'd have just turned the wrong way into a one-way thoroughfare and if you'd done that and hadn't noticed then the agency might just start to wonder why.

Then, a little later, having survived the close attentions of all those irate cabs, you'd taken a left from that same street onto First, maybe heading for FDR, then the agency really would be getting jumpy. Now this guy sounds like he's doing a tail job courtesy of an out-of-date street map as opposed to the tail job he's actually being paid to do out on those self-same streets where he wouldn't need to be told you can't take a left from 27th onto First.

Detail, detail, detail. Never missing a single thing. Never letting yourself become tripped up on the smallest little fact. Occasionally a client would complain about the pages he had to wade through to get to the meat, but Con never complained. He knew it wasn't the steak that sold, it was the sizzle. As he'd proved time and again in different courtrooms the length and breadth of the city as he literally bombarded a hapless petitioner with detail after detail of the trip he claimed never to have made – or the illicit, evening excursion about which he'd previously disavowed all knowledge.

The cab pulled up a few moments later outside Number 222, West 23rd Street, better known as the Chelsea Hotel.

The Chelsea had always been something of a Manhattan

landmark. Opened first in 1884 as a private co-operative it had been designed in a style that, so an architect friend of Beth's had once told us, was either Queen Anne Revival or Victorian Gothic.

In other words, just plain damn ugly and not even the flower-ornamented balconies on the façade could hide that unpalatable truth.

I'd been inside just the once. The main feature was the grand staircase which extended upwards for twelve floors. Not even the paintings that decorated its each and every twist and turn could hide the fact the staircase was just plain damn ugly too.

The private co-operative didn't last too long and the building went bankrupt a few years after opening before re-opening as a hotel in 1905. It had played host to many a literary celebrity over the years, including the legendary Mark Twain and, today, a guy from across the water called Thomas. Artistic types sure seemed to like it, but for the vast majority of the rest of this city's population it was one thing and one thing only.

A flophouse.

Give me the Cornish a few steps along the street any time. OK, it didn't have the boho appeal of the Chelsea but it didn't have its prices either. 'Modern Accommodation At Moderate Rates', proclaimed the billboard above the entrance and no-one was going to be able to argue with that. Some guy – a cabbie I think – once told me it was so-called because it originally welcomed new Cornish arrivals to the city, but I'd never had the time or inclination to check that one out.

Miss Reitell escorted Subject Thomas inside where he was greeted extravagantly by the bellhop, suggesting he'd been the recipient of a more than usually generous tip sometime in the not-so-dim and distant past. Subject Thomas hardly seemed to see him. Instead some dispute seemed to be taking place about the room.

I moved into the lobby and picked up a paper. At the desk, Miss Reitell, who seemed to have a fairly intimate knowledge of all the different rooms in the hotel, was trying to change the accommodation that had been allotted to her charge. Subject Thomas, it seemed, liked light and air and the room he'd been given was at the rear of the building and would therefore be small and dark. The receptionist kept trying to point out that the hotel was full, that she could hardly evict another of the residents from their rooms and that she'd try to do something about the requested room change in a day or so's time.

Subject Thomas hardly spoke but even across the lobby you could feel the agitation coming off him in waves. For some reason this issue of the room seemed like a really big deal to him.

As Miss Reitell continued to press for what was patently impossible, he wandered to the entrance. I thought at first that he might be off on another search for raw eggs and beer, but he just paused in the doorway instead taking in great gulps of air. It was the closest I'd been to him since I'd first seen him coming out of Idlewild and I'm no medic, but the man really did not look well.

Strictly speaking, it wasn't all that germane to my report but it went in anyway. He seemed to be gasping for breath even though he was out in fresh air, or what passed for it in New York, at least. And his shirt was sticking to him, large patches of sweat were clearly forming under the armpits, visible even through his jacket.

After a few moments he turned back inside to be told by Miss Reitell that there was nothing that could be done, that he'd have to take the accommodation on offer and negotiate a move at some later date. He nodded back at her meekly and then, equally meekly, allowed himself to be led upstairs like a small boy submitting to the will of a mother.

I'd expected, given the fuss about the accommodation, that he'd be back out on the street within moments but he wasn't. He remained in the small, dark hotel room for the next few hours, uninterrupted by room service, the concierge, the bellhop, maintenance, house-keeping or any stray inquiry agent detailed to keep track on his movements for the next few days.

Either he was working on a new poem or something else was going on to detain Subject Thomas and distract him from his surroundings right now.

Miss Reitell stayed with him the whole time too.

Dedicated lady.

As the afternoon melded into evening, the unlikely-looking couple appeared again in the lobby. Miss Reitell went outside to hail a cab while Subject Thomas made rather more genial conversation with the receptionist than he'd managed on his arrival. Then his escort came back to collect him. I headed outside while he was trying to remember where he'd left his room keys before his companion produced them from her bag. Then I followed them as they journeyed the few blocks down Eighth Avenue to Hudson and 11th, stopping at the White Horse.

Now they had something approaching my grudging approval. OK, the White Horse might have been garnering a reputation lately as a gathering place for those of the bohemian persuasion but it was still, at heart, what it always had been; a retreat for longshoremen and factory workers. There wasn't exactly sawdust on the floor, but it was a close-run thing.

Through the window I could see Subject Thomas being greeted extravagantly again by a couple of the staff behind the bar and even more so by the suited owner who came out from a small office at the rear. He was wearing the kind of smile that recognized a sudden and welcome increase in profits. Something in the way his visitor dealt with the first of the succession of drinks he was handed suggested he wasn't destined to be disappointed, even if this initial reunion was something of a flying visit. Within a few moments, Miss Reitell was outside again, once more on cab duty. But the suited owner didn't look too concerned. What he was thinking was written all over his smiling face.

'You'll be back.'

As I waited for Subject Thomas to clamber into the cab I looked round. The neighborhood was changing, that was for sure. Up to then if you were of an artistic leaning you'd tend to stick to places likes Romany Marie who ran three, always dimly-lit, tearooms and taverns offering a fairly irresistible combination of cheap eats and gypsy music. She'd even been known to throw in the odd free meal for those who had talent but no cash. Myself and Beth had been to her Christopher Street joint once in the early days and Beth had loved it. Rumor had it she'd also just opened up on Minetta Street as well as somewhere around Washington Square.

I followed Miss Reitell and her charge but the cab rides were now getting shorter and shorter. From the Chelsea down to the White Horse wasn't more than just a few blocks but the hop to the next port of call was almost literally that. A hop. The cab had barely shifted up through the gears before the driver came to a halt outside Herdt's.

George Herdt's was a cocktail joint at 284 West 12th Street although the two neon signs to either side of the corner door described it as a lounge. It probably sounded classier. Above the door there was another sign – vertical this time – with the single word 'Bar' flashing on and off while just around the corner, half-hidden by the street lamp another neon sign read 'Restaurant'. George obviously liked to cover all bases.

This time Subject Thomas lingered a little longer although he did now had rather more in the way of an incentive to stay. Previously in the White Horse he'd had the company of working men and the occasional artist. Here in Herdt's he had rather more exalted company in the shape of actress Shelley Winters and actress Marilyn Monroe.

And no, as I later felt impelled to point out in my log to Con, I wasn't shooting a line.

Subject Thomas's two new companions were tucked away at the back of the restaurant for perhaps obvious reasons. They were also facing away from the door and the large plate glass windows for even more obvious reasons. New Yorkers don't like to appear fazed by anyone or anything, but these were two seriously hot and famous women and they were certainly soon warming up the sickly-looking Subject Thomas. He was facing the window making it easy, even through the fogged-up glass, to see the bottles coming and then, ever more quickly, disappearing again. In the course of a single hour Subject Thomas drank a bottle of red wine, a bottle of white wine, a six-pack of beer and six Martinis, the latter being consumed for some reason through a straw.

Miss Reitell was more circumspect, as if she knew it was going to be a long night. Miss Winters and Miss Monroe didn't seem to be drinking at all. Miss Winters had recently given birth to her first daughter after her second marriage the previous year, which may have explained her somewhat uncharacteristic abstinence. But maybe she also suspected it was going to be a long night. Maybe Miss Monroe did too. Or maybe they didn't get too much opportunity. As soon as a drink appeared – any drink, of any description – a hand would reach out to claim it and it wasn't the elegantly manicured hand of a movie star.

With some guys who drink like that you can almost see the alcohol sucking the life out of them but that didn't happen with this one. If Subject Thomas had been feeling fragile on arrival he seemed to have well and truly put all that behind him now.

Another half an hour on and Miss Reitell was on cab duty again. Subject Thomas was now drawing sketches on a napkin for his appreciative companions and had to be virtually frogmarched from the restaurant towards the impatiently waiting cab driver, who soon forget all about his impatience when he saw the companions accompanying his latest fare.

The two movie stars had been keeping a fairly low profile in the restaurant but they clearly weren't going to be able to keep the same low profile out on the street, particularly when the driver insisted on a picture because his wife, as he pointed out, was never going to believe who he'd carried in the back of his cab that night if he didn't provide some kind of proof.

And while they were sorting out all that, would Miss Monroe mind signing something, he wanted to know? And now the cab driver whipped out a copy of *Life* magazine from the year before with a smiling Miss Monroe on the cover under a headline, 'The Talk Of Hollywood'.

For a moment, and from the look on her face, Miss Monroe clearly feared she was going to be confronted with a very different and more recent publication, a calendar that featured – or so it was alleged – a nude photo of herself, although she'd vehemently denied it. Why she would do that was lost on most of the audience who'd, somewhat hungrily, viewed it. Anyone who had a body like that had nothing to be ashamed of was the general and heartfelt view amongst almost everyone I'd encountered.

The long-suffering Miss Reitell was put on camera duty – the camera in question being provided by Herdt's – and she proceeded to take a succession of pictures as the driver decided that maybe his friends in the office, not to mention an old uncle who lived in Brooklyn Heights, would really like to have a memento of that night as well. All of which gave Subject Thomas ample time to steal his cab.

No-one realized what was happening for a few moments. No-one had even registered the fact that Subject Thomas had climbed inside. And sure, the driver really shouldn't have left his keys in the ignition like that, but then again he could hardly have expected the companion of two movie stars to try and drive his cab away. Subject Thomas didn't exactly get too far, only a few feet or so, before he mounted the pavement and came to a more or less gentle halt at a street lamp that was already bent at a slight angle anyway so no-one was going to be too upset it was now bent at a slightly more acute angle again.

Apart from the cab driver of course. With his curses now ringing in her ears, Miss Reitell hailed another taxi before shepherding Miss Winters, Miss Monroe and Subject Thomas into the back. Miss Winters realized, after just a few feet, that she still had the camera from the restaurant and, having no wish to add to any other possible charges that evening such as accessory to grand theft auto, wound down the window and threw it back at another of the restaurant staff who'd come outside along with several of the diners to investigate the commotion.

By that time I was behind them as they headed up Sixth Avenue, crossing Broadway before heading for the Lincoln Tunnel. Around fifteen minutes later the cab was pulling up outside a smart – a very smart – townhouse in Ocean's Gate where, if the sounds coming from inside were anything to go by, a party seemed to be going on.

The party, I was to discover a few moments later, was being hosted by a man who'd announced his intention to leave the US permanently just one year before. But he'd recently returned for a very specific purpose, which was to sell his lifelong dream. The man in question was called Chaplin, first name Charlie and no, as that same log to Con again later made clear, that wasn't another line.

Years before, in 1917 and at the end of his contract with his former employers, Mr Chaplin had decided to build his own studio which he did complete with developing plant, cutting room and offices in Los Angeles on the corner of Sunset and La Brea. I'd been there myself when I'd done some work in LA a couple of years before.

Mr Chaplin's intention was to live in the northern part of the property while the motion picture plant was housed in the south. For the movie plant itself he built six buildings in the style, as he called it, of a typical English village. The *Los Angeles Times* had called it fairytale architecture but it just looked like something out of *Peter Pan* to me.

Mr Chaplin had never actually lived there even though the grounds included all the usual home comforts including stables, a swimming pool and tennis courts. But he shot many a movie on the site including some of the classics – *The Kid*, *The Gold Rush*, *Modern Times*.

But the modern times had certainly turned against Mr Chaplin this last year or so. Senator McCarthy – and whisper the name quietly because who knew who might be listening – now had him well and truly in his sights. Part of his movie studio had already been sold to construct a supermarket and he'd just negotiated the sale of the remaining lot to a real estate developer from New York. The party that night was to celebrate the severing of Mr Chaplin's final link with the US before he started a new life in Switzerland.

All of which went some way to explaining Subject Thomas's welcome drink with two of Hollywood's finest. They weren't in New York just to welcome a rhymester. They were there to bid goodbye to a legend too.

Subject Thomas, Miss Winters and Miss Monroe were met at the door by a man I didn't recognize but who was later identified to me as the German novelist, Thomas Mann. Like Mr Chaplin, he'd also made his home in the US during the Second World War from where he'd made a series of anti-Nazi radio broadcasts. Like Mr Chaplin too, he'd left the US a year or so before but had obviously now returned to mark this final farewell from his friend.

Behind the fairly elderly Mr Mann were two other legends of the silver screen, actress Greta Garbo and actress Marlene Dietrich. I'd read somewhere that the last screen test Miss Garbo had done was at the studios owned by Mr Chaplin. But Subject Thomas seemed more transfixed by Miss Dietrich, whom he immediately began to molest, although she seemed more amused by his fumbling attentions than anything else. Miss Garbo – who seemed as amused as her companion – attempted to intervene, but only succeeded in diverting Subject Thomas's attentions onto herself. Perhaps acting out of a misplaced sense of chivalry, Mr Mann attempted to engage him in a discussion of literary matters only to suffer some of the self-same attentions.

'Hey! You!'

A hand rapped on the window. It didn't carry a nightstick but the tone was the same.

Hostile.

Seeing something it really didn't like and about to say so.

I wound down the window, intending to play the part of the hapless movie fan out on an autograph hunt. But before I could say anything the owner of that hostile voice nodded at me.

'Are you with the caterers?'

At times like that any sort of hesitation is fatal. Ask any operative. It's what separates the good ones from the dross and, without wishing to claim kinship with some of the real greats in the field, I was far from dead wood.

I nodded back, prompt.

'Just got here.'

The security guard eyed me, sourly. He was at the start of what was quite clearly going to be quite a night and he really didn't need small-time irritations like this.

'The kitchen's round the back.'

'On my way.'

I swung around the side of the property, another security guard opening a gate at a signal from his companion back on the drive. I parked next to a couple of catering trucks and followed the sounds of clanging pots and pans to a kitchen that was surprisingly small for a house of that size and which was certainly working overtime right now.

And then I paused. For a moment I just stood in the doorway, listening to the sounds of the party coming from the other side of the far door as I had what I'd heard described somewhere as an out-of-body experience.

OK, maybe that was overstating it a little. I wasn't exactly floating in the night sky looking down at myself. But as I stood there I still, briefly, marveled.

Here I was, a kid from Long Island in the house of a movie star, a movie legend no less, other movie stars – including other legends no less – all milling around him and I was about to watch all those beautiful people doing things they really shouldn't be doing.

And as for my man, the main man at least so far as I was concerned, something was already telling me that Subject Thomas was going to be Numero Uno, the top of the tree, the worst of the very worst and as I stood there in the doorway of that small, overheated kitchen I kept thinking over and over, I just *love* my job.

'OK, we're looking at six different highballs.'

The harassed waitress was called Iris, surname not known because she hadn't told me. She just nodded at me as I stood before a worktop littered with every drink known to man. I just hoped I knew them too. Having bamboozled the security guard outside I didn't want to fall at the first hurdle once inside. Whoever heard of a cocktail waiter who couldn't mix a cocktail?

'We need a Cuba Libre.'

I nodded.

Rum, cola and lime juice. I'd made a good start.

'Jack and Coke.'

Tennessee's finest, Jack Daniels. And a splash of cola if you've a serious deficiency when it comes to taste buds.

'Greyhound – and make it a salty dog.'

Used to be gin, now more often vodka, mixed with grapefruit juice and add a salted rim.

'Seven and Seven.'

Whiskey and Seven Up, but not any old whiskey, Seagram's 7, garnished – the all-important touch – with a lemon wedge.

'Bloody Mary.'

No explanation necessary.

'And a Car Bomb.'

And now I felt my forehead start to prick with sweat and that wasn't due to the steam pouring from the nearby stove.

A Car Bomb?

What the hell was a Car Bomb?

Iris eyed me for a moment.

'Problem?'

'No.'

I turned to the bottles, hoping against hope that inspiration would strike from somewhere.

Iris smiled, wry, clearly taking pity on me.

'Guinness with a half-shot of Jameson and a half-shot of Baileys.'

I stared back at her as she shook her head, wry again.

'It's OK, I'd never heard of it either.'

Then she nodded towards the far door, the sound of the party rising in volume all the time.

'It's for that poet guy.'

I didn't pick up on it straightaway, just turned to the bottles and started mixing liquid in the tall glasses stacked to the side. It was the second of the golden rules, the one that comes straight after never hesitate.

Never approach the mark head-on. Always circle around them first. Talk about anything and everything and then – and only then – steer any conversation back to the real matter of the moment.

'And what about the soft drinks?'

I was rewarded with a barking laugh. No further response necessary, although there was more in the way of instruction to come.

'And while we're out there, if any of the guests start speaking to us, we answer. Apart from that, no talking.'

'Pictures? Autographs.'

'Sure. Feel free to pester them as much as you want on that front.'

I put the Cuba Libre and the Jack and Coke on a tray, broke out some salt for the rim of the Greyhound, trying to sound just as casual as the door opened and closed in front of us, waiters ferrying drinks inside.

'Not too much talking going on out there anyway from what I can see. Plenty of drinking though.'

I put the Greyhound down on the tray too, same tone.

'Especially by that poet guy.'

And then it happened. She was in a house racked wall-to-wall with movie stars and her voice actually started to grow husky as her mind suddenly filled with a short little fat man.

'I wonder what he's like?'

She looked, quickly, towards the door.

'Do you think he speaks like he writes?'

The third golden rule, never get involved, don't get riled, doesn't matter what you say, what you hear. Who cares? You're not the judge or jury, you're just the recorder, the dispassionate observer, taking it all down, committing it all to print or tape, nothing more, nothing less.

But I couldn't help it. Look at the guy. I didn't care what fine words he might have scribbled in his time, he was one thing and one thing only in my eyes and he'd already proved that time and again from the moment he tried to stand on that sidewalk outside Idlewild in his doomed attempt to track down two raw eggs in beer.

The man was a bum.

'You mean he writes as well?'

But Iris was still away with whatever fairies he'd managed to sneak behind her eyes and hardly heard me.

'How's he find the time?'

All I got was the same dreamy response. She'd even stopped chopping the crudities for the dips.

'He's a genius.'

And what did that mean? OK, I'd never read any of his stuff and OK, maybe it wouldn't mean too much to me if I did. Aside from the reports I'd submit to the office, or to any client who'd care to hire me, words weren't exactly my thing. In my world they were there to communicate the facts of any given situation and sure, Beth might enjoy her novels but they provided some sort of escape, some kind of entertainment.

What did a poet do? Especially one who went around sexually molesting movie stars? I just couldn't help it.

'Looks like a bum to me.'

For the first time Iris registered the single chord of dissent, the jarring note.

'Yeah well, where I come from you don't judge a book by its cover.'

'Unless you're my Uncle Eddie.'

Too late, I was trying to lighten the mood.

'He can't read.'

Iris was still eyeing me, meaning it was very definitely too late.

'Who are you anyway? I've not seen you before.'

She eyed me more closely.

'You're not like the normal guys the agency sends along.'

And in that moment, I made up my mind. Let's do it. Let's perform one selfless act of charity that night at least. Iris might have worked her way up to head honcho in some mobile catering outfit but she was obviously still just a star-struck kid at heart so maybe it was time to open those blinkered eyes a little. Time to introduce a little iron into that sweet little soul.

I picked up the Car Bomb.

'What are you doing?'

'Special order, right? Let's give it priority.'

'Maybe we should leave it to the waiters.'

I nodded at her, smiling all the while now.

'Come on.'

Then I nodded towards the door.

'Meet your hero.'

You've heard the stories, right? Everyone has. When Hollywood parties, it parties like no other animal so I was hoping for the usual and then some.

Movie actresses tottering round on the thinnest heels this side of an ice-pick, wearing nothing but imitation horsehair tails belted to their naked butts.

Old men paying young studs of waiters to ride them while they themselves looked on.

Crimes against nature committed with actresses – and actors – of rather more minor renown.

No-one leaving until the very last moment lest they miss the main event of the night, a powder blue Rolls Royce given away by its owner in exchange for the perfect highball, a condo on the Strip auctioned for a pittance, a drunken extra stripped and upended in the Jacuzzi, a general invitation sent out among the stragglers to take their turn at buggery.

On those counts the party was something of a disappointment. Whatever excesses might have been expected to trail in the wake of the guests from Tinseltown, no outlandish endeavours seemed to be gracing this particular outpost of the land of celluloid dreams. Small knots of people chatted among themselves. A pianist tinkled ivories in a corner. A giant screen played some of Mr Chaplin's more famous screen moments, not his idea but that of his brother, Sydney, who was also there I was to discover.

Who wasn't there – or who didn't seem to be there right now anyway – was Subject Thomas.

Iris hovered nervously behind me. She'd been put in sole charge of the evening by her boss and really didn't want anything going wrong. She'd been so blindsided by hero worship back in the kitchen she hadn't been alerted to anything amiss, but now her antenna was twitching big-time. She could smell a loose cannon about to go off.

'Mr Thomas.'

I called round the room, conversation pausing briefly as I did so.

By my side, Iris hissed.

'Hey.'

'Drink for Mr Thomas.'

I nodded at the tray I was carrying.

'Choice of drinks for Mr Thomas, Car Bomb, Seven and Seven, Greyhound.'

'Would that be the cocktail or the bus?'

I turned to see Miss Winters eyeing me. In strict contrast to the warm and happy figure she'd presented to the world some couple of hours ago she didn't look all that happy or warm right now. In fact – and not to put too fine a point on it – she looked seriously pissed.

'We can arrange both.'

That was Iris, defusing things with a smile and a brave attempt at a merry quip.

'Make it the bus and do me a favour, make the ticket one-way.'

Behind her a figure hove into view.

Actually make that, stumbled.

Shambled.

Shook, maybe.

And he just remained in the doorway for a moment too, before his fingers began to fumble with and then explore his crotch.

Miss Winters turned that cold stare of hers onto him but Subject Thomas didn't even seem to see her. Then again he didn't seem to be seeing anyone right now. He just continued fumbling with his crotch. I really couldn't work out what he was doing at first but I soon would.

We all would.

Miss Winters glanced down at her frock. It was difficult not to follow the look. Miss Winters always did have the keenest instinct for an outfit that would flatter her natural assets but tonight those assets were somewhat obscured. Her frock wasn't in the most pristine of conditions either. For the first time I could see that someone had just thrown up all over it and from the way Miss Winters was eyeing Subject Thomas you really didn't need to be Albert E. to identify the culprit.

Miss Winters followed my look and nodded.

'I was trying to steer him into a closet.'

Beside me, Iris tensed. Subject Thomas had now unbuttoned his crotch and was reaching inside.

'We got distracted as he tried to touch up my tits.'

Across the room, conversation was grinding to a halt as more and more party-goers began to register the unfolding antics of the guest from the land across the sea.

'Touching them I'd have settled for, but throwing up over them, that's something else.'

Then Miss Winters herself paused as she too tried – and largely failed – to take in all she was seeing. Across the room, Subject Thomas, who didn't seem to be aware where he was, who he was with, maybe even who he was, had extracted his flaccid member and was now pointing it downwards towards a plant pot by the door.

By now an awed hush had descended making the sound of the splashing urine a moment or two later echo even louder round the room. Subject Thomas didn't notice, he just threw back his head as he continued to piss on the plant, the yellow urine splashing off the leaves before snaking its way across the floor.

Miss Winters gave up. She went into the kitchen to sponge herself down and fix herself a much-needed drink. Several of the other guests melted, diplomatically, into the next room. A couple of the waiters looked at Iris, unsure what to do for the best while all the while Subject Thomas – his eyes still closed – continued to direct his piss over the plant pot with more or less reasonable accuracy.

Iris kept staring at him.

'Oh my God.'

Then Subject Thomas, finally, came to a halt.

I took a glass from the tray, nodded back at her as I began to take it over to him.

'He's entitled.'

Subject Thomas looked round the room blearily, for the first time seeming to register where he was.

'He's a genius.'

3

DAWN WAS BEGINNING to break by the time I made it back to the apartment. Beth was still sleeping. She had a job in a hospital a few blocks away, in the records department. Her sister, Nora, was a nurse there and she'd had a couple of words in the right ears on her behalf.

Beth made sure she looked grateful, which in one sense she was. It wasn't exactly Westchester but our new apartment in Stuy Town was still a fair step up from where we'd been living before and neither of us wanted to go back there. Finding the rent each month was always a struggle so the contribution supplied by the hospital every four weeks or so was more than timely.

I parked my car, made my way along the communal walkway towards our apartment. At one time this area had been the Gas House District. The whole place had been dominated by huge storage tanks most of which leaked making it a somewhat less than desirable place to live. The local – and dubiously-renowned – Gas House Gang who preyed on any dwellers unlucky enough to live there didn't exactly add to the general appeal.

What changed everything was a road, the East River Drive, recently re-christened FDR. Once people were driving past the place on a daily basis the clamor started for something to be done about it.

What followed was called urban renewal although to some it more resembled forced evacuation on a scale to match that of the famed Highland Clearances thousands of miles and thousands of lifetimes away. Six hundred buildings including three churches, three schools, five hundred stores and two theaters were razed to the ground. For more than three thousand families it was goodbye to everything they'd ever known. To others it was the chance of a fresh start.

Priority was given to military personnel returning from the war – the only reason Beth and myself had managed to get our foot on the first rung of that particular ladder. On the first day of opening the new-build housing development had received more than seven thousand applications from couples and families desperate to live in the country in the heart of the city as the Mayor at that time, the somewhat legendary LaGuardia, had termed it.

Once inside, I decided to grab a quick shower and head across town to see Con. He was renowned for getting in early and leaving late but maybe he didn't have too much choice given the heat perennially blasting around those Times Square offices. On the way out I picked up a copy of the T&V – *Town and Village* – the local newspaper covering not just Stuy Town, but Gramercy Park as well. I unlocked my car, looking forward to finding out what my fellow residents in what passed for our version of dreamland had been up to this last week or so.

One eye on the headlines, I didn't see him for a moment. He was just another down-and-out who'd somehow slipped past the eagle-eyed security guards but who sure wouldn't escape their gimlet-like appraisal for long. These boys were on top dollar and I knew that for a fact. Part of our monthly service charge went to pay their wages.

Then my visitor opened his mouth – clearly a reflex action even now – before closing it again as he made no sound, save for a strange, strangling noise.

I paused, then nodded at him.

'Hi, Rick.'

And there they were, back again before my eyes.

Those images unbidden and unwanted.

Impossible to dispatch.

Five years earlier, I'd been traveling west. I'd been given money for a train ride although that cash advance didn't stretch to journeying on the Pullmans; no such luxury for a lowly operative in those days. Besides, the point was to merge in with the crowd and there was usually quite a crowd too, keeping each other company on those long and draughty rides.

A few years previously I'd made a fairly intimate acquaintance with a land far away across the sea while fighting a war that was still being called honorable and just, where so many before, and so many to come, would not. That land was lush and verdant. This land was anything but.

It was the first time I'd seen this land – my land as the songster Woody Guthrie had christened it. I wasn't traveling from California to the New York Island in the words of his famous song but I was still traveling deep into its heartland, seeing sights I'd never seen before.

For the first time I was looking out onto the flat stretches of the Great Plains before coming out onto the Rockies. For the first time too I was seeing small train towns, mining camps and isolated farmhouses where homesteaders clung, often heroically, to existence. It sounds trite I know, but I'd never realized before that trip just how big this land – my land – really was. And then I'd disembarked at one of those small mining towns and began my work.

The first port of call, as always, was a local boarding house. Back in the city I had a small apartment I called home but for the next few weeks my home was the Gladstone valise of the commercial traveler.

Sometimes the food was good, sometimes not. Sometimes the company and conversation was good, more often not. Rooms were usually around a dollar a night, each a temporary home to a stranger passing through, usually young men hopping trains, picking up work however and wherever they could.

It was in such a boarding house in Butte, Montana, that I heard the voices. Male voices, hostile, accusatory, bombarding the redoubtable but increasingly ragged female owner of the boarding house with the same question repeated over and over as if on a loop.

'Where is he?'

'Where is he?'

'Where?'

Followed by a name, his name, the name of the mark, the quarry I'd been detailed to follow, the object – quite clearly – of some considerable interest to others right now too.

The redoubtable owner of the boarding house knew trouble when she saw it, indeed she'd have to have been blind, dumb and stupid not to espy the dark malevolence in the eyes of her unwanted visitors or to recognize the deadly threat in their voices. She wasn't blind, dumb or stupid but she didn't want trouble either, certainly not this sort of trouble, not on her patch and not during her watch and her voice kept rising in volume all the while, repeating the name of the mark time and again as they pressed her, alerting not just him but the rest of the boarding house to the clear and present danger now within.

Sure enough, from the room next to mine came a scraping sound as a sash window opened but if I could hear it then so could his pursuers and a second or so later came the sound of splintering wood as the door to his room was forced.

A second or so later again there was a single howl that was swiftly silenced – so I was to later discover – by a sheet from the bed that had been torn in two and wrapped round his face, stuffed deep into his mouth, choking off any further attempt to protest what he now knew was to be his inevitable fate.

A door slammed. Then there was silence. A couple of the other boarders tentatively opened their doors, but then closed them again. They could do nothing and they knew it and so didn't even try.

Dawn broke the next morning on a grotesque tableau. A makeshift trestle had been erected opposite the boarding house, directly in front of the entrance to the local mine. The object of the previous night's attentions was hanging from a noose suspended above the trestle, a handwritten warning on a piece of thin board stapled to his naked chest. His leg – broken as he was carried from his room the previous night – was bent at an impossible angle beneath him. Just below his chest and the stapled sign was an angry bright-red stain where his balls had once been.

Traveling into the town those few days before I'd picked up the local paper and read the words of the mine owners as they fulminated against the local agitators as they called them, malcontents who:

'... snarl their blasphemies in filthy and profane language.'

'... advocate disobedience of the law and insult our flag.'

'... disregard all property rights.'

'... seek to destroy the institutions which are the safeguard of society.'

In another article the next day they'd further railed against those who'd shown themselves, in the view of those self-same mine owners, to be bullies, anarchists and terrorists.

The police had arrived by now and were debating how best to remove the display up on the trestle, but the debate was hardly urgent. The victim was clearly beyond any help any local medical man might bring and besides they'd already been proffered a not-so-small consideration to make sure this lesson remained on full view for the longest possible time so that the lesson might be absorbed by others.

And they weren't the only ones. I looked across the street and met a pair of eyes staring back at me.

A pair of eyes that held my stare.

The lightest of signals dispatched and understood.

In a small bar on the main street of Butte the previous evening I'd been joined by the owner of that pair of watching eyes. Rick, another of the operatives from the agency, had arrived some three or four days before. To anyone else we would have looked like two young men striking up a simple conversation. Two lone travelers journeying a common road. But there was nothing simple about this conversation because the rules of engagement had been altered either by the office back in the East or by this particular operative out in the field.

In truth it hardly mattered.

There was a new situation now.

That's all that did.

And that new situation was simple. Previously the role we'd been sent out to perform was the usual sort of thing. Surveillance. Infiltrate a body of men who presented a threat to a client and use various time-honored methods to defuse that threat. Identify the ringleaders and isolate the opinion-makers. Report back to the office in the East the names of those who were most closely identified with the forces arraigned against our client and let that client decide how best to deal with that new threat.

Only now there was a new deal on the table. And the deal came with an astonishing price tag attached. Five thousand dollars. I could have stayed in that boarding house, had I been so inclined, for five thousand nights for such an amount. I could have bought the boarding house indeed several times over. It came with a condition attached of course, because this wasn't about the simple breaking of a strike anymore. This was about the breaking of a collective will and it was to be achieved by another time-honored method, whether that was in Montana in peacetime or in the wilds of Tuscany in a time of war.

By force.

By the simple demonstration of a superior show of violence.

The agents were not to trace and track the quarry anymore. They were to kill him. Then they were to display his body for all to see as a warning to those who might be tempted to walk in his often-troublesome footsteps. Those followers were to look on the mutilated corpse and then realize what would happen if they too chose such a path.

Rick must have seen in my eyes my deep unease and the offer was withdrawn almost as quickly as it was proffered. Somehow he – and perhaps the office back in the East – had got this wrong. I wasn't going to be of use to them in what was to unfold over the next few hours so I was excised from the frame, removed from the sphere of conflict. Left alone to assume the role of spectator in all that was to follow.

I stood in that square that morning before the corpse of the union leader, watching as the police milled around, feeling the silent eyes of a growing crowd look upon a man who, up to the previous evening, had been their potential savior, feeling at the same time a collective will ebbing away.

Across that same square, Rick's eyes never left mine. And as he maintained that stare he nodded again, a clear instruction dispatched once again against the backcloth of an image of medieval barbarity.

This is what we do.

This is what is in store for those who oppose us.

Choose your side and choose it now.

Stay silent or speak out.

And I stayed silent. I watched as the police finally cut the body down from the makeshift trestle, the dried blood from the corpse staining the shirts of the officers deputed to carry out the grisly task, spreading the stain of death as it did so. Then those same officers moved back into the crowd, carrying the mutilated corpse, their part in the all-too public spectacle completed.

I'd left the agency soon after that by more or less mutual consent, but still kept tabs on all my old colleagues. So I found out pretty quickly what had happened to Rick a short time later. Later, when it was all over, when all that happened had happened, Rick had shown me his diary – he always did keep meticulous records – which gave a flavor of his typical day back then.

Rick had been in another small mining town in the Midwest, working in a local smelting company. At 9 a.m. that morning, Rick been visited by one of the union officials who'd told him there were a car-load of Italians being shipped in to break a strike that had just been called. The union official and Rick agreed that they'd send a couple of men down to meet them to see if they couldn't be persuaded to turn back.

Then Rick had grabbed a quick lunch in the works refectory where he completed a couple of applications to join the union on behalf of some other workers who'd approached him, those workers being unable to read or write themselves.

After lunch, Rick had visited the various pickets that had been established thus far before joining the men deputed to meet the arriving Italians who – thus far also – hadn't shown.

In the afternoon it was decided that a strike committee

should be formed. Rick had been co-opted onto that committee along with four others. Three of the committee, including Rick, had been picked out as captains to look after the different shifts of pickets.

Had Rick arrived at his new place of work earlier there would have been no need for any of this, but the owner of the large smelting works had been tardy in recognizing and responding to the approaching danger as he himself had been forced to acknowledge. A year before an agent of the Western Federation of Miners had visited the works and had secretly organized the Mill and Smeltermen's Union, No. 125.

Rick had arrived at the works a couple of months later as just another of the guys. As the newly-formed union grew in power and influence – and given his reading and writing skills – Rick was quietly approached one evening and invited to join. After displaying the customary and expected show of reluctance as he affected to consider the matter, Rick finally signed up.

From his new position on the inside, Rick had been able to speedily identify all the other union members. One by one a pretext was found for their dismissal.

After another month or so, Rick had been appointed secretary of the new union, leading the owner of the smelting works to proffer grateful thanks to the Gods of Commerce and Industry because he now had access to that union's records and papers. The mass dismissals continued apace.

But the owner overplayed his hand and attitudes began to harden. A strike was called with Rick right in the vanguard, so it seemed, of the developing protest but that was to be his undoing too.

Previously, Rick had been able to send his daily reports back to the agency by post. Locked in his small room in a local boarding house his night-time scribblings attracted no attention and if anyone saw him posting regular letters out on the main street a reference to a family back West – or to a much-missed lady – ensured no undue interest was taken.

But now the owner wanted more frequent updates. With the announcement of the strike the situation was changing virtually hour by hour. If the owner waited for the mail at least a day or so would be lost.

And so Rick began spending more and more time away from the works at exactly the time – as a member of the newly-formed Strike Committee – that his presence was required there more and more. A couple of the other guys started to notice his absences. Either he was now sweet on some local lady or something else was going on.

The next day he was followed. Maybe Rick had begun to lose his touch or maybe he was getting over-confident. Either way he didn't register the tail. He was observed spending an inordinately long time in a phone booth on the other side of the town and seemed to be constantly referring to a large sheaf of papers he was bringing out from a bag.

His followers returned to his room in a local boarding house. They turned it upside and down and even though they couldn't find any direct link back to the agency they found plenty of evidence that he wasn't just a simple, ordinary, itinerant smelting worker like themselves.

They found all the evidence they needed that he was, in fact, a paid spotter for the company.

When Rick returned an hour or so later there was a welcoming committee. They didn't wait for him in the room, nothing so obvious. He could, and would, have bolted the moment he saw them – and they made sure they'd straightened that same room too so Rick wouldn't be immediately alerted to anything being wrong or out of place. They just waited in an adjoining room instead.

When they heard Rick return, they knocked on his door. Rick opened it to a fellow member of the Strike Committee and welcomed him inside. The other members of the committee immediately piled in behind. They'd agreed beforehand that they were to share joint responsibility for all that was to happen next.

While two of the committee held Rick down, a third brought out a Bowie knife. The fourth – a great bull of a smelterman – yanked and held open Rick's mouth. Then his tongue was sliced out at the root.

Then they left him behind on the floor, blood pumping out from his mouth. He was alive but only just and from that moment on he'd be what they intended; a living, breathing, testament to treachery.

Rick just looked at me. Then he held out his hand. I hesitated, but only for a moment before I reached inside my pocket, closed my hand on a couple of coins and bills.

There but for the grace of God and all that.

Ten minutes later I was outside Con's office. All around, deliveries were being made, to hotels, fast-food joints and stores. The city that was reputed to never sleep was waking up, but the light shining in Con's office meant he'd still beaten most of the early risers.

Five minutes later still and Con was wearing the kind of smile that was never going to steal across Rick's face again. A smile that told the whole wide world that all his dreams had just come true and life was turning out just fine and dandy.

A couple of times Con had paused in his reading, a silent, quizzical question in his eyes as he'd looked up at me. All

I'd had to do was nod back at him. It didn't matter if some of this sounded like some of the wackier adventures from Wonderland, every word of it was true.

Con knew me better than that. I'd never have invented even half this stuff. Apart from anything else I didn't have the imagination.

Con finished and laid the papers down on his desk, looked across at the tape machine and the camera I'd placed down by my chair. Then he looked up at me again.

'All this was the first day?'

I couldn't work out whether it was incredulity or envy in his voice.

'No. All this was the first twelve hours.'

Con looked back at the profile open on his desk. Now I couldn't work out whether he was amused or just plain bemused.

'And the guy's got the nerve to sue us?'

I shrugged. That was none of my business. In fact none of this was going to be any of my business from now on, at least so far as I was concerned.

'Looks to me like all your Christmases and birthdays just rolled into one.'

I stood.

'And mine.'

Con looked up at me as I nodded back down at him.

'Bye, Con.'

'Where are you going, Jimmy?'

I paused, now halfway to the door, looked back at him.

'Job done.'

'Job what?'

I kept staring at him, ever more puzzled.

Con never used to be this slow.

'What more do you want? What else can the guy do? Read

the log, Con. Look at the pictures I took on that neat little camera you gave me.'

I reached down by the side of the chair and put it on his desk in front of him.

Con didn't even look at it.

'You're not exactly going to need a hanging judge here, put even half this little lot before Gandhi and there'd only be one verdict, this guy is toast.'

'We'd still like you to stick with this a little longer.'

Outside, the morning rush was beginning to build. I'd had fantasies of getting home before it started, maybe even cooking Beth breakfast before she went to work. It had been a while since I'd been able to do that for her, but it was beginning to look like it might be a while longer yet.

'What the hell for?'

I picked up the magazine, still on Con's desk, flicked it open at page forty-seven, the original, offending profile.

'If anything, all this is looking a bit mild now, wouldn't you say? I'd say so and just about everyone who reads this report or takes a look at these pictures is going to say exactly the same too.'

His eyes had never left mine.

'This is news, Jimmy.'

That was a fresh one on me.

'A drunk making a fool of himself is news?'

'A famous drunk makes it news.'

Con corrected himself.

'No. Even better. It makes covers.'

Instinctively I glanced round at the walls again, at all those faces staring down at us.

Smiling faces, sad faces, faces with eyes that seemed to have lived forever, some already fading from memory but all famous in their own way in their own time.

Con hunched forward.

'OK, I don't exactly know how our august employers reacted when they first heard this scribbler was going to sue us, but let me make an educated guess.'

Con moved closer still, his voice dropping all the time, swirling the words around on his tongue like a sommelier savoring a particularly fine vintage.

'Raised their eyes to the skies and thanked whatever Good Lord may reside in whichever Heaven, and now you see why.'

Con tapped my log.

'Think about it, Jimmy. This guy has been here for twelve hours and already we've got the sort of copy that could keep the *Enquirer* going for a whole month. And the guy's due to be here for at least another month too.'

Con tapped the log again, nodded at me, shrewd.

'Now if our famous poet's going to do all this in his first twelve hours in the good old U S of A – .'

I nodded back at him, well and truly up to speed now on this particular flight up the flagpole.

'What the hell's he going to do in the next four weeks?'

'I don't know, Jimmy. But I know one thing. I'm going to have a hell of a lot fun finding out and if I'm going to have fun finding out then every John and Jane Doe out there is also going to have a hell of a lot of fun finding out too.'

I couldn't help it. I felt a big grin start to spread across my face. It was beginning to sound like fun to me too.

Con spread his arms wide.

'These are tough times, Jimmy. All over this great country of ours. And we, my old friend, have a chance to spread a little happiness, to sprinkle some stardust, to make everyone smile.'

Con regarded me, his supplicatory hands still spread wide.

'Now wouldn't you say we'd be failing in our patriotic duty if we didn't do just that?'

I nodded back.
What else could I say?
'If you put it like that.'
Con nodded back at me.
'I do.'

Half an hour later I was back out on the street and still grinning. The traffic was now racked. I'd miss Beth before she set out to work but there was some compensation in the shape of a tasty little advance from Con for the extra duties that had just wafted my way.

He'd told me to treat Beth to something for her birthday. I didn't even know Con knew when her birthday was, but maybe there was a file on the two of us somewhere in that office of his. Maybe, somewhere, there was a file on everyone.

I cut up to Times Square again and this time headed on into the Astor. Across the street a small gang of kids were being moved on by a cop. A supersized statue of a nude woman had recently been erected on a store opposite in a bid to grab attention and it was certainly working for the under-tens and a fair few over-tens too from the way the passing traffic was beginning to slow and bunch outside.

I cut into the lobby, looked at the menu displayed outside the restaurant, mentally reviewed the number and denomination of the notes Con had just handed over to me. Then I made a booking for Beth's birthday the following week.

The maître d' wrote the details of my booking in the ledger with a flowing hand. Just something about seeing my name and our address in there made me feel good. What kind of exalted company had Beth and myself just joined? Then I walked back out of the lobby and saw a poster for a new movie that was opening the next month; *How To Marry A Millionaire.*

Feeling not unlike one myself right now I collected my car and headed back home to Stuy Town.

4

'IF YOU ASK me, I think he sounds unhappy.'

I stared at her. Beth was washing dishes in the sink. I was drying before stacking them back in the small cupboard I'd shoehorned in behind the even smaller table and sink. Living in Stuy Town made you something of an expert in the ancient art – in that old English phrase – of squeezing quarts into pint pots.

'He sounds what?'

Beth looked back at me.

'Don't you think so?'

Behind her, framed in as many windows, a thousand different men, women and youngish couples were all doing the same, looking out over the communal walkways and gardens, washing up, making up, falling out, a million and one different stories playing out as night fell.

I considered the proposition as if it was some sort of philosophical treatise. In other words – and Beth had used exactly those words at different times in the past and with increasing frequency lately it had to be said – I was playing the wise guy.

'Well, let's see. He's been partying non-stop since he landed.'

I took another plate from her, polished the slightly off-white front and back that had been called a certain shade of cream when we bought the service, which was the color of the year that year, or so we'd been assured.

'He hasn't paid for a single drink, hasn't stopped chasing skirt or popping pills.'

I put the plate back in the cupboard, nodding down towards

those same communal gardens and walkways, at families escorting small children, at returning office workers grabbing the last of the sun on the benches dotted throughout the gardens before heading for whatever home awaited them.

'Throw a stone, Beth, most guys out there would think they'd just been handed the keys to Neverland.'

'Especially you, right, Jimmy?'

If she expected me to fall into that one then she really had started to seriously underestimate me. OK, we'd had our moments these last couple of years and I know those moments had been multiplying in their frequency, but give me a break.

'Leaving out the chasing skirt bit. The rest doesn't sound so bad.'

Beth nodded as if some sort of point had just been proved. I didn't think it had and I could now feel a familiar prickling beginning on my scalp, the start of an all-too familiar frustration.

'I just don't see what the guy's got to be unhappy about.'

'I thought that's what you were finding out.'

Time and again, she'd do it. This should have been a simple conversation about the events of the day, the sort of conversation going on in almost every one of those thousand and one other apartments right now as dishes were being washed and stacked, as one person recounted to another the detail of their previous few hours. Something to be reviewed and dismissed, not analyzed and forensically dissected. But then all our conversations these days seemed to end this way.

'I'm not finding out anything. It's not what Con pays me for. He doesn't care if the guy's happy or unhappy, all he's paying me to do is watch the freak show.'

'It's what you used to like. The working things out, the finding out why.'

See what I mean about forensic?

'Yeah well, maybe I don't do *why* anymore.'

I should have left it at that. Beth didn't seem in any frame of mind to respond anyway so I should have just kept on stacking the dishes, maybe picked up a magazine, put on some radio show.

NBC were carrying the *Grand Ole Opry* and if we weren't in the mood for all that toe-tapping along with the rednecks there was always *The Red Foley Show*. Another twist of the dial would have brought Jack Benny into our sitting room or Jimmy Durante or even Groucho Marx if we really wanted to surf with the surreal. Or, if we were feeling low down, mean and dirty, we could have sampled some of Henry Morgan's caustic sarcasm as it coruscated across the airwaves.

There were, in short, a million different distractions I could have sourced in just that one small kitchen. Maybe I could even have read the sales pitch delivered by a slimy salesmen the day before who'd tried to entice us to join the ten million or so other Statesiders who'd apparently just invested in their first television set and which had come a long way, so we'd been somewhat breathlessly assured, from the dark days of '47 and the infamous RCA seven-inch screen.

All right, everything was still largely in black and white although there were rumors of color being just around the corner – and yes, the black and white was really various shades of grey – and OK, you received your pictures through some kind of antenna which was a big ugly thing that stuck straight out from the window of your apartment which didn't exactly make you popular with the window cleaning contractor. And OK, the thing had to be sited with pinpoint accuracy to receive anything like a picture, meaning someone usually had to stand by the window until that pinpoint accuracy was achieved; but it was still, so we were told, the future. Forget that tinny little contraption in the corner from which only sounds could emanate, from now on we'd all be loving Lucy instead.

But that prickling feeling on my scalp was spreading all the while and I just couldn't help pushing this now.

'Why should I?'

'I thought you didn't do *why*, anymore.'

So now who was playing the wise guy?

'Not exactly what you talked about when we first met, was it Jimmy?'

By now the dishes were being put back in that small cupboard with just a touch more force than previously, the drying just that little bit more vigorous.

'Meaning?'

If I'd hoped the tone in my voice was sending out the right sort of message – just leave this alone, change the subject – it wasn't working. Or maybe Beth was beyond listening to those sort of messages now.

'Wasn't the life you told me you wanted back then; spying on lowlife and losers.'

So things hadn't quite worked out as I'd imagined. Throw another stone. Ask any one of those commuters out there who crowded the morning subway on their way into the city. Had their lives worked out as their teenage selves envisaged? Were they in the land of milk and honey where angels blessed their each and every endeavor?

'And you know the worst thing?'

Beth had now abandoned any attempt at any more washing of dishes. She was turned back towards me and the look in her eyes was something harder than anger to absorb, there was something else there instead, something softer, something more resembling sorrow.

'You're actually starting to enjoy it.'

'Oh sure, I really enjoy camping out on some sidewalk all

night, wondering if I dare get out and take a leak. Or sitting in some dingy downtown bar watching some fool make even more of a fool of himself.'

'I can just hear you back in his office.'

'What?'

'You and Con, cackling away like a couple of witches as he reads all that purple prose you send him.'

'Facts, Beth, cold, hard facts, leave the purple prose to those novelists you like so much.'

'Anyway, this isn't about facts Jimmy, it's about you, what it's doing to you.'

'Everyone's got to eat, Beth.'

'What it's turning you into.'

'I've got to eat, you've got to eat.'

'It's like everything's just one big joke to you these days.'

But I was just rolling on.

'This kid you're always telling me you want has got to eat.'

I nodded at her, the drying forgotten now too, one object and one object only now on my mind, attack; always the very best form of defence.

'So tell me, Beth, how are we all going to do that without the likes of the cackling Con and the troublesome Mr Thomas?'

Beth just kept looking back at me for a moment, but if I imagined this was objective achieved, the objector silenced for once, I was about to be swiftly disabused of that fond notion.

'This kid *I* want?'

Too late, there it was, all I'd successfully skirted around before, the trap opening before me, the abyss into which I'd just dived, headlong and reckless.

Beth kept looking at me and if there was sorrow in her voice before it was multiplied a million times now in those wide, staring eyes.

I didn't reply for a moment, didn't know what to say.

'Look – Beth. I didn't mean – .'

Beth turned away from the sink.

'I'm going to bed.'

'Beth.'

'Goodnight, Jimmy.'

'Beth?'

Then the door closed behind her.

I crossed to the window, looked down onto the gardens again. Then I looked uptown, towards the top Manhattan House between Second and Third, thrown up like Stuy Town in the last couple of years and the resemblances didn't end there either. The whole edifice was clad in white brick, giving it a stripped-down, functional look, like a huge chain of slabs rearing up from the sidewalk. Half a century before every New Yorker had hoped to live fabulously. Now, it seemed, it was enough just to live.

I kept looking out of the window and there they were again. More images from a different place and time.

As unbidden and unwanted as the first.

As impossible to dispatch.

Ten years before, I'd been in another land completely, a land far away, across the sea. But there were no doubts about my companions here. Fear might have filled their eyes but there was no hint of treachery, no suggestion of mendacity. Every eye was focused on one object and one only, the summit of a twin dome in the Italian countryside, a German machine gun astride one of the knolls, another encamped on the other.

Those eyes, steadfast and loyal, belonged to an unholy combination of Bible-belt Southerners and apprentice Mafiosos from Queens and they followed me, every single one of them, as I ran under the fire from the enemy guns which wasn't as synchronized as intended, leaving a jagged avenue through which a body might run without – hopefully – being cut to pieces.

I threw my carbine down onto the ground as I ran, the fire of my companions covering me all the while, yanked a grenade from each of my shirt pockets, pulling the rings as I did so and released the spoon handles. With the fuses now lit I sailed the two grenades away in separate flights.

I turned and picked up my discarded carbine just as the first of the German gunners came running from a bolt-hole that had suddenly turned into an inferno of blood and body parts and scored a direct hit right in the middle of his chest exposing a cat's cradle of bone and tissue. I was aware of something tearing at my leg but as yet the pain hadn't kicked in because now there was another distraction, another German gunner advancing from the second of those encampments. The first of the gunners had already scored a glancing hit on my left leg as I was to discover later, but for now the only thing on my mind was downing the second target which I did, aiming at his chest again, the largest, widest possible target but he ducked at the last moment, some reflex attempt at self-defence perhaps, only for his face to suck in on itself as the bullet hit that instead. A second mouth appeared in the very middle of that face, spreading in milliseconds to obliterate every other feature before he fell at my feet.

'Medic!'

One of the Bible-belt Southerners, or perhaps one of the young Mafiosos – I didn't know, I was beginning to drift into unconsciousness – was yelling at my ear. For a moment I wondered why a medic should be summoned to treat an enemy quite clearly already well beyond saving but then I realized he was being summoned for myself.

With the rest of the small company securing the twin-domed hill and the two machine guns, I was carried out on a stretcher to a field hospital where an X-ray revealed a fracture of the pelvis. The bullet fired by the first of the Germans had struck a glancing blow before it had ricocheted behind me, avoiding the advancing reinforcements and embedding itself harmlessly in the earth.

From the field I was evacuated to a base hospital before being sent back to New York where I was later visited by a four-star general on a morale-boosting mission who informed me I was being awarded a Distinguished Service Cross, no less, for my role in leading that Tuscan ambush.

My war was over, only mid-way through '43 but my duties were far from finished. For the rest of the year and most of the next I was pressed into service on similar morale-boosting missions. Myself and other war heroes as we were now, somewhat bewilderingly, being described, called in on regiments about to be sent to a multiplying series of new battlegrounds and fronts.

At the time there was no chance to think, to reflect on just what had impeled me across that small window of opportunity into an open trench where the bullets, thankfully, couldn't intersect. Perhaps I'd never have reflected on it at all had I not stumbled upon the scene of that macabre lynching some five or so years later.

Since then those two sets of images had danced together inside my head. I was a war hero who'd later chosen to act the coward. Why? Maybe that was the reason those two sets of images floated through my head like that. Because I didn't understand it myself.

Maybe it was because, in that land across the sea, that lush and verdant land that wasn't my land, there was nothing at stake at the time and so nothing to lose.

Later, in that land that was my land, there was a relationship at stake and so something and someone to lose.

Or maybe it was something else, something I couldn't as yet

grasp and that's why those images gnawed away at me instead, a puzzle that demanded to be solved.

Or maybe people were just plain strange.

Take that guy.

Take Subject Thomas.

I picked up some stale bread from the trash, went out onto the small balcony. There was just about enough room for one person out there or, as in right now, one person and a bird.

I didn't know what type or breed of bird it was. All I knew was it was small and cute and seemed to have befriended me. Because every evening it appeared, flapping its wings as it perched on the iron guardrail, looking in through the window, waiting for me to appear and respond to its silent signal.

I'd open the balcony door, although not as cautiously as I used to because now it seemed nothing and no-one was going to scare him away. Or her. That was another thing I didn't know and there was certainly no way I was going to try and find out. Then I'd put the stale bread – or a cookie – or whatever I could find – down on the rail and the bird would hop a few steps along to the offering and dip its beak time and again into the now-regular supper while I'd stand and watch.

Once, to the considerable and vocal amusement of Beth it had to be said, I'd tried heading back inside before the bird had finished. There was a radio show I wanted to catch, featuring the lampooning talents of Stoopnagle and Budd. The bird had stopped eating and just looked at me through the window. And it hadn't started starting eating again until I'd taken the all-too clear hint and gone back outside to keep it company.

I'd met Beth when I came home from the war. While I'd spent those eighteen months or so on that so-called hero circuit, one question had been gnawing away at me and wouldn't go away. I felt like I'd lived a hundred years in the last three and in a sense I had. I'd taken at least two lives away from those who'd lived them in that time too. But I was still only in my early twenties. So what the hell was I going to do with the rest of my time?

The war had provided a convenient excuse to postpone any decisions. For those three years my every movement had been determined for me. I'd been inside a giant machine that had directed my every action. But all of a sudden that machine had stopped moving. The wheels that had previously provided the forward momentum had stopped turning. Now it was time to do something for myself.

Previously, all that had been on my mind had been escape. Growing up on Long Island at that time tended to do that to you and it was an impulse that wasn't confined to the young. My parents had always dreamed of life in Free Acres in New Jersey, a place where everything – back then anyway – was radical and new and exciting.

My father was a painter. Not an artist, nothing so prosaic, although he did help out at the local theater from time to time, painting scenery and getting ribbed from the rest of the guys on his watch for mixing with those of a theatrical persuasion.

My mother came from Nova Scotia, about as far out of town as seemed possible in those days. I'd gone back there once with her as a kid, to visit family. They lived in a modest clapboard house owned by her uncle, a retired sea captain. The whole family was shot through with sailors and marine engineers. At the end of the street was a cemetery where she'd taken me to look at the headstones of people who'd drowned on the *Titanic*.

Stray birds aside, my main interest had always been the law. Don't ask me why, we didn't have any lawyers in the family and there was no possibility of my going to college to study it, before the war anyway. But so much had changed in the last few years. Those self-same colleges were now beginning to open doors to those they'd previously have debarred. I still didn't have a hope of making Ivy League but in the last couple of years education was suddenly no longer for the rich or for the élite, helped in part by legislation such as the GI Bill of Rights, and the number of college students had doubled.

The radio had played its part too. I'd listened to a couple of shows related to the law that had been broadcast back in the Forties and even now they lingered in my mind. *I Was A Convict* and *Criminal Case Book*, for example, had taken the real life testimonies of convicts in an attempt to explore why they'd turned to crime. The broadcasts were initiated and hosted by a lawyer called Edwin Lukas who was something of a pioneer in the still-fledgling field of crime prevention. He'd joined the New York Society for the Prevention of Crime in '42 and was largely credited with changing its direction and focus from one of prevention by detention – still the favoured route of many – to prevention by concentrating on the social, political and economic factors that might have led to the committing of those crimes in the first place.

After the radio broadcasts I found out that he'd written some books on the same subject. The next day I traveled across the river to the City Library and took out two of them. *The Adolescent's Court Problem in New York City* may not have been the raciest of titles although the later *Crime Takes But A Moment To Commit* promised more of a zing.

A week or so later again I went down to New York University. I still wasn't ready to go the whole hog and trek up to Columbia even though I'd found out by then that Lukas had recently taken up a teaching post there. I wanted information about a couple of courses, as I told the fresh-faced girl on the desk. She spent the next half-hour sourcing that information for me. I walked in a single man looking for a direction in life and walked out a married man with a wife.

OK, maybe that didn't all happen in the same day. But that was still the day myself and Beth, that fresh-faced girl on the desk, first met and talked – and then talked some more as she kept finding more information on yet more courses for me – and talked some more later that night over coffee in the Village – and then talked some more that weekend when we took in an off-Broadway show.

Beth also told me of her own hopes for her future which lay, she'd decided, in teaching. I talked of my new interest in criminology. A few months later I'd proposed and she'd accepted. The intention was we'd both find work and save and we'd use those savings to, firstly, fund my way through law school and, secondly, her path through training college. We'd have to scrimp and save in our twenties we agreed, but in our thirties and with our respective qualifications achieved and our studies behind us, we'd be set up for life.

Beth left the university. It was only a temporary job anyway and not well paid and, via her sister Nora, secured her current and permanent post in the hospital record department. I joined the agency. At the time it seemed a useful preparation for the courses I hoped to follow. The majority of the people I'd be reporting on in my new calling had to be of the criminal variety. Why else would they have attracted any sort of attention from inquiry agents? Even a few, short, weeks later I was already starting to realize how naïve that sounded.

I watched as the bird feasted on the last of the scraps, then flew away. I turned back to the door catching my reflection in the window as I did so. To my eyes I still looked exactly the same but that wasn't how Beth saw me. She thought I'd changed. In her eyes I'd come to resemble one of the creatures I'd been deputed to track down.

OK, maybe that was overstating the case again. But in her book the kind of work I was now doing was corrosive.

In my book, this kind of work was just that – work – something to do – a means of earning a daily dollar and what the hell was wrong with that? And OK, if the dream of law school had slipped a bit – I sure wasn't going to be starting in any college this side of thirty, not now – well, that's what dreams do too, isn't it – moderate into something more real?

I settled back on the only chair we'd managed to find that was compact enough – in the words of the manufacturer – to fit on the small outside space and closed my eyes. I hadn't intended to actually fall asleep, just rest for a short while but sleep I did. And for a while too. Normally the temperature dropping as night set in would have woken me but this was one long and hot fall. The mercury hardly fell a degree or so in the couple of hours I was out there. And when I woke I had a clogged-up feeling in my nostrils and at the back of my throat.

The smog was definitely getting worse by the day or, in this case, the night. There were rumors that people had already died from respiratory-related difficulties but the city authorities were pouring cold water on those sort of claims. Mindful of compensation proceedings perhaps. Maybe that was going to be my next job. Sitting up all night measuring air pollution in the service of some court case or other. Sometimes this job was all glamour.

I stood, stretched my aching arms and legs, then turned and slid back the bolt, just catching a voice from the other side of the kitchen door as I did so.

Beth's voice. Followed by a soft ping as she replaced the phone. At least that's what it sounded like to me, but it seemed I must have been wrong. I opened the door to see Beth about to head from the bathroom to our bedroom.

'You been talking to someone?'

Beth turned, looked at me. For a moment she just stared,

those blue eyes I'd first fallen in love with back in that university admissions office clear and steady.

'Who would I be talking to, Jimmy?'

Beth nodded at me, those eyes still clear, untroubled.

'This time of night?'

Then Beth turned back into the bedroom and closed the door.

5

EARLY THE NEXT morning it was the same phone that was again the matter of the moment. Only this time it was ringing. It started ringing at a few minutes after six according to the time on the new alarm clock Beth had bought for me for my birthday the previous year. We were assured it kept perfect time. I'd checked it several times in the first few days and, much as I hated to give the man from Macy's credit, he was right.

So it was definitely just after 6 a.m. Which meant we might have some sort of family emergency on our hands and some family member on the other end of the line needing to tell us all about it. Who else would be calling at this time in the morning?

Which was another stupid question and as I blinked my way out of the small bedroom into the even smaller hall, I already knew the answer.

Con.

And I was right.

'What did I tell you, Jimmy?'

He sounded as bright as ever. In fact he sounded even brighter. Behind me, Beth stood in the doorway, as concerned as I'd been roughly two seconds before. In another two seconds she was going to feel much the same as I was feeling right now which was seriously pissed.

'Con.'

My tone was flat and unwelcoming. Con didn't even seem to notice. Beth turned back to the bedroom and closed the door. I was right about her being pissed.

'What did I tell you?'

'Con, do you know what time it is?'

'Didn't I say? Didn't I just say?'

Con also didn't even seem to hear me. His tone was exultant.

'Six a.m., Con. That's as in six in the morning, where the hell's the fire?'

'This is better than any fire, Jimmy.'

Con leant close to the phone, his tone conspiratorial again.

'This is news.'

I was back in his office half an hour later. I'd said goodbye to Beth but she hadn't replied. Maybe she was already asleep. Or maybe she was still just pissed. Either way the unseasonable heat of the last couple of days had suddenly turned a little chillier and in more ways than one.

On the drive from Stuy Town to Con's office I passed a news stand. The latest Kinsey report was dominating all headlines again. Every time the guy came up with a new survey, the papers all ran it as the lead. I didn't know anyone who'd actually read any of the original reports but who needed to when the results were reported in such minute detail? All across the nation, it seemed, everyone was fascinated by the private lives of others. Their premarital and extramarital affairs. Their experiments in group and same gender sex. We just couldn't get enough of it.

Beth had picked up *Harper's* the previous week and a guy called Albert Deutsch had said that Kinsey was exploding all traditional concepts of the normal and abnormal, the natural and unnatural. The man, so the article argued, was holding up a mirror to the nation. If that was true, then maybe Con didn't have any reason to sound so excited. According to Kinsey, everyone was living life on the edge.

As I walked into his office, Con was wearing his now-habitual sunshine smile. Habitual, that is, since Subject Thomas had first decided to grace our shores. I wasn't feeling all that sunny myself. Our esteemed current Mayor, the so-called unbought and unbossed Vincent Impellitteri, had recently decided to raise the city budget and to do so he'd increased the bus and subway fares to fifteen cents which didn't affect me all that much. In my line of work I had to keep rather more mobile, right? If a mark hit the subway I'd have to follow but more usually any tail job would be done courtesy of a car.

But Mayor Impellitteri – who'd also famously celebrated his election with no band or tickertape – hadn't been content with just increased bus and subway fares, not to mention also increasing the sales tax, he'd started to site parking meters on more and more streets of the city in a bid to claw back even more revenue. I'd found a new one outside Con's office that morning. Now I was lighter in the pocket as well as feeling deprived of some much-needed sleep. As starts to the day went, it wasn't one of the best.

Con, again, didn't even seem to notice. Quite clearly he had other things on his mind.

'What did I tell you?'

'Con, you're sounding like a broken record.'

'Doesn't matter what I sound like, Jimmy. All that matters is this.'

Con tapped my log, delivered the previous day.

'That stuff you dug up on our visiting poet.'

Con's tone became so dreamy it was like he'd gone into some kind of rapture.

'Gold dust.'

'Just told it like I saw it.'

And now his smile became almost beatific.

'And no-one sees it better, Jimmy.'

OK, I couldn't help it, I admit. Despite the early hour, despite the disturbed sleep, despite the seriously-pissed wife now –

hopefully – sleeping again back in Stuy Town, I was beginning to feel flattered.

'Nice to know someone appreciates me.'

'Not just someone, Jimmy. And not just me.'

Con pointed upwards.

I followed the arc of his finger.

'You've had word from God.'

'The next best thing but don't tell him that. He hates to be second in anything.'

'The great man himself?'

'None other.'

Con was talking about Roy Alexander. He'd commenced as managing editor in '49 and looked set for a long stint at the helm as well. He was sharp with a real eye for a story. And it seemed, according to Con anyway, that he'd spotted an absolute peach of one here.

Con hunched forward again in his familiar, almost-conspiratorial, pose.

'The magazine wants to open all this out a little, Jimmy. Up to now they've just been getting some high-level dirt to throw at some slimy prosecutor, but not any more. Now they want to do a new profile.'

I blinked, trying – and largely failing – to get my head round that.

'What's to say after the last one?'

'This is going to be bigger than the last one.'

Con nodded at me.

'Better.'

'Meaner? Nastier?'

Con smiled, the smile illuminating his lips, not quite reaching his eyes. A killer about to devour its kill.

'You catch on quick Jimmy, no wonder we use you all the time.'

My mind was still on that original profile, page forty-seven of the magazine, those florid phrases already running around inside my head.

'I still don't see what else there is to say, you've hung the guy out to dry already, what more do you want?'

'It's not just the guy, Jimmy. I told you, we want to open this out a little, broaden the scope.'

'Meaning?'

'Meaning we need background. We don't just want to know what he does although thanks to you we're getting a pretty good picture of all that, right? We want to know who he is, where he comes from, what about his family – he's got a family, did you know that Jimmy? Your tail's a good old family man, not that you'd know it from the way he behaves.'

Con shuffled some papers in front of him. More information to feed the machine. More juice to keep the wheels oiled.

'So what makes a guy – a family man – with a wife, kids, the whole caboodle – act like this, what does the little woman think about it?'

I broke in.

'You're going to tell her?'

'She's going to be reading about it soon enough. But no, we don't want to actually tell her, obviously.'

Obviously. Tell a mark in advance or at least too far in advance and they might do something seriously sneaky about it, like go to a lawyer, try and have some sort of gagging order put on it all.

Far better to delay till the last possible moment, say, the night before the story appears. That way you can get an initial reaction from the wife, husband, lover or even the kid of the mark which can be inserted as late copy. The best of both worlds in fact and everyone's happy.

Well, apart from the mark. But who cares about him? He

shouldn't have been doing what the whole world would soon be reading about in the first place, should he?

'We want you to dig around a little. Find out what their home life's like back in – .'

And now Con paused, puzzled.

'Laugh – .'

I looked at him.

'Laugh?'

'That's what it says.'

'He lives in town called Laugh?'

'Not exactly a town. Smaller, more of a village. But yeah, it's called Laugh – something.'

I looked at the piece of paper in front of Con.

It was too.

'It's in England.'

Con peered again at the paper.

'Well, near.'

'So how am I going to do all that?'

Con looked at me as if I was stupid and maybe I was. I was obviously seriously underestimating the effort he and the magazine was about to put into all this. Mainly because I really couldn't see the point. Some two-bit poet from a small and strange-sounding town, well, village, from England, well near.

Who cares?

'You're going over there.'

I stared at him.

'It's all fixed up, you leave on the last flight tonight.'

'Just a minute.'

'Come on Jimmy, if I said hop on the greyhound to 'Frisco, you'd do it, if I was telling you to take the shuttle down to the Keys, you'd do that too, so what's the difference?'

'Tonight?'

'We are paying you for the week, Jimmy, and that's as in

minimum and we've paid upfront, I think we're entitled to a say in how you spend the time we've already paid for don't you?'

I kept staring at him.

'Anyway, you said it yourself and you were right, what more do we need on him? We've got it in bucketfuls already, now it's time to cast the net a bit wider.'

'So this was all my idea?'

'Maybe she's the key.'

Con wasn't even listening.

'This guy's heading for the rocks, hell, heading for them, he's throwing himself onto them, so maybe she's the reason, something she's doing, something she's not doing, I don't know, but that's your job, Jimmy, and if anyone can find out you can.'

Con threw a ticket across the desk at me.

'You've got three days. And you'll need all of them too, seems it's not just a simple flight, there's a few train journeys too.'

Con grinned.

'In fact it's a bit of a close call which is longer, to tell you the truth, the flight or the trains once you land.'

'Terrific. So the guy not only acts as if he's from a different planet, he actually lives on one.'

He wasn't listening again.

'Then I want you back for this.'

Con threw another piece of paper across the desk at me. I looked at it. It was some kind of flyer.

'What is it?'

'It's his new play. The one they're putting on in that fleapit up on 92nd. Opens in four days' time.'

I looked again at the caption on the top, read it out.

'A play for voices.'

I looked back at Con, puzzled.

'So what other kind is there, a silent one?'

Con shrugged.

'Maybe he's been living on that different planet of his so long no-one's told him talkies have been around since the Twenties. Hell, maybe the talkies aren't around where this guy comes from. Maybe they don't even know the war's over yet.'

I was still reading the flyer. I'd just got to the title of the play. Under Some Wood or Other. I waved it at Con.

'And what the hell does that mean?'

'How do I know, Jimmy?'

'It's all set underground? And no-one talks?'

Con shrugged.

'Sounds like a barrel of laughs to me, maybe I'll take my wife. Honey, I'll say, you know I was going to take you to that new production of *Oklahama*? Well can that, we're going to watch some play written by this drunk that takes place six feet under and all you're going to hear are voices. Oh yeah, that's really going to go down a treat.'

Con dismissed the flyer with an impatient wave.

'OK, Jimmy, I know we're asking a lot. This isn't exactly going to be a pleasure trip, but compared to some of the ones you've done for us it's not going to be too bad either.'

Memories of Rick swam before my eyes, the silent Rick, the man who'd now be silent forever, the man who went out to do his job and paid that kind of price for doing it.

Con was right.

This wasn't too bad.

'I've got a feeling about this one. I've got a feeling about her, about the little lady back home.'

He nodded at me.

'You know how it is, Jimmy. If there's a guy in the gutter there's usually a woman who put him there.'

Con nodded at me again.

'Right?'

ON THE SHORT drive back I channel-hopped the radio, finally settling on WJZ. It boasted a fifty-thousand watt clear channel signal and covered the whole of the Tri-state area of New York, New Jersey and Connecticut and it was always as clear as a bell. Some Canadians had even claimed they could hear it at night.

They were running down the latest hits. Tommy Dorsey had just finished singing about 'The Most Beautiful Girl In The World' and then Eartha Kitt followed up with 'Santa Baby'. By the time I pulled up in Stuy Town, Hank Williams had just started warbling about 'Your Cheatin' Heart'.

I called Beth in work and explained about the trip. She said she'd try and get back before I went to say goodbye. I had the impression she would, but not too hard. I didn't know why. It wasn't anything she said. Just something in the way she didn't say it.

As I packed my bag for the trip I put out food for the next three days for the bird and a note for Beth to remind her not to forget her night-time duties in respect of our feathered friend. Beth herself had still not shown. It looked like my instincts were none too rusty. As I was on expenses I'd called a cab to take me to Idlewild and a buzz on the intercom alerted me to the fact it had arrived. I made for the door, bag in hand but then – on a sudden impulse – paused and picked up the phone.

I dialled the service number for NYTel and a young, female voice came on the line.

'Operator.'

I gave her our number. She'd have it anyway, but she'd still need any caller to confirm it as a security check.

'I want to check my call records.'

'For the last billing period?'

'No. Just the last twenty-four hours.'

'And would that be all numbers?'

'Yeah. All of them.'

Then I heard the sound of a key fumbling in the lock and I spoke again, hurriedly.

'If you could just send them through.'

As Beth came through the door, I held onto the receiver.

'Yeah. I'll call back.'

That wouldn't have made a lot of sense to the operator, but as I'd cut the call a moment before, it wouldn't exactly cause her too much concern either.

A harassed Beth looked at me.

'Problem on the subway.'

'You shouldn't have bothered.'

'You didn't want me to bother seeing you off?'

'I didn't mean it like that. I just meant you shouldn't have put yourself out.'

Beth paused a moment, then nodded at the phone.

'So who are you calling back?'

I shrugged, affecting unconcern.

'Airline messed up my booking.'

I gave her a quick kiss, picked up my bag.

'All fixed now.'

Beth left it till I was almost through the door.

'If it's all fixed, why do you need to call them back?'

'I'm running really late, Beth.'

On the way to the airport I asked the driver to swing by Columbia. He left the engine running as I headed into the university bookshop. Something told me the concession in Macy's wouldn't have stocked the particular tome I was seeking, but maybe I was wrong. Maybe it was Book of the Week or something. Maybe all over the city commuters were riding the subway engrossed in it.

If they were it wouldn't have taken more than a few stops to get to the end of it all. The tome in question was called *Deaths and Entrances* which didn't sound to me like the snappiest sort of title and sort of the wrong way round as well. Shouldn't the entrance bit come first followed by the long goodbye? According to the print history on the inside cover it was first published in '46 although this was the second edition so presumably it had sold pretty well.

I leafed through the list of contents as the driver negotiated the traffic and headed for Queens. It wasn't just the afore-mentioned 'Deaths and Entrances' I picked out in there, there was, 'Unluckily for a death'; not to mention, 'Among those Killed in the Dawn Raid was a Man aged a Hundred' and 'A Refusal to Mourn the Death, by Fire, of a Child in London'.

I looked out of the window just catching sight of the first of the big silver birds as they came in and took off from Idlewild and thanked the heavens I'd never been the superstitious type. Did this guy write about anything apart from death?

There were some other outpourings in there that seemed to be about something else though. 'On the Marriage of a Virgin' seemed worth a look, but it was a small note of cheer in what looked to be a pretty downbeat collection. Not exactly feeling in the mood to get to grips with it just yet I put it back in my bag, looking out of the window again as the terminus hove into view.

I had a choice of three airlines for my journey across the water – Pan Am, the new upstart TWA, and BOAC. The latter had introduced a new luxury Monarch service to New York a couple of years previously using something called a Stratocruiser which offered sleeper accommodation. I'd asked Con if I was booked onto that and he told me not to be so unpatriotic. Pan Am was American and proud.

Yeah, and a hell of a sight cheaper too.

I paid the cab and checked in, filled out the checklist for clipper passengers and went through to the observation deck to wait for the call to the boarding gate. Then I settled back and opened the slim book I'd picked up from Columbia. Selecting a poem at random I started to read.

On almost the incendiary eve
Of several near deaths,
When one at the great least of your best loved
And always known must leave
Lions and fires of his flying breath,
Of your immortal friends...

I raised my eyes, looked outside. A plane was docking, Pan Am livery. Looked like my chariot had arrived. I turned back to the slim volume, tried again.

Who'd raise the organs of the counted dust
To shoot and sing your praise,
One who called deepest down shall hold his peace
That cannot sink or cease.
Endlessly to his wound
In many married London's estranging grief.

OK, call me stupid and obviously I was. But could I get my mind round even one single line of that?

Could anyone?

I bent over the book again, really trying to concentrate this time, read again the last line.

In many married London's estranging grief.

Then I straightened up again, no more enlightened the second time round. I had a feeling I wasn't going to be too enlightened on a third reading either or maybe even a fourth.

Or maybe at all.

A call came over the Tannoy summoning passengers for the Pan Am London flight to the gate. Then another voice, closer at hand this time, cut across as I stood, packing away the book.

'Any good?'

A sweating figure beside me nodded at the thin volume I'd just put away. He was about fifty, clad in a cheap-looking belted coat and was clutching a briefcase. One of the new breed of businessman. A couple of decades before he'd have been tramping the streets of Des Moines or Phoenix pushing whatever product he was currently carrying in that clutched case. Now he was hopping across to England. The world was changing day by day.

The sweating gent nodded at a book he was also now putting away. *The Case Of The Green-Eyed Sister*, a Perry Mason mystery by Erle Stanley Gardner. I'd read a couple of Mr Gardner's earlier efforts and this one, from a summary I'd also read, seemed much like the others. In other words, not bad.

In this latest outing, Perry Mason lands the toughest case of his career when blackmail leads to murder – and he's a suspect. The police, perhaps understandably given their joint history, are licking their lips at the prospect of finally roasting Mr Mason. His key witness also doesn't help. The key witness in question is a private eye with all the moral fiber, so the blurb on the dust jacket made clear, of Al Capone.

Like them all, right? OK, there were one or two honorable exceptions in some of the books I'd dipped into over the last couple of years, usually in the lulls that came with the territory on most tail jobs. But most of them seemed as venal as the lives they investigated.

'This is the pits.'

I fell in step with the sweating gent as we both headed for the departure gate.

'I worked out who'd done it on page six. Flicked all the way to the end just to make sure, and guess what?'

'You were bang on the money.'

'Maybe I should ask for a refund. This was going to see me halfway through the flight, now what am I going to do?'

The sweating gent nodded at me.

'So how about yours?'

'It's not a book.'

He looked at me.

'So I was seeing things. Those pieces of paper inside a dust jacket, that was something else?'

I smiled. It was going to be a long flight and maybe this guy was going to be in the next seat and those seats weren't that wide and he was packing a fair bit of weight around those shoulders.

'Not a story anyway.'

I paused. For some reason I felt foolishly embarrassed at the admission.

'It's poetry.'

I could almost feel the chill settle over the departure gate as, passports and boarding cards checked, we headed down onto the tarmac before climbing up the stairs into the waiting aircraft.

'Poetry?'

'It's a sort of work thing.'

Why was I explaining myself? Like I'd been caught with a girlie mag or something?

Now my new companion was looking at me even more suspiciously.

'You a poet?'

I shook my head, squashing that one pretty damn quick, rolled on.

'And you think you're disappointed – hell, reading this stuff, it's like dipping into something scrawled in Swahili.'

The sweating gent shot me a sympathetic glance.

'Pretty difficult to get your head round, right?'

'Someone, somewhere in the world, might understand what he's talking about. Not anyone in any world I know.'

'He sounds like my wife.'

I followed him up into the cabin, didn't reply.

On the flight over, I picked up the Gardner book. The sweating gent wasn't sitting next to me, but he was close enough for me to reach over and take a look when he fell asleep with it open on his lap. He was right about cracking the mystery on page six. In fact the only mystery was what had taken him so long. But it wasn't the story I was interested in. It was the private eye with the moral fiber of Al Capone. From the few pages I read – and from the small flavor of his antics I could glean – it seemed something of an insult to Mr Capone.

OK, a lot of our work wasn't exactly palatable. Just ask Rick. A lot of us really didn't want to work on what might be called the industrial side of the business but there was never actually that much choice. That was where the real money was for the agencies, so that's where most of us were sent.

And the guys who ran the agencies would pick carefully. There weren't too many operatives working in the field with private fortunes to fall back on. Most of them were just regular guys looking to earn a crust.

The entry criteria were simple. If you were married, you were of special interest to the agency. A married man usually meant there was a commitment of some kind to honor, usually to some landlord somewhere. Single men could just up and go wherever the fancy took them. If you were married, life was usually more complicated.

If you were hard up and married then you were of extra interest. If you were hard up, married and already had some debts to take care of, then the agency really began to lick its corporate lips.

The first approach was never direct. There'd be some story that the company you'd just joined represented some bankers or bondholders or maybe an insurance company and their clients needed a little information. What you actually had to do was never spelt out, at least not until you started work anyway. More usually, not until you'd received your first pay check and had spent it and were already eagerly looking forward – along with your wife or girlfriend – to the next.

And, once started, if the guy started to sicken of the whole thing, there were always a couple of neat tricks they could employ to keep him in line. In his mind the new operative probably thought he could get out at any time, maybe even deny any involvement at all if challenged.

Think again. Remember the receipt the company asked you to sign for that first pay check? Put that alongside that first report you wrote for them. Same handwriting, same slant to that word and that one too.

Sometimes the approaches were made in an even more indirect way. You'd pick up a paper and see an advert for a rubber worker on Sundries and Specialities. You could make up to a dollar an hour depending on production. You'd be invited to detail the machines you could work, your age and your phone number and then it would be suggested you contact, for example, Box 7372 in the *Cleveland Plain Dealer*.

Or maybe you'll see an advert for a planer hand. It would be heavy work on an expansion program and the highest hourly rate would be paid to producers. All you have to do is give details of experience, references and phone number to, say, Box 13772, same august newspaper.

Once you replied, your response was carefully vetted, not by the personnel manager as you might imagine, but by representatives of a detective bureau. If any qualifications were detailed on the application form they merited only a cursory inspection. What mattered much more was anything they could glean about the character and personal and financial circumstances of the applicant.

The applications would then be graded as carefully and conscientiously as a professor assessing a college student. And it didn't matter which detective bureau had instigated the trawl – William J. Burns, Corporations Auxiliary, Pinkerton's of course, or Railway Audit and Inspection – they all employed exactly the same recruitment methods.

You'd receive a reply on a letterhead from some company or other. The name wouldn't mean much to you but that didn't matter. All you were interested in was the job. You'd turn up for the interview where they delved into your home circumstances and asked you to do a literacy test. Then, if all that stacked up, you'd be called for a second interview where you'd be duly offered the job. Then – once you'd actually started – the real deal would be outlined.

In addition to the dollar an hour, or whatever remuneration had been agreed, you were going to be paid another fifty dollars a week – fifty a week! – for a simple report. And this wasn't going to be anything too onerous either. You simply had to report on the men you were working with, let the company know whether any of them were complaining about the conditions, make clear their attitude to their pay, all the while making sure the names and ages of those men were detailed along with their opinions. If discontent among the workforce rose to the extent that union activity was contemplated, the operative – who by now was well used to his monthly bonus – would be told, Rick-style, to join that union too.

In other words you'd just enlisted in a private army.

Back in the office, your reports would be analyzed by

the first of the four main divisions in any bureau, Clerical, Criminal, Operating and Executive; usually by the Assistant Superintendent. He'd not only tidy the reports for the client, he'd analyze it for the benefit of the agency itself too. It wasn't just his fellow workers who were going to be spied on at this stage of the game, but the operative himself. From that kind of study, the agency's going to know what time that operative got up in the morning, where he worked and at what times during the day, what time he quit his work that night, when he had his supper, what he had for supper in all probability, whether he spent the evening trying to obtain information or whether he'd decided to shoot the breeze in some local bar instead – as well as how much money he spent at different times during that working and non-working day and what he spent it on.

So now it's the watcher who's being watched. Now it's the spy who's being spied on and by now there were a lot of spies too. Even back in the Thirties, the eighteen-volume report of the sub-committee of the Committee on Education and Labor – popularly named the La Follette Civil Liberties Committee – had uncovered more than two hundred and thirty different agencies with a workforce totaling over one hundred and thirty-five thousand operatives.

By now most of the passengers were asleep. The sweating gent was sweating even more. By the time we landed his shirt was going to need wringing out. For some reason I couldn't sleep despite the fact I had an onward transfer of some two hundred or so miles.

Beth was right. It wasn't what I'd talked about when we first met. This was always going to be a stepping stone and the truth was I hadn't done too much by way of stepping anywhere lately. But I'd found something I was good at. I had a nose for the hidden, an instinct when something was being kept from me and then I worked hard – damn hard – at bringing it out into the open.

Or maybe it wasn't instinct. Maybe the simple fact was that most people had something to hide, something they'd rather the rest of the world didn't know about, a secret life in fact. Beth thought it had made me jaundiced, but she was wrong. She was still an idealist where I'd become a realist, that's all.

I looked round the plane at all those sleeping travelers and wondered how many of them had secrets they were hiding from their wives or husbands or employers. Previously, such a thought would never have occurred to me. Now it was the first thing that came into my head whenever I met anyone new. Beth didn't like that either but there had to be some reason I'd become so good at my job in these last couple of years. There had to be some reason the likes of Con employed me time and again. And if I kept on like this, then maybe I could even open my own agency one day.

I'd never said that to Beth. But these last couple of years I'd been thinking, why not? Con was right. When it came down to sniffing out the lowdown and the lost there weren't too many better.

So why should I keep thinking of it as a stepping stone? Maybe it was time to make a real career out of all this.

TWELVE HOURS ON and I'm in a different world again, one question and one only now on my mind.

What the hell was this guy doing writing all that stuff about lions and fires and organs and dust or whatever the hell he was writing about, the sort of stuff that just made no sense? Why the hell wasn't he just looking out of his window and writing about plain and simple things like everything he could see out there? Because it all looked pretty damn good to me.

After the flight I'd caught a west-bound train. For the first few hours it was much as I expected – town after town, suburb after suburb, some fields, some nice mansion-type houses dotted in the hills, but all pretty well what you'd see anywhere on any train ride. Then the west-bound train came to a halt and I transferred onto a smaller train along with a gaggle of locals. The seats were cramped, there was barely room to stash my holdall in the overhead galley and there was just the one john for the whole of the train so, all in all, I thanked my lucky stars it was only going to be a fifty-minute hop down to the next stop on the line. A few minutes later I was wishing it could have lasted a lot longer.

The train came out onto the beach. For a moment I wondered if all those hours of traveling wasn't making me hallucinate or something, but the rails actually ran alongside the edge of the sand. A wide estuary led down, in the distance, to the sea. The tide was out and a small army of women were on the sandbanks accompanied, somewhat improbably, by panniered donkeys. The women were digging, so I'd later discover, for something called cockles, although back in the US we'd probably have called them clams. The sun was up and the sand was bleached a pinky-gold.

The train ran on past a succession of small villages, all hugging the sides of cliffs. All the time the beach kept us company, the estuary sometimes contracting so we could almost lean out of the window and touch the other side, sometimes widening so you could barely see the opposite bank.

At one point a ruined castle looked down on us, not remote or forbidding but homely somehow, as if it had been built to protect all that lay below it rather than keep it in check. All the time more women crowded the sandbanks, great sacks by their sides, more and more cockles – or clams – being loaded inside, all ready for transportation on to the fine restaurants of cities, close and far.

I stared out of the window, not moving for the whole of that fifty-minute trip, forgetting where I was, even what I was supposed to be doing. For once I didn't take any notes so Con – should he be so minded – could check on the progress of my journey once I'd sent in my log. I didn't need to. Every moment felt like it was burned into my memory.

I felt like even I could pen something about all this and, facts and observations aside, I was no wordsmith.

So just look out of the window, buddy. Pick up your pen. Everything you want to write about is right here, smack in front of your eyes.

I guess it couldn't last. What does? That warm glow inside that somehow matched the pinky-gold glow outside – the pinky-gold glow that kept company with me all the way down to the small market town that was the next stop on the journey – that was just a distant memory once we'd reached journey's end.

Because it wasn't journey's end. Journey's end was still

another fifteen or so miles away but it didn't matter how many timetables I consulted or how many times I tried to access the closed booking office – it was more usually closed than open I'd later discover – there didn't seem to be any way of accessing that final fifteen or so miles aside from picking up my holdall and walking which, after a transatlantic flight and an eight-hour train ride, wasn't an option I was about to embrace too eagerly.

I walked out of the small station, looked across a bridge towards a large, strange-looking building being constructed up on the hill. Even though it wasn't finished, it already looked vaguely French-Canadian, as if it had been dropped down out of the sky onto its current location and couldn't work out why. It looked alien and out of place and I knew exactly how it felt.

A train driver passed, heading onto the small platform, about to take the train from which I'd just alighted back along the line.

I stopped him.

'How do I get here?'

I showed him the name of Subject Thomas's home town or village – or at least his adopted home town or village. Apparently he was born around thirty miles away, in one of the towns I'd passed through, so why the hell couldn't he have stayed there I briefly wondered? Then again, if he had, I wouldn't have just experienced that rock and roll ride along what looked like the edge of Paradise.

'What train do I get?'

He studied the name on the piece of paper, then looked up at me.

'You don't.'

'I don't what?'

'Get a train. Not to there anyway.'

'Why not?'

'Because there isn't one.'

He looked at me, half-pitying, the kind of look a teacher might give a slightly backward child, then nodded beyond me towards a set of buffers cutting off the track.

'This is the end of the line.'

Then he turned and was gone.

I looked after him for a moment, looked at the buffers, then looked round again.

End of the line?

End of the world more like.

Then I saw it. Salvation, or at least what might just pass for it in this forgotten corner of a blasted land. A taxi. Or at least a car with the word 'Taxi' hand painted on the side. Either the fates were playing a cruel trick on me – I'd heard that a different language was spoken by some in these parts – or I'd come across something that almost resembled civilization.

'Taxi – hey – taxi!'

The car swung lazily in a loop, not because the driver was taking his time but because the car just seemed to be built that way. Everything it did it seemed to do at roughly half the normal pace of almost every other car I'd ever seen. It just seemed that kind of car in that kind of place.

The driver, a great hulk of a man, wound down the window and looked at me, lazily again.

'That's what it says on the door.'

A wise guy. A taxi driver who's a wise guy. I could feel myself starting to relax, some small part of the universe already beginning to re-align itself back into balance.

'And you're for hire?'

'I'm for what?'

'Only you haven't got a light.'

He just looked at me.

'Where I come from the cabs have lights. If it's on, they're for hire. If it's off, they've already got someone inside.'

'You can't see if they've got someone inside?'

I paused. Now he came to mention it you probably could.

'We've got a slightly different system over here.'

'Which is?'

'If you want a ride, you just ask.'

Which sounded reasonable enough to me.

'I need to get to – .'

I peered at the piece of paper again and this time attempted to manipulate the strangled vowels.

'Laugh – something.'

The driver, who'd later introduce himself to me as Maddox, a Christian name I'd not come across before, looked at me. It was that same look the train driver had given me too, the kindly old schoolteacher gazing on a more than slightly-retarded child.

'Laugh?'

I nodded.

'Something. Laugh – something.'

For a moment a light twinkled in his eyes.

Maddox took the piece of paper from me.

'Laugharne.'

'As in Larne?'

I spelt it out and Maddox nodded.

'As in Larne.'

I smiled, couldn't help it, he just had that sort of effect.

'Well, if you say it that way, why not spell it that way?'

Maddox didn't reply, just smiled back and I got in the back of the cab feeling that somehow, and in a way I didn't quite understand, some sort of bridge had just been built.

'This to do with our world-famous poet is it?'

I looked at him warily, his eyes studying me via the rear view mirror.

'Excuse me?'

'Your trip to Laugharne.'

Maddox did a pretty good impersonation of my mangled effort to pronounce the name. I had the impression he was the kind of guy who picked things up pretty quickly.

'What makes you say that?'

'You're a Yank.'

See what I mean about quick on the uptake? What was it, the accent, the clothes, the New York pallor on my face, the way I looked out of the window as if I'd just landed on Mars?

'What else would a Yank want in a beat-up, broke-down backwater of a place like – ?'

I joined in, mangling the vowels at the same time.

Maddox grinned, not at the attempt, more at the gesture. He seemed to give me some credit for it at least.

'Maybe I've come for the view. The scenery.'

I looked out of the window.

'It's sure pretty. All those hills.'

And it was. The road was now winding in and out of small villages with rolling fields on either side.

'You don't have hills back in America?'

'Where I come from they're called skyscrapers.'

And now Maddox rolled that word round his tongue too, savoring it as if it was an exotic treat, which maybe it was. If they built anything above a couple of stories in these villages and towns I sure hadn't seen it.

'And yeah – your poet guy – he's sort of why I'm here.'

I hesitated.

'I'm a journalist. Doing a piece on him. Where the great man comes from, that sort of thing.'

Maddox stopped to let a farmer escort a herd of cows across a lane. Then he turned to look at me. The guy really filled that front seat. For not the first time I was feeling pleased we'd made some sort of friendly connection.

'Actually we're getting more and more of you boys over these days. Disciples following the trail. Not just from America either, all over, we even had a couple of gentlemen from the Far East the other day, Japan or somewhere.'

'Is that right?'

Maddox nodded.

'But the Yanks. They're the best in my book.'

I nodded back.

'The special alliance, hands across the water and all that, right?'

'Generous tippers.'

I paused. Something told me I'd do well to bear that in mind.

The farmer doffed his cap towards the waiting cab. Maddox honked his horn by way of a response before putting the car into gear and moving on. And now his shoulders hunched as if he was really concentrating on something.

'Actually I've had a little idea in connection with all that, I'd be interested to know what you think.'

I nodded, cautious.

'Go on.'

'Well, you're here – and it feels strange probably, you don't really know what you're coming to, not too many references to this place in the guidebooks and you can't even pronounce the name of the town, so that's not going to help either, is it?'

Maddox smoothly circumvented a stray duck that wandered across the road.

'So I was thinking, if we could make it a bit more like home – well, a bit more like your home anyway – then that might just help.'

I looked out on more rolling fields, not a house or farm now in sight.

'Make this more like Manhattan?'

This should be good.

'Go on.'

'My cousin's got a van.'

Even in this early stage of our acquaintance, he was already demonstrating an unerring ability to wrong-foot me. That could have been accident or design, but something was already telling me that little the large Maddox did was ever accidental.

'A van?'

And even at this early stage in our acquaintance I was also developing an unfortunate habit of repeating every left-field grenade he'd lob into any exchange.

Maddox looked at me again through the rear view mirror.

'You have vans in America?'

He prompted me.

'Big things, bigger than this, still got wheels at the four corners though.'

'We've got vans.'

Maddox nodded.

'He does a roaring trade out of it when the pubs close too, although I don't suppose you have that do you, pubs closing, or anything closing really, isn't that what they call your home, the city that never sleeps?'

'That's what they call it.'

'The Big Apple. They call it that too, right?'

'They call it that too.'

'An expression first used by Edward Martin in his book, *The Wayfarer in New York*.'

I looked at him.

'Is that right?'

Could you believe it? I'd lived there all my life and didn't know that.

'First published in 1909.'

'Well, there you go.'

'He said New York was merely one of the fruits of that great tree whose roots go down in the Mississippi valley and whose branches spread from one ocean to the other, but the Big Apple, New York, gets a disproportionate share of the national sap.'

Maddox nodded at me.

'We've got the same problem here. Outsiders grabbing more than their fair share. We call them the English.'

I really was going to have to watch this guy, wasn't I?

'Anyway, my cousin does a roaring trade like I said, mainly fish and chips, something of a national dish around here, but I was thinking, maybe we could adapt it a little for our overseas visitors, especially the Yanks, something a little more suited to the culture and then it came to me, in a flash.'

Maddox paused, maximum effect.

'Burgers.'

I nodded.

'We like burgers.'

'With a twist.'

'Always good to vary the mix a little.'

But all of a sudden he was off on another of his tangents again.

'We could roll it out too – extend the franchise as I think you Americans might call it – Fern Hill Fancies, maybe.'

I stared, not replying, not needing to, my face saying it all anyway.

Fern Hill what?

'Liquorice Laments.'

I kept staring.

'We could even try Countryman's Candy for those of a sweet-toothed disposition, but just to kick it all off – .'

I was still just staring as Maddox paused, just about resisting the temptation to parrot all that back at him

'The Boat House Burger.'

Then he nodded at me again, seemingly genuinely curious now.

'As a Yank yourself, how do you think that would go down?'

We arrived in the small village twenty minutes later although, according to Maddox, it was actually more properly described as a town. A very small town from what I could see, fringed by an estuary. You dropped down into it from a single road that led you in at one end and spirited you out the other, taking the traveler on to more villages hugging the bank of that same estuary until it opened out into the sea.

On the drive down into the town, Maddox told me a little about the corporation that seemed to govern the place, presided over by the Stateside equivalent of a Mayor, only here this head honcho was called a Portreeve. This Portreeve, apparently, wore a traditional chain of golden cockleshells, one added by each succeeding Portreeve in turn with his name and the date of his tenure stamped on the back.

According to Maddox the corporation held a court twice a year, dealing with land disputes and even some minor criminal cases and every three years they also presided over a Common Walk which had something to do with preserving the old boundaries of the town. It seemed that in older days – and not just in that small town, but throughout Europe too – there were few maps or documents to define ownership, so boundaries were walked instead with key points along the way physically touched by the walkers so everyone knew where they were.

I didn't quite get it if truth be told. Imagine that happening in NYC, right? But I did pick up on the fact the local pubs opened at five in the morning to provide the walkers with the liquid sustenance apparently required to fortify them for the rigors of the day ahead.

I also recorded – for Con's later delectation and to prove that I really had been soaking in all the local atmosphere and gossip – that at different significant historical landmarks one of the walkers would be asked to name the spot. These included, according to Maddox again, such places as Spring Mead, Merry Moor, Beggars Bush, Knave Lane, Mackerel Lake, and Oaten Cake And Cheese. They all sounded pretty memorable to me but, apparently, there were those in the village who'd forget where they were at the time of asking, although maybe that was something to do with those local pubs opening at dawn. By way of admonishment the forgetful miscreant would then be hoisted upside down and beaten three times on the rear.

I checked into a small bed and breakfast on the main street opposite a pub that, so I was told, was something of a second home to our visiting poet. There was a path at the rear of the pub that led to a lane at the end of which was his house, but I didn't do any exploring in that direction that night. Instead I wandered round the strange little town for a while before I spotted a phone booth on the edge of the small estuary inlet. I checked my watch and did some calculations. Beth really should be home by now.

Heading inside I dialed the operator and negotiated the equivalent of the plane fare over the Pond for a few moments conversation with my wife. A short time later – time spent watching a couple of local women spin flatfish up from the bed of the estuary into pots with their bare hands – Beth's voice wafted across the ocean.

'Hi.'

It was weird but it happened every time. Whenever I was away from her all she had to do was speak just one simple word of greeting and it felt like someone had reached inside and twisted my guts.

We caught up. I told her about the journey – especially the last bit on the train along the beach – and about the town I'd reached.

'I'm looking back at the Square. Only it's not really a square at all. And the town's not really a town either. And there's this smell too, not unpleasant, sort of tangy coming from this small factory along the street and there's a boat, well the ribs of it anyway, sticking up out of the mud.'

I looked round, wishing I had more of Subject Thomas's facility with language even if I still couldn't understood a single word he'd written.

'It's a strange place, sort of cut-off from the rest of the world.'

Beth's honeyed voice came down the line again.

'Sounds nice.'

'Yeah, it is. I wasn't too sure when I first got here, but – .'

I paused, looking round, not quite able to get my head round it all, not quite sure why I liked it in truth.

Then I remembered a home-made flyer I'd seen on the wall of a school some few moments before, a forbidding-looking building with windows set high up in those walls, ensuring – presumably – that once inside, no daydreaming student could look out.

'Oh – and there's some kind of carnival taking place tomorrow.'

I looked round again.

'But right now it's quiet. Real quiet. Can actually hear yourself think.'

Back came Beth's voice again but this time there was something new in it, something questioning, slightly wary, something that once again I couldn't quite place.

'And that's good is it, Jimmy?'

I looked at the phone. For that moment it was just Beth and myself in the universe, nothing else, just a man in a phone booth three thousand miles away from home and a woman in a city that the wildlife fringing these shores would never recognize as anything built by the hand of man.

'What does that mean?'

'Sounds a simple enough sort of question to me.'

I let the silence stretch. An old investigator's trick. Let the mark do the talking and they usually did so for the simple reason that they're the ones with something to hide so they're usually the ones with something to say. The guilty rarely take refuge in silence despite the protection afforded by our famous Fifth Amendment.

'A package arrived today from the phone company. A print-out of our calls.'

And now, on the bank of that estuary, I was the one who started to feel edgy, sweat beginning to prick my scalp, a damp feeling stealing under my arms and that wasn't due to any unseasonable heat, this place certainly wasn't defying the conventions of the seasons; we were now well into the fall and this place was cold.

'Yeah, I wanted to check the bill.'

Was it my imagination or was my voice beginning to affect a stammer, my tone sounding just that little too stridently self-righteous?

'I think we've been over-charged.'

Beth let the silence stretch.

And stretch.

An old investigator's trick.

Let the mark do the talking etc., etc.

'Look – Beth – .'

Finally I spoke but I wasn't destined to do so for much longer. A succession of pips suddenly sounded, signaling the approaching end of the conversation.

I tried calling for the operator in case she was listening in on the last few seconds of the call as I knew they sometimes did, at the same time as hunting in my pockets for coins that might prolong the transatlantic contact for at least a few more moments.

'Beth – Beth?'

All the time I called out her name, receiving only silence by way of a reply. I could almost feel her listening but she didn't say a word as I flapped around the booth. Then the line went dead.

I stood in the phone booth, receiver still in hand. Outside, a large bird I'd later identify as a heron stared at me, unblinking as if I was some sort of exotic visitation. Later again I'd discover the booth was its regular place of shelter on cold nights and the heron was now waiting for the intruder to vacate it.

Which I did. A minute or so later. And headed back up a short hill, past a large clock set into a small tower, past three-story houses crowding the small main street, back to my simple bed, all the time with the sound of silence from across the ocean ringing in my ears.

8

THE NEXT MORNING dawned, but it wasn't Beth I was thinking about. Now there was only one thing on my mind and that was my employer.

The day began with Maddox. I was fast beginning to realize that he wasn't just the local taxi driver and inventor of strange-sounding schemes to relieve passing tourists of their unfamiliar notes and coins. According to my talkative landlady he also ran the town's electric generator as well as a vehicle repair shop. But he seemed to be some sort of unofficial Master of Ceremonies as well and it was in that capacity that I first heard his booming voice the following morning.

'Off and on, up and down, high and dry, man and boy, I've been living now for fifteen years, or centuries, in this timeless, beautiful, barmy – .'

And now Maddox broke off, his face splitting into the largest, widest grin.

' – both spellings – .'

Then he resumed.

' – town, in this far, forgetful, important place of herons, cormorants – known here as billyduckers – castle, churchyard, gulls, ghosts, geese, feuds, scares, scandals, cherry-trees, mysteries, jackdaws in the chimneys, bats in the belfry, skeletons in the cupboards – .'

Each phrase was greeted with a resounding cheer, a swelling cacophony of approval and I was becoming impressed. Maybe it was a touch lyrical for some ears but Maddox certainly had a turn of phrase at his disposal.

I headed outside only to realize that he was reading from a piece of paper. And a quick interrogation of a neighbor standing next to me in the appreciative crowd established that this composition wasn't of Maddox's making. This was an out-take from some radio broadcast recorded by Subject Thomas before his latest trip and given to Maddox to open his home carnival in his absence.

I listened on, now with renewed interest.

'Whatever the reason, if any, for our being here, in this timeless, mild, beguiling island of a town with its seven public houses, one chapel in action, one church, one factory, two billiard tables, one St Bernard – without brandy – .'

Another great cheer from the watchers.

What the hell did that mean?

' – one policeman – .'

Who now duly took a bow.

' – three rivers, a visiting sea, one Rolls-Royce selling fish and chips, one cannon – cast-iron, one chancellor – flesh and blood, one Portreeve, one Danny Raye – .'

Which heralded another bow from, presumably, the named dignitary standing on the other side of the street and which provoked another great cheer.

' – and a multitude of mixed birds, here we just are, and there is nowhere like it, anywhere at all.'

Yet another great cheer sounded, but now I wasn't looking at Maddox any longer or watching the delighted reactions of the swelling crowd.

All of a sudden I saw her. Across the street. Standing in the middle of all the other attendees, but a little apart from them as if they were giving her room which maybe they were.

Subject Thomas. Female. A striking woman in her mid to late thirties. Sharp features, hair tied back accentuating those features all the more. A woman who looked as if she wasn't to be trifled with. A woman – in strict contrast to the rest of the audience for that impromptu rendition that morning – who didn't look as if she was taking the slightest amount of pleasure in listening to a single word of it. Indeed, as Maddox continued and as the roars of the appreciative crowd swelled more and more, her face seemed to darken with each word. And as Maddox's retelling of their famous son's tribute to his adopted town continued, she just seemed to become ever more embittered. At the same time those around her allowed her ever more space as if increasingly fearful of an explosion of some kind. Then, as Maddox came towards the end of the recitation, but before he could intone the final flourish, she turned and was gone.

Through the crowd, I saw her heading away past the local pub. For the next fifteen minutes or so – as the preparations for a carnival procession took place – I paced the main street unsure what to do. The carnival should have been a bonus, a chance to see Subject Thomas, female, at close quarters, out in public, among her companions. How the hell was I even going to begin to get close to the little lady back home as Con called her, if she'd now locked herself inside that home, upset in some way by the talk she'd just listened to out on the street?

Then, as the carnival procession made to move off to travel the half-mile or so from one end of the village to the other, she reappeared, a little more strained in the face perhaps, a little more tense, but aside from that she seemed to be the same woman who'd absented herself just a short time before.

Until the crowd parted and I could see her a little more clearly – and it became all-too obvious that if Maddox had afforded Subject Thomas his all-too public stage earlier that morning, she was about to stake her very own claim to that same all-too public stage now too.

My log to Con, typed up a little later that same day and wired over from the nearest large town, sort of said it all. I was going to send an accompanying note. It was going to read something along the lines of – 'Did I say all your Christmases rolled into one? And your birthdays and every Thanksgiving too, Con' – but then decided just to send the log unadorned by anything else.

Reading it again, it didn't seem to need it.

Report, Subject Thomas. Female.

1300 Hours. Grist Square in Laugharne.

And yep, that's the name of the place, Con, pronounced Larne and don't even ask why they spell it one way and say it another, no-one seems to know and no-one seems to care.

Opening ceremony, the town's annual carnival.

Subject Thomas, female, arrives dressed in full Moulin Rouge costume.

I didn't know how else to describe it. I didn't know where the hell she'd got it from and most of the onlookers seemed pretty bemused by it too. Maybe it spiced up the long evenings back home with Mr Poet. It certainly spiced up that carnival that day.

Subject Thomas, female, proceeds to dance a can-can.

She wasn't bad either, had clearly had some sort of professional training of some kind.

– for a full half-mile –

Not that any of the onlookers were even remotely interested in her technique.

– wearing no panties.

I didn't realize at the start. It was the growing noise from the drinkers outside the various pubs that first alerted me but even then it took a few more moments to sink in. What the hell was she doing? Actually, as questions go, that was one of the dumbest that could have floated through my disbelieving mind. It was pretty obvious, after all, what she was doing. She was putting on the kind of floorshow that wouldn't be forgotten around those parts in a hurry, that was for sure. Why she was doing it was going to prove a little more difficult to explain.

And she wasn't finished yet.

By now most of the villagers had packed into the bar, some even overflowing out into the street but most with a view of the inside if only through one of the open windows. I'd managed to squeeze into a small gap by a dartboard that some of the enterprising locals had apparently managed to sell around twenty times over to gullible admirers of their local scribe. There was some kind of talent contest going on inside but that wasn't the main focus of attention right now. As a few hours previously, all eyes were on one woman and one woman only.

Subject Thomas, female, lines up twelve men along the bar.

For all the world as if she was a Sheriff in the Wild West lining up some kind of makeshift identity parade.

Subject Thomas, female, moves from male to male, assessing and inspecting each in turn.

Now perhaps more in the manner of an auctioneer assessing prime cuts of beef.

Subject Thomas, female, selects one man in particular, takes companion outside into a small alleyway at the rear of the pub –

To the accompaniment – need I mention it – of yet more raucous cheers from the onlookers.

– where she proceeds to entertain him.

Con would have enjoyed that last touch particularly. Less was always more when it came to those sort of reports. Some rather more lurid description might have gone down well in the clubby environs of Con's office but if this ever came to court it wouldn't sound too good being read out before some judge somewhere. It was always better to appear calm and measured, in fact the more outlandish the events detailed, the calmer and the more measured the reporting the better. It seemed to immediately award the high ground to the recorder of the excesses. One of the tricks of the trade I'd learnt fairly early on and one that was still standing me in good stead.

Report, Subject Thomas, female.

1900 Hours. Victoria Street. Laugharne.

Which was just round the corner from Brown's Hotel. Subject Thomas, female, was about to head home but first there was another distraction to deal with. A woman, soon to be identified as the common law partner of her previous chosen companion – they didn't seem too hot on actual marriages in this part of the world – was barring the way. She didn't seem too happy that her partner had become that chosen companion. And within a few moments there was some fresh cabaret to savor.

A fist fight involving Subject Thomas, female, and another local female.

And there was only going to be one victor from the start. The common law partner of the chosen companion might have had right on her side but Subject Thomas, female, sure had a mean left hook on hers.

Subject Thomas, female, wins the exchange. The other local female departs for the local County Hospital in an ambulance with a severe head wound, requiring stitches and, later, surgery.

And now, in respect of her next trick, it was difficult not to append some sort of accompanying note, to put something in the report to alert Con in some way even if it was never going to be read out in court. Apart from anything else, Con might have thought I'd lost my mind or taken up some new life as a cheap novelist as opposed to the supposedly-dispassionate observer of all-too human foibles he thought he'd employed.

Because did this beat everything Mr Poet was doing back in the Big Apple, or did it not?

I'd noticed some construction work going on in and around the village when I'd first arrived. It had caused some bad feeling locally according to the landlady of the bed and breakfast under whose roof I was currently encamped. I found out about it as initially she thought – with my somewhat exotic accent – that I might be associated with the construction company in some way.

The company had been employed to lay down the pipes that would bring the first mains water to the town. Up to that point the residents had relied on a series of old brooks and even older wells for their drinking and bathing. But the company – called Watson and Horrocks, a name I'd included in my report for added verisimilitude – had shunned the local workforce for reasons known only to themselves and had instead recruited a party of laborers from Ireland who were brought in each day from an outlying town to carry out the work. The laborers – some twelve in total and their work over for the day – now joined the carnival crowd, some of whom clearly didn't like their presence among them and made little attempt to hide their hostility.

But not everyone had a problem with them.

Subject Thomas, female, seems to get a new lease of life at their appearance. Within thirty minutes –

And here I felt the need to repeat the last two words, even in this, the official report, knowing how a mind can sometimes take time to absorb these finer details.

– that's thirty minutes, Subject Thomas, female, has taken up residence in the same rear alley as previously. This time she entertains all twelve gentlemen, one at a time while the rest form an orderly queue.

You want the truth? Everything else might have contained within it an element of cabaret. Everything else Subject Thomas, female, had done that day might have been entertaining in some way even if the common law partner of the chosen one might have been hard-pressed to see the joke. Everything else she'd done that day might, in some way, be put down to the intoxication of the proceedings, an over-exuberant abandonment in the moment.

But there was no fun here. Nothing about this even remotely attained the status of cabaret. There was something else going on instead, something that withered any smile on the faces of those who witnessed it – and there were plenty. Even the laborers waiting patiently in line seemed to sense they were taking part in something they really didn't want to contemplate too deeply. Something dark and subterranean. Something hidden they really didn't want to bring to the surface.

Subject Thomas, female, didn't even seem to be there. Her body was going through the motions as each man approached and as he concluded his business. You really couldn't call it anything else. But all the while she looked beyond the next man who then mounted her, looked beyond the dwindling line of men waiting to do the same, beyond the expanding line of men recovering from their efforts on the other side of the lane, beyond the fast-retreating crowd of onlookers, beyond the small lanes and smaller cottages of that small town, beyond the estuary and out at something I couldn't even begin to divine.

I also couldn't even begin to work out what was driving her to do all this, in much the same way as I couldn't understand what was driving her husband to his own catalogue of excess some three thousand or so miles away.

What the hell was going on here? Was it some weird game of one-upmanship? Anything one can do the other could do better – or worse – in some way? Did they swop notes each night, did she make that same transatlantic phone call from the same phone booth I'd used to contact Beth, did he tell her the events of his days and nights and she returned to their home, determined to match him in some way, surpass him indeed if the events of that day, including its inglorious end, were anything to go by?

But I doubted it. At least then there would have been

some element of enjoyment in it all, some triumph in a task that, however twisted in conception, was successful at least in execution.

This was bleak. This was barren. This wasn't a woman setting out to prove any kind of point or win any kind of battle, this was a woman who'd seemed to have hit the depths only to find there was further to go and determined, for reasons I still couldn't understand, to plunge those depths even further.

None of that went in the report by the way. I just stuck with the facts for Con. Something told me he wouldn't have appreciated those sort of embellishments.

'This is it.'

Maddox had met me outside the Town Hall. It was the morning after the carnival and most of the other residents were still indoors. Recovering from their exertions the previous day, no doubt. Subject Thomas, female, hadn't been seen since her spectacular floorshow. No-one knew when she would be seen and no-one was going to enquire too deeply either. She was that kind of woman and this was that kind of place.

We'd taken a left after heading back towards Brown's Hotel which, like the rest of the town, was closed right now. Turning by another pub called the Three Mariners, we'd paused outside a tall, three-story house that had – according to Maddox – been the first home in the area for the male and female Subjects Thomas.

'Landlord was Tudor Williams.'

Was that supposed to mean anything to me?

'Brother of the landlord of Brown's.'

Or that?

'Seven shillings and sixpence a week they paid him in rent.'

I did a quick mental calculation, swopped pounds and

pennies for dollars and cents, stared at what looked like a mansion before me, compared that to the small rabbit hutch myself and Beth inhabited in New York and began to see some point to it after all.

Taking a gentle left at the bottom of the street we came onto a narrow lane. On the right the blue of the estuary could be seen through the overhanging trees, along with the odd house clinging to the cliff leading down to the bank. Bushes and hanging plants trailed all the way down the cliff face.

Halfway along the lane – and having survived the determined attentions of assorted low-lying branches to bar our progress – we stopped outside a small shack, built onto a tiny promontory looking out over the water.

I looked at Maddox, repeated his own words back to him.

'This is it?'

My official taxi driver and – for today – unofficial guide nodded back.

'This is where he works.'

I looked at the unprepossessing structure. For some reason I expected more. Decorated friezes studding the walls. Engraved angels around the door. Something more befitting the endeavors of a poet at least. Beth's uncle had a similar place to this back in Nova Scotia. He did a roaring trade from inside, repairing motorcycles.

'A little shack on the side of a cliff?'

Maddox didn't seem to hear me.

'It's been here since the Twenties. Dr Cowan – died before the war, he did – he spent his holidays here and he bought it to house his car. A Wolseley. Very nice car it was too, caused quite a stir in these parts.'

Then Maddox looked at the small structure, quite clearly still unable to get his head round what was obviously a local monument to astonishing extravagance.

'The shed cost five pounds. But he paid seventy-five pounds to have it put up.'

Maddox shook his head.

'Seventy-five pounds for a garage when you could buy a house for less than two hundred.'

'He must really have liked his car.'

'Billy Williams from Meidrim, he built it in sections, then brought it over on a horse and cart.'

Maddox nodded inside.

'Of course the stove wasn't in there then or anything else.'

There was a window let into the door and I peered inside. Two further windows at the far end looked out onto the estuary, additions to the original structure, I later discovered, that had been carried out at the behest of Subject Thomas's wife.

As I picked out some details – a chair pushed back at an angle – papers screwed up and thrown under a desk jammed up against the far window – Maddox pushed against the door which swung open.

'Go in if you like. It's never locked.'

Inside, the walls were lined with various photographs and cuttings torn from magazines. Walt Whitman was there along with some more obscure figures identified by captions under their faces – Louis MacNeice, another poet, so I discovered – along with William Blake and W. H. Auden. There was a reproduction of a painting by some artist called Modigliani and some nudes chosen more for their visual appeal than any intrinsic artistic merit they may have possessed, at least to my, admittedly untutored, eye.

I moved up to the desk, although it was more of an old table. There were lots of different scraps of paper on there too, all covered in spidery writing, sometimes lines, but more often just words, sometimes the same word, repeated over and over, list after list it seemed of variations on a theme.

There were also letters or beginnings of letters, at least five or six that I could see, all decorated with strange drawings and odd little faces as well as various magazines. There was something called *Horizon*, as well as what seemed at first glance to be an Italian offering, *Botteghe Oscure*.

There was also – another surprise – a small collection of dime-store edition detective stories.

I looked back at Maddox, suddenly aware he'd been watching me all the time from the door. For a large man he had a disconcerting ability to meld into the background.

'And this is all there is?'

I nodded round.

'Some bits of paper, a table and a chair?'

'What more does a poet need?'

Maddox pretended to consider his own question.

'Except maybe a pen.'

I looked out through one of the two windows, paused.

'Great view, though.'

Maddox joined me, nodded at what I was to discover later again was the east window.

'Look out through there and you'll see the ferryman.'

Another large figure – large indeed even at this distance – was visible down on the estuary.

'That's Booda, he works the ferry path across to Llanybri. Just been released from custody he has, some numbskull in the police got it in his head Booda had killed an old lady a few miles down the road, Pendine way. All nonsense of course, but how could Booda deny it with him being deaf and dumb?'

Then Maddox nodded over the water.

'Those are the fields of Pentowin and if you look through the other window – .'

Next, Maddox nodded to my side.

' – that's the Llanstephan peninsula and if this was a fine

day you could see all the way down to Worm's Head which our famous poet once commemorated in a poem.'

But I kept looking out over the water, at the hills to all sides, hardly listening.

'Really is some view.'

Maddox looked at me, amused again.

'You don't have views in America?'

'Not like this.'

I nodded directly ahead at a hill opposite, small buildings hugging the side. Then again, every building everywhere I looked right now seemed to be hugging the side of some hill or other.

Maddox followed my look.

'That's Sir John's Hill.'

'So who's Sir John?'

But Maddox seemed to have something else in mind.

'And that farm on the top?'

I followed his nod, could just about make it out, some distant figures visible, moving between outbuildings.

'Just above the woods?'

Maddox nodded, gratified, as if I'd just fed him some sort of punchline and for good reason.

'That's the local dairy, keeps the whole town supplied with milk.'

I looked at him, blank. For some reason he seemed to think I'd find that significant in some way.

'Under Milk Wood.'

Fragments of my last briefing with Con swam back through my mind. That play, the reason – or the ostensible reason – the resident of this small shack had come over to the US in the first place, the play for voices.

I stared around some more. The guy was writing about his home. He was writing about the view from outside his window. He'd traveled three thousand miles to put the home he lived

114

in and the people he lived among day in, day out, on a foreign stage, which seemed sort of curious.

A bit like the behavior of his wife. A bit like his behavior too, I guess. All building the developing sense I was experiencing of a world more and more out of step with itself. Something wrong – maybe rotten even – at its core.

I moved closer to the window, taking in more details of the landscape outside as well as Subject Thomas's home, now just glimpsed along the lane, a three-story structure adorned with balconies and verandas and boasting what looked like a stepped garden.

And now just one question dominated.

'Why would a man ever want to leave a view like this?'

'Maybe he doesn't.'

I looked at him, work mode kicking back in and maybe it was time too. Spend too much longer daydreaming out of riverbank windows and Con really was going to start thinking I was losing my grip.

'He has, hasn't he?'

'And you've never done things you didn't want to do?'

It was like he was trying to tell me something, but wasn't going to do anything so obvious as come straight out with it.

'No-one made him, did they? He's a free man.'

'I think that's what you Americans might call the sixty-four dollar question.'

I was impressed. It was a well-worn catchphrase back in the States. It had its roots in the CBS radio quiz show *Take It Or Leave It* which ran in the Forties, hosted by Bob Hawk and then Phil Baker. I didn't realize it transmitted in the UK as well but maybe it didn't. Maybe Maddox was just well up to speed on all matters Stateside. Maybe Subject Thomas had debriefed him and the rest of the residents after his previous US trips.

I took a different tack. If any sort of regular debriefing had taken place, it was time to find out what else Mr Poet might have let slip.

'He's certainly enjoying himself too from everything the papers back in my country are saying.'

'We don't get the American papers.'

'Take my word for it.'

He just looked at me. I had the impression he wasn't too inclined to take my word about anything and something in the look stung me.

Who was the one acting badly round here? Why should I feel as if I was the one who had to apologize for something?

'While the cat's away, right, Maddox? Fun and games.'

He didn't speak for a moment and for a moment I thought he'd drifted off somewhere across that estuary, over those fields, maybe even along the lane to that house by the water. Maybe it was an occupational hazard, living in such close proximity to a poet. Maybe at times it transported a body and soul to some other place entirely.

'So it's true what they say about you Americans, then?'

'Which is?'

'They talk a lot. Don't listen too much.'

There wasn't actually any hostility – or even criticism – in the simple observation. It sounded a little like Beth. There just seemed something resembling sadness behind it instead.

I stared at him.

'Is that supposed to make any kind of sense?'

Maddox just inclined his head towards me, softening the words with a smile just in case I was inclined in turn to take any offence.

'Point made. Wouldn't you say?'

Maddox leant down to the floor, picked up a book that had been discarded or dropped from one of the makeshift shelves and handed it to me. I looked at the front cover. It was another collection of poems written by the great man.

'Here – take one of his books. There's always lots lying around.'

I was about to say I wasn't much of a man for poetry but stopped myself just in time. Then again, I didn't know why. I knew he hadn't remotely bought my story of being a journalist on some sort of fact-finding mission anyway.

Maddox looked at me as if he could read my thoughts and once again I had the strange and disconcerting suspicion that maybe he could.

'You might surprise yourself.'

I didn't open the book. Instead I went for a walk. I crossed the cliff top to another bay and then another. It was low tide and I rounded a point that had been previously hidden by the sea. Across the estuary – at its widest now – the small train I'd traveled down on those couple of days before, chugged its way back up the line.

I came out onto a small beach tucked in between two cliffs. A house looked down onto the sand, a small slipway leading from the house onto what looked like a private beach. Out in the bay the ever-present cockle gatherers were at work again, their ever-patient donkeys at their sides, the cockle gatherers scooping their catches into large canvas bags.

I sat on the beach and stared out over the water. I'd be leaving in the morning and for some reason right now I just wanted to be alone. I had the long flight back to the States to write my log for Con, to devote to what you might call business.

Instead I looked out over the water and imagined Beth and myself, sitting here on this beach, a million miles away from everything and everyone we knew. Part of that terrified me. Part of it excited me beyond anything I'd care to admit or explore.

It was strange. Unsettling. Not that I actually wanted to leave NYC and settle in this strange and out-of-the-way place. I had no desire to suddenly turn this work trip into anything more permanent even if it might have allowed me to crack the deepening mystery that was my erstwhile companion, the enigmatic Maddox.

Not to mention my absent companion, Subject Thomas.

Not to mention his equally puzzling wife.

So what was it that kept me on that beach long after the light had faded and the tide returned meaning I'd have to find a different way back to that strange little town and my bed for the night?

What was it that made me postpone even that delayed return, taking in more moonlit bays on the long walk back, exploring every one before moving on again, keeping company with assorted rabbits and foxes that dashed past me in the dark?

I still didn't know in the morning and I still hadn't opened the book that Maddox had handed to me either. But whatever the answer, I had a shrewd suspicion I wouldn't find it among those pages.

9

BUT PLANE JOURNEYS are long. Like, really long. Not helped by the coldest of cold snaps that had frozen the wings of that west-bound aircraft into a solid mass and delayed my departure back to the States by five hours. Add that to the fourteen-hour journey ahead of me – and that was minimum – and that was a lot of time to kill. Small wonder then that at a certain stage in that journey I'd run out of magazines to read, reports to complete and airline safety messages to absorb.

At which point I did what I thought I'd never do when Maddox first picked up that dog-eared volume from that rubbish-strewn floor and handed it to me. I opened up some more of Subject Thomas's poetry and began to read, and read properly too as opposed to the somewhat bewildered scanning I'd managed so far.

Which I'd like to say was a life-changing moment. I'd like to report light breaking into that small silver cabin as the celestial heavens illuminated a thunderbolt of understanding deep inside my head. I'd like to say the rest of the journey passed in a blur of new-found self-realization as my eyes were opened to a world hitherto obscured from my now-grateful view.

But it didn't. Yes, I had experienced something of a sea change in my attitude to the natural world on my night-time walk the previous evening; I'd always been something of a city boy and had never understood till then the more simple delights of the great outdoors. But I wasn't, it seemed, destined to experience the same sort of about-turn when it came to all matters poetic. In that regard I'd always been much more of a dime store story kind of guy and so, it appeared, I would remain.

I opened the pages at random and was initially encouraged

in that at least I was able to just about understand the first line I encountered. After my experiences on the way over I really was beginning to wonder if this guy was perpetrating some kind of gigantic confidence trick on us all. The Emperor's Clothes and all that.

Now as I was young and easy under the apple boughs...

But hey, breakthrough time. Yeah, I'd felt pretty easy when I was young and I guess I'd have felt even more so if I'd been looking up and seeing apple boughs rather than roofs of Long Island tenements.

I hunched over the slim volume, more energized now.

About the lilting house and happy as the grass was green...

But now I was beginning to get that all-too familiar cold feeling creeping into my stomach, the feeling that everyone else was in on some kind of joke and I was the fool, excluded.

Happy as the grass was green? What the hell did that mean? And what kind of house lilts and what was a lilt anyway?

Less encouraged, I scanned down some more, pausing briefly at such offerings as – *the sabbath rang slowly in the pebbles of the holy streams* – what? – pausing again as I read about some owls that were *bearing the farm away* – like, how?

From down the aisle the stewardess approached, pushing a trolley. Most of the travelers in the cabin were sleeping now which was what I should have been doing, and soundly too. Instead I bent to the slim volume before me and tried one last time.

Nothing I cared, in the lamb white days, that time would take me

Up to the swallow thronged loft by the shadow of my hand...

A voice cut across, the stewardess, her practiced eye registering one pair of eyes awake and more or less alert in the middle of all those slumbering mouths.

'Anything to drink, sir?'

She smiled, practiced again, but warm enough.

'Coffee? A soft drink? Maybe a beer?'

I nodded back.

'A beer, thanks.'

I was beginning to feel as if I needed it. The stewardess – who clearly had a practiced hand as well as those eyes and that smile – whipped the top off the bottle with a smooth motion, placing it down on the small tray in front of me, nodding at my book at the same time.

'Must be good.'

'What makes you say that?'

'There must have been about fifty people reading books on this flight. You're the only one still awake.'

'Cramps.'

'Excuse me?'

'They keep me awake too. Nothing good about them though.'

She rippled a soft laugh. Maybe it was part of the training. How to laugh without waking any nearby snoozing souls.

'Head colds always do it for me. One of those little beauties and I may as well be on a red-eye for a week.'

She made to pass on but on an impulse I stopped her.

'Can you do me a favor?'

She eyed me, half-amused, half-wary. How many propositions had she fielded on just that flight alone? Her expression was saying it all. Here comes another.

'Can you read this?'

Her stare faltered a little.

'Not the whole thing, just a couple of lines maybe. I've been trying to get my head round it for the last half-hour.'

I hesitated.

'I'd really like to know if it's just me.'

She hesitated for a moment too, then looked round the cabin

but no-one else seemed to want anything. So she looked back at me and shrugged.

'Here to be of service. Isn't that what the airline always tells us?'

I handed over the book, nodding at the last verse.

'Just that one.'

And she began. Straightaway, no hesitating, no faltering, no stumbling over the unfamiliar cadences or the strangely juxtaposed words.

Nothing I cared, in the lamb white days, that time would take me

Up to the swallow thronged loft by the shadow of my hand,
In the moon that is always rising,

And now her voice was growing in confidence all the time.

Nor that riding to sleep
I should hear him fly with the high fields
And wake to the farm forever fled from the childless land.

I nodded, approvingly.

'Hey, not bad.'

I was rewarded with a dazzling smile but she didn't pause, just kept straight on.

Oh as I was young and easy in the mercy of his means,
Time held me green and dying
Though I sang in my chains like the sea.

I looked at her as she came to a halt.

'You understand that?'

'No.'

She shrugged.

'But maybe you don't need to.'

Now it was my turn to stare at her.

'Excuse me?'

'Maybe you just need to feel it.'

She smiled at me as she handed back the book before moving

on, another passenger on the far side of the cabin having just woken up.

I looked back at the book, the brief lifting of my spirits occasioned by that whispered exchange between two strangers now well and truly behind me. For some reason I actually felt like scowling.

Yeah, I muttered, under my breath, let me show you the guy who wrote it.

Let's see how you feel then.

For the rest of the flight I didn't think about slim volumes of poetry. In among the pile of papers I'd brought with me from the apartment – mostly Subject Thomas-related – there were some papers that were very definitely not. Papers I hadn't looked at in years. Papers that, at one time or another, I'd contemplated throwing out but had never quite managed to do so. Maybe that was just plain indolence, maybe it was because I always had been a hoarder. Maybe it was something else.

A few years previously I hadn't been content with just scraping some money together for what myself and Beth had called the college fund. OK, I couldn't actually enrol on any courses back then – some of the organizations to which I was going to apply had a reputation for being relatively generous, but none were prepared to take on a prospective student for a great, big, not-so-fat zero which pretty well described the state of our finances at that time. But no-one could stop me conducting my own researches into the thorny issue of crime and the law, which is what I did via various libraries and the occasional free course at the odd night school that would open its doors to those who sought a better life for themselves and their own.

I began with history. One phrase from my early researches had always resonated with me. Because historical analysis, so the primer declared, was simply the application of logic, the kind of logic you might employ in any other investigation.

And that appealed to me. As if, in some way and by working my way through those dusty volumes, by sitting in a cold classroom before a tutor already exhausted by the demands of his or her day not to mention those additional evening duties, I might feel close to some kind of ongoing tradition. As if I may, somehow, become part of it all.

But it wasn't the dry retelling of facts that enthralled me. Even then it was the personalities that really engaged my imagination. History as lived by the characters who created it. Men – and women – who'd become heroes in some way through their achievements in their chosen field. Men and women I'd sought, at one time anyway, to emulate.

Men like Jonathan Wild, although maybe here there was less to emulate than most. Wild, I guess, became the world's first private investigator. He was a buckle-maker in rural England who moved to London but who soon spotted a very different gap in the contemporary market.

Wild established a new business whereby he would charge a fee for locating stolen property and returning it to its owner. In those crime-infested days his new business flourished. He soon expanded from simple property to the apprehension of actual felons as well. A new law awarded him up to forty pounds for the capture of the really juicy villains of the day.

The problem being that Wild's ethics left something to be desired because he wasn't just a thief-taker, he became something of a thief-maker as well. When trade was slack he oiled the wheels a little. He'd encourage those of his acquaintance to become involved in theft in order to later apprehend them and claim his subsequent reward, although not before fencing the goods appropriated by the same illicit activity.

It didn't end well for Wild. After years of pursuing those who stole from others he was finally convicted of robbery himself and hanged. He was hardly a role model but he had identified a specific and pressing need for law and order and it was a mantle picked up by a man who began as his biographer but who soon became his successor.

Henry Fielding had previously chronicled Wild's life in a satirical book. But he'd become obsessed by the same issues that, initially at least, entranced his mentor, and Fielding established a police force to deal with what seemed to him to be a total breakdown in law and order.

There were three divisions, a foot patrol that worked in the city, a horse patrol that monitored the outlying areas or suburbs as they came to be known and – the most interesting of all to me anyway – the detective unit, successors to Wild's thief-takers. This latter creation formed themselves into a plainclothes unit and didn't only concern themselves with pioneering such modern-day techniques as paying informants, they also probed into crime causation. Fielding was an early pioneer in that field as in so much else.

The plane banked and I reached out my hand, stopped my beer – long forgotten – rolling into the lap of my still-slumbering neighbor. The bright young stewardess was behind a curtain fixing juice for serving before the descent. On my lap was the next stage in my trawl through the strange and wonderful world of crime in all its many forms and the character who probably, out of them all, had really captured my imagination.

Crime and how to fight it wasn't just an English preoccupation at that time. All over Europe different countries were grasping the same thorny nettle and none more so than France where a former convict called Vidocq was about to rise to prominence.

Vidocq was the classic example of poacher turned

gamekeeper. A habitual criminal, he'd escaped from prison many times but on one notable day had actually sought out the local police rather than fleeing from them. Maybe he was just plain tired of running.

Whatever the reason, Vidocq proposed a trade. He knew just about everyone and anyone in the Parisian underworld. So he offered to become an informer if the police dropped all ongoing charges against him.

The deal was too good to resist and Vidocq went on to put some eight hundred people behind bars. But he didn't stop there. He was made head of the Paris Sûreté in 1827 after establishing his very own investigative unit with a unique proposition at its core – that serious crime can best be fought by criminals. He rounded up twenty convicts – men much like himself – from which he created the nucleus of the French Criminal Investigation Department, inveigling men into prisons to obtain information about their fellow convicts as well as exploiting numerous other undercover techniques.

The wily Vidocq did everything. Police investigation, private investigation – even, later in life, counter-terrorism activities for no less a personage than Napoleon III. He also found time to write several books, one on the criminal classes of France, still a classic. I'd raced through it after the class devoted to Vidocq and his colorful activities. I was due at work at six the next morning but simply couldn't put it down.

Over in the UK, one Robert Peel was also placing police activity on a more organized and official footing, establishing the Metropolitan Police Force in 1829. A Criminal Investigation Unit soon followed as did the first use of the term 'detective' in print, by Charles Dickens no less, who wasn't destined to exactly fade away either.

Then came the Special Branch, formed in response to what was then called the Irish threat and modern-day crime fighters were born. No longer were they closely associated with the criminals themselves – one of the reasons the general public were slow to fully trust them. Now they were drawn from other classes and ranks of society such as non-commissioned, army officers. But back in the States it was a private rather than any public initiative that was changing the face of crime.

One man, one name. Pinkerton. He was actually a Scot but he came to bestride the US criminal scene like a latter-day colossus. Other private investigators were already at work, so he wasn't a pioneer in that sense. But Pinkerton put everything on an ultra-professional basis, instituting a proper wage system for his employees – or private detectives – as well as banning the practice of working for rewards.

Pinkerton also instituted the system of information-sharing, principally with Scotland Yard in the UK and the Paris Sûreté in France, the foundation for what, in later years, became Interpol.

Pinkerton was also a technology freak, embracing the new and occasionally dark art of photography, establishing the practice of handwriting examination and helping to centralize criminal identification records.

Like Vidocq in France, Pinkerton also became something of a personal hero. Maybe that's why I was so quick to embrace the latter-day incarnation of the work he'd instituted some fifty or so years before.

Thomas Byrnes of the New York City Police was another celebrated character who came under my night-time spotlight, instituting the famous Mulberry Street Parade where all criminals arrested in the previous twenty-four hours were marched before the city's detectives so they could be memorized and, later, described. Byrnes believed in getting personal and intimate with his criminal contacts, often using those thieves to catch thieves. If something tasty went missing from one of the houses of his up-market friends, Byrnes would put the word around the streets. The valuables in question, he made clear, would be returned by the end of the day. If they were not then the harshest retribution would follow. The valuables, invariably, would be reunited with their grieving owners.

Then August Vollmer took all Byrnes was doing and added science, pioneering the lie detector and setting up a police laboratory, as well as a college for police officers, liaising with leading scientists of the day on particularly baffling cases.

Over the speakers came the announcement that we would be landing in half an hour. The smiling stewardess began handing out the wake-up juice. All over the cabin passengers started to hunt among their possessions, getting ready to begin their day.

I remained stock-still, almost frozen, my research papers still open on my lap. It was a feeling I hadn't experienced for longer than I could remember. All I'd done was leaf through some old notes culled from a combination of even older books and the ramblings of tired professors. So why did I feel more alive than at any time in the last few years? It didn't make sense.

But maybe it didn't need to make sense. Maybe it was like the smiling stewardess and the poem by Subject Thomas. Maybe I didn't need to understand it, just feel it somehow.

But then the plane jerked as it landed and I jerked back to the land of the living at the same time – and put away my old lecture notes. I'd like to see how that would go down with Con.

'Don't read the log, don't try and understand it, just feel it, Con.'

Yeah, right. The next thing I'd have felt would have been his boot on my butt kicking me out of his office.

Kicking Beth and myself all the way back to where we came from.

10

THE CAB DROPPED me outside Stuy Town a couple of hours later. There'd been no visiting poets disturbing the officials on the arrivals gate this time, so everyone went through smoothly enough. The smiling stewardess was escorted off the plane by the captain. He was smiling too. Maybe they were going off somewhere to read poetry together. Maybe that's why she'd been so well disposed to my slim volume on that flight over from the UK. Or maybe it was something else.

I let myself into the apartment. It would be touch-and-go whether I'd catch Beth if she was working her usual shift. I hadn't been able to get through to her for a couple of days and didn't know. It did change pretty regularly though, as Beth often volunteered to do a few hours for some colleague with childcare problems. She'd tell them they could repay the favor sometime. She'd been saying it for quite a while now.

I paused as I came inside, immediately registering something amiss. The apartment looked the same – it was always kept as neat as a new pin, whatever the hell that was – but something was still different and I soon realized what. There was a different smell as I came in, something apart from the usual. It was perfume, that was for sure, but it wasn't Beth's perfume, so who the hell did it belong to? Had we had visitors, some female caller or other trying to sell something?

A few seconds later a larger version of Beth appeared in front of me as her big sister, Nora, came through from the bedroom, a small case in hand.

I nodded at her, puzzled.

'Nora.'

She called over pretty frequently. There was about eight years between them but Beth and herself had always been close. It wasn't that unusual seeing her there although she didn't usually carry a case. Her apartment was just Uptown so she rarely felt the need to stay over.

Then I realized she was carrying one of Beth's cases, not her own, and I began to suspect that staying over was probably the last thing on her mind right now.

'What are you doing?'

'Collecting some of Beth's things.'

Nora moved past me into the sitting room, picking up some more of Beth's underwear from a drying rack we'd put out on the small balcony to catch some rays as the sun, briefly given the proximity of the surrounding apartments, blessed our small part of the great outdoors.

I followed, floundering.

'What for? What do you mean, collecting some of her things, what's going on?'

Nora's tone remained calm, neutral.

'She's staying with me for a few days.'

Nora opened the bag which was stuffed full, I could see now, of quite a few more of Beth's clothes. We'd journeyed across to Montana the previous year, a four-week trip, part work, part vacation and Beth hadn't packed as much for that excursion as Nora was currently stuffing into that case right now.

'And what does that mean, she's staying with you? Why?'

Nora just looked at me for a moment and a chill feeling suddenly spread through me.

'She is OK, is she?'

She just looked back at me.

'Nora?'

But Nora didn't reply directly, just reached into her own smaller – much smaller – bag and extracted a sheaf of papers, handed them over to me.

'She asked me to leave these for you. I didn't know if I'd be seeing you so I was just going to leave them on the table.'

I took them, now more puzzled than ever.

'What are they?'

There were just lists of numbers on the pieces of paper, most of which meant nothing to me, not at first glance anyway.

For a moment Nora seemed tempted to just head away, leaving me to enlighten myself but then she hesitated. Maybe she was taking pity on me. Or maybe – knowing Nora – she couldn't resist that age-old pleasure of kicking a man when he's down. Particularly when that man, in her mind at least, had clearly been doing something of the same to her own sister.

'That's the number you were looking for, right?'

Nora prompted me as I stared at one of the numbers towards the top of the list.

'Beth's call, late Monday night?'

All of a sudden I was back in that phone booth on the banks of the estuary, Beth's voice floating out of the ether from three thousand miles away.

Nora nodded at me again.

'That was to me. Asking if Big Sis could put her up for a few days.'

And now I really was floundering and from the expression on Nora's face I had a shrewd suspicion I wasn't going to get any more in the way of enlightenment from that quarter.

'She never said anything to me.'

'Oh I think she did, Jimmy.'

Nora picked up her sister's case, moved past me.

'Maybe you just weren't listening.'

One hour later and I was walking. Not walking anywhere in particular, just walking, not thinking about anything, just letting my legs take me, trying to work things out without trying to, if that makes any sort of sense; just taking in the sights.

Things were changing almost daily in the city. And some of the biggest changes were being ushered in via the new hotels that were springing up on almost every corner. I walked past the Hotel Tudor just a block away from the latest hot spot to visit, the United Nations. Singles – with bath – at just over three dollars a night, complete with innerspring mattresses, maple furniture and even a Venetian blind according to the billboard high above Tudor City itself.

I walked on, passing the Biltmore which was right next to and built at the same time as Grand Central Station. Here a room was going to set you back over six dollars but they threw in an indoor pool as well – one of the first in the city – as well as the chance to don your smoking jacket for a highball and cigar in the Men's Bar and then maybe sample a lobster served by a pretty girl in the Madison Room.

I then passed one of the newest of the new, the Edison with its dining room air-conditioned with circulating ice water, followed by the Park Sheraton with a television in every room and, even though there were almost fifteen hundred of those rooms, there was still a good chance, so they claimed, of bumping into well-known and regular attendees such as Jackie Gleason, Mae West and, even, Eleanor Roosevelt.

I paused outside the Barbizon on 63rd and Lexington, the city's hotel for women only where all nice young ladies stayed when they came to New York. Seven hundred tiny rooms, just enough space for a desk, a bed and a dresser but very definitely no space for men, who weren't allowed above the second floor.

Then I moved onto the Algonquin where I could almost hear the exchanges of the glitterati from the Rose Room inside and smell the enticing aromas from the Oak Room and Round Table as the diners inside tucked into house specialities such as rolled pancakes stuffed with chicken hash. And on your way out to one of the concierge's recommendations – maybe the NY Yacht Club or the Princeton or Columbia Clubs – make sure to stroke the resident cat for luck. The Algonquin had taken one in since the Thirties.

All the time I tried working all this out without approaching the matter directly. Why had Beth decided she needed a few days away from the apartment? Meaning a few days away from me? I'd been away three days already but presumably that hadn't been enough time and space for her right now. On my return she apparently needed to quit our apartment for the considerably more cramped accommodation offered by her sister, leaving no note, no phone message, nothing to give me any sort of clue as to why.

Apart from that one enigmatic parting shot from Nora, her pithy observation that Beth had told me but I wasn't listening.

I walked on, now swopping hotels for different sort of sights, first taking in the occasionally strange inscriptions on a variety of local six-story walk-ups. One of the most puzzling was on a tenement in Hell's Kitchen, just four letters carved into the façade.

'ELSW.'

What was that all about? The name of the builder? Some arcane building term whose meaning had become lost in the decades between its construction and the present day?

Or what about the more understandable but still puzzling inscription on the arch I'd once seen above the walk-up in Astoria?

'PROGRESS.'

I guess, compared to the kind of housing the local residents would have lived in before this type of old law – or dumbbell – tenement hit the scene, it would have been progress of a type. But it still seemed a pretty strange inscription to carve into the façade, almost as if the whole building was trying just that little bit too hard.

And what about the name carved into the tenement on St Mark's Place?

'Juliette.'

There was a local tale that the tenement was built by the same contractor who'd built the Puck building and that it was his habit to continually reference Shakespeare. The teller of this local tale was unsure if that was due to his deep admiration of the Bard or whether he simply wanted to demonstrate his learning. But whether it was the former or the latter, you'd have thought the gentleman in question would have checked his spelling.

Puzzling signs or inscriptions weren't just restricted to buildings. On the corner of 17th and Avenue C, east of Stuy Town, there was a little spit of land called Murphy's Brother's Playground. So who was Murphy? And why did his brother get a playground named after him?

Local legend – once again – had it that it all went back to the days when Tammany Hall ruled Manhattan politics. John Murphy lived in the area at the time, the son of poor Irish immigrants. He made his fortune in construction but owed a lot of his good fortune to his brother, a bigwig called 'Silent' Charlie Murphy.

But it still seemed a pretty strange thing to do. Why not Charlie Murphy's Playground if that story was true? Why not use his actual name? Who wants only to be known as someone's brother?

Beth and myself used to go there in the evenings when we first met. It was usually deserted back then, the only sense of a world outside coming from the cars as they surged up or down the nearby incline on the East River Drive. Of course, we could have opted for the more scenic option of a bench overlooking the river but the playground was more private which suited us just fine at the time.

Finally I stopped my wanderings. Something told me it wasn't going to unlock anything that particular night. I let myself back into the apartment instead. A tapping on the window alerted me to one constant presence at least, as my adopted bird came calling. I took some stale bread from the basket, went out onto the balcony.

As I stood there, I looked out over the city, still a million miles from working out what the hell was happening here.

11

IF CON LOOKED as if he'd died and gone to a better place before, now he looked as if he'd just joined the innermost hosts of angels and archangels. I could swear he was almost salivating as he scanned my latest log – which wasn't a pretty sight, but was still a whole lot prettier than the figure Subject Thomas, female, had cut in her home village – or town – a few days before.

Con's eyes widened as he mouthed my own lines back at me.

'A can-can – for a full half-mile – wearing no – .'

A rhapsodic Con read on as if unable to credit the good fortune that the gods – or more accurately myself – had just delivered into his grateful lap.

All the time I kept quiet, partly because the log was doing all my talking for me.

And partly because – and for reasons that were nothing to do with Con – I really hadn't slept too well.

'A fist fight – common law partner of the chosen one – .'

Con looked up at me. He didn't know it, but he was still on the entrée. The main course in this particular smörgåsbord was just over the page.

'This is pay-dirt, Jimmy.'

'Told you it was good, didn't I?'

I'd wired Con from the airport in London just to give him a sneak preview of the upcoming treats. Now he had those treats literally in hand he knew I wasn't just blowing hot air across the ocean.

'Good?'

Con shook his head as he turned over the page.

'Twenty-two carat, solid as it comes.'

Con read on some more, eyes widening again as he reached

the highlight of the day, at least so far as I'd witnessed it. Maybe even more had gone on later that night but by then I was back in my small bed and breakfast writing up all I'd witnessed so far, something telling me that for the magazine's purpose it was already more than enough.

'Shame she didn't ravage a couple of choirboys as well. Then we really would be dancing a jig.'

Con's eyes didn't leave the page.

'I'm dancing anyway.'

Then, for the first time, there was the hint of doubt in his eyes.

I didn't blame him. If I hadn't seen it with my own eyes I wouldn't have believed it myself.

Con intoned the words carefully, enunciating each one.

'Twelve Irish laborers?'

'No partridge on a pear tree though. Couldn't quite manage that one.'

Con kept looking at me, doubt now being replaced by something else, something more wary as he picked up something in my tone.

'You OK, Jimmy?'

'Top of the world.'

Con kept looking at me.

'Long flight, right?'

'Right.'

Con nodded again, then he almost vaulted the desk, enveloping me in the sort of bear hug that promised a nice little cut of that extra-special little bonus he was probably going to get for delivering the latest epistle to his Lords and Masters.

'You're a genius, Jimmy. A one hundred percent proof, walking, talking legend.'

Again, I couldn't help it. Who could? I started grinning back – last night – Beth – Nora's cool eyes – all fast being banished back to a place I didn't want to visit anymore. Hell, a place I didn't even want to acknowledge existed. Why shouldn't I bask in all this a little? I'd worked my butt off on this one and produced something really good at the end of it all too.

Didn't that count for something? Didn't I deserve some sort of credit for it – rather than an empty apartment and a wife who seemed to think I'd done everything wrong even if she didn't have the decency to explain just what that might be?

'So that's it, right?'

My voice was muffled, my face still buried in Con's exuberant, celebratory embrace.

'Job done. Come on, Con, do not tell me your guys want anymore, they haven't got a story here, they've got a syndicated serial.'

Con stepped back, shook his head.

'Not even close, Jimmy. You're on this for the duration, no parole, no time off for good behavior, just you and Subject Thomas all the way to the drum roll.'

He reached back towards his desk, brought out a file, thin at the moment – a little like the Subject Thomas file was thin at the start of all this – but destined, like that file, to become more than a touch fatter in the next few days.

'It's time to take a look at the third piece in this jigsaw. The Girl Friday. The oh-so-willing helpmate. The producer of that play of his, Under Some Wood or something.'

Instinctive, out it came.

'Milk.'

'What?'

'That's what it's called.'

Con hardly seemed to hear me.

'Who is she, what is she to our main man, is she just another bit of skirt or something else, someone he picks up when he's over in the Big Apple, forgets about when he goes home?

She's not the first, Jimmy, we know that much. Forget the one-night stands, hell, most of those didn't even last a night, there was someone before Miss Reitell, some broad called Kazin or something, she was a junior editor on some magazine or other, that's how they met, she got Mr Poet to write a story for them a couple of years back.'

Con pushed a sheet of paper across the desk, a brief biography of the lady in question along with a photograph. She didn't look unlike Miss Reitell, the same willowy figure, a similar shock of dark hair.

'She was on the scene for a while according to one of the friends we talked to, seemed to think it might even develop into something more permanent but then his wife found out about it and went into orbit although what she's got to beef about when she's back home doing things like this beats me.'

Con tapped my log again, shrugged.

'So is Miss Reitell just the latest in the line or is she actually going to last the distance? Is she the reason he's back, he only went home a few months ago and now here he is again and OK, I know he's got this play of his to put on but is all that just an excuse?'

Con shook his head.

'I don't know but I've got a feeling about this one, Jimmy. I've got a feeling about her. He doesn't seem loved-up exactly – look how he was at that party, right – look how he was with Miss Monroe and Miss Winters – it's not like he only has eyes for her but there's still something going on between those two, something I want to know more about and something the magazine's readers are going to want to know more about as well.'

Con eyed me, sage.

'I told you before, Jimmy. Take a look at the lady. Nine times out of ten – .'

I finished it for him.

'That's what's wrong with the man.'

Con eyed me, a slight cloud descending over his eyes, that same touch of wariness now creeping into his voice.

'You sure you're OK, Jimmy?'

I let myself out of the office a few moments later. Con had arranged a backstage pass for me for the premiere of Subject Thomas's play that evening. For that one evening only I was going to be a showbiz journalist writing a feature that might be picked up by various radio stations for wider broadcast coast-to-coast. It wasn't exactly going to be Pulitzer Prize stuff – little more than low-level backstage gossip in truth – but it should still be enough to shift a few extra seats at any subsequent re-staging of the play, so the theater had accepted the request readily enough. There'd be a few other stringers working the same evening for much the same purpose and the intention was I'd merge into the background, giving me ample time and opportunity to do an in-depth study of Miss Reitell.

Con was right. Was this relationship serious or was she just another star-struck kid? It seemed strange to talk about poets as any kind of stars, but Subject Thomas was fast attaining that sort of status, at least in the States. One of the reasons the magazine had become interested in him in the first place, I guess.

Even a few years ago his sort of trade had been positively staid. Something to be studied in the rarified avenues of academia. But Subject Thomas was one of a new breed of scribblers who were changing all that. Taking words from the confines of slim, dusty volumes and putting them center stage in the concert hall. Heady stuff it seemed, so was Miss Reitell just the latest in a line of admirers who'd had her head turned by it all? Or was there, as Con suspected, something else going on?

I passed the Hotel Astor on my way back to Stuy Town. With a jolt I remembered my booking, debated briefly whether to go in and cancel, then decided against it. Nora had said Beth would be gone a few days but maybe she wouldn't stay away that long. Maybe she was already heading back to the apartment, missing me as much as I was missing her, despite the distractions offered by new hotels, odd inscriptions above six-story walk-ups and curiously-named playgrounds.

On an impulse I dived into a phone booth, fed the slot with a dime. Back in our apartment the phone rang – and rang – and rang. I replaced the receiver and immediately dialed Nora's number. Once again the phone rang out a few times but then Nora's cool voice wafted down the line. I didn't speak – didn't really know what to say. I'd been hoping that Nora might be at work, that Beth might have answered. But despite the silence that was greeting her on the other end of the line, Nora still seemed to know who was calling.

'Leave her alone, Jimmy.'

I didn't reply.

'Just let her work a few things out.'

I could have asked her what she was talking about, what things, told her I didn't know there were any things; but I knew it wouldn't have done much good. If I didn't know, then Nora wasn't going to tell me. Clearly, in her eyes, I really should have been able to work it out for myself.

The problem being I couldn't work anything out at the moment, but again I didn't say that. I had the impression from our last exchange back in the apartment that any confession of that sort would only have stacked the counters even more heavily against me.

So for now I just replaced the receiver, exited the phone booth and headed home to change.

12

I ARRIVED AT the theater with about six hours to go to curtain-up. I'd expected all sorts – fraught producers – nervous actors – strained stagehands doing final checks for lighting and sound.

What I didn't expect was no play.

As in nothing to perform.

A grizzled old rigger updated me on the whole sorry situation within a few moments of my showing my fake pass which accessed all areas – in this case meaning the small backstage area and the rabbit warren of even smaller offices and rehearsal rooms at the rear of the building.

Apparently, Mr Poet had left the manuscript of his latest *magnum opus* in a pub in London – the Helvetia in Old Compton Street – just before he boarded his flight to NYC.

It wasn't the first time he'd been so forgetful either. A few weeks previously, so I also discovered, he'd left the same manuscript under a bar stool in another pub in a small seaside town a few miles along the coast from his own, a drinking den called the Coach and Horses on the somewhat exotically-named Upper Frog Street in a place called Tenby.

On this latest occasion, in London, a radio producer called Douglas Cleverdon had delivered duplicate copies to him at the terminal before embarking on an extended search for the missing original, perhaps galvanized by a drunken promise from Subject Thomas that, should he find it, he could keep it.

But that resolved crisis only precipitated a fresh one in its wake. Because the duplicate manuscript was, it seemed, an older draft of his play and Subject Thomas hadn't been all that happy with that version. There was, it seemed, one whole lot of stuff to do on it and Subject Thomas had been locked in one of the rehearsal rooms since dawn trying – with the help of Miss Reitell and some agent of his who'd flown down from Boston – to do all that stuff, to actually finish it in fact, while the actors prowled around nervously outside.

They'd managed some sort of rehearsal earlier in the afternoon when they ran through a half-finished version of the whole thing, but all that had achieved, according to the same grizzled old rigger, was to highlight the fact there was still one shit-load of stuff missing or, in some other way, not quite fit for purpose. So Subject Thomas had retreated into what seemed to have become something of a self-imposed exile to put that right.

In roughly six or so hours.

Not to mention coming up with an actual ending because that also seemed to be missing at the moment too.

I checked out the auditorium which would be packed to bursting in just a few hours' time. It wasn't the largest in the world but it wasn't exactly intimate either. The stage was pretty bare save for six stools which were to be individually lit. The six actors – including Subject Thomas – would take their places on those stools and that was pretty well that. No fancy effects, no claps of thunder, no forks of lightning, no stunts, not even much in the way of a backcloth.

Nothing to distract from the performances or the play.

Which, at the moment, didn't exist.

I next checked out the performers currently milling about the stage, liaising in huddles, looking at their watches and checking out the wings, hoping at any moment to see a guardian angel arrive bearing something that might at least resemble some sort of finished drama. But no such angel bearing any such beast had appeared as yet.

These guys were up against it from the start even without this last-minute complication. I'd done some checking up on them before I came in and the actors – two women and three men – were hardly household names. In fact the majority were amateurs and office workers, culled from the Poetry Center's own staff. It wasn't exactly a wealthy institution and couldn't afford to employ professional actors and actresses, even for a play written – or hopefully written – by a visiting celebrity. The union scale of pay made that impossible, so this strange system had come into play with unemployed actors and actresses hired as temporary help in the theater – running the switchboard, helping out backstage – and, when the occasion arose, stepping out onto that stage to perform.

I still hadn't caught sight of Subject Thomas. But I managed to stop the harassed agent from Boston as he returned to the rehearsal room with some ginger ale. The agent was something of a dandy, dressed in a neat suit and a bow tie and sporting a balding head that was currently glistening with sweat. And, despite what were his fine and reassuring words, the guy was clearly in something of a funk.

I showed my pass and asked how things were going.

Things were going fine, he replied.

I pointed out that it was curtain-up in just a few hours and the cast didn't seem to have had anything like a final rehearsal yet.

He replied that they would, and all would be good.

I pointed out that everything seemed to be a little last-minute.

He replied that the author liked it that way. Then he hurriedly exited into the rehearsal room where I just caught a glimpse of the great man himself, surrounded by dozens of scraps of discarded paper.

Another guy was also with him, a short, punchy, barrel-chested man I hadn't seen before. Discreet enquiries identified him as a doctor summoned by Miss Reitell herself, an NYC physician by the name of Feltenstein, first name Milton. There was rumored to be some kind of family connection here, although exactly what connection – and how close he and Miss Reitell might be – remained unconfirmed.

But even from the little I could see of him, he seemed to be lacking the usual bedside manner. In fact he seemed more than a little pissed that he'd been summoned there at all. As I kept watch he wrote out a prescription – more than a little hastily – and then headed away to resume what I'd later establish was an interrupted lunch date.

With the main protagonists in that night's drama otherwise distracted, I next checked out the rest of the backstage offices. I found a producer's office where the agent had left his briefcase which was neat and new, a little like the man himself. The briefcase was unlocked and I looked inside to find two pieces of paper. The first was a speech he obviously intended to give that night, welcoming the audience to the play and saying a few words about the performance they were all about to enjoy. He obviously had something of a way with words as well.

The second piece of paper was an alternative speech, announcing the cancelation of that night's performance, pleading illness on the part of the play's creator and apologizing for any inconvenience caused or disappointment suffered.

I went back to the stage and talked to one of the actors, a large and kindly-looking man who was rigging up a small portable recorder to catch the evening's performance on tape; an act of faith if ever there was one. He told me, in a hushed and rather scared tone, that he and his fellow actors had only actually seen anything like a complete script that very morning, only to find out within moments that it wasn't anything like a complete script at all, something like half a script instead and that was erring on the generous side.

I moved to the back of the stage, stared out over the

currently empty auditorium. I just didn't get it. Why was the guy putting himself through all this? He must have known the performance was looming. It was, supposedly, the main reason he'd returned to the US. So why travel thousands of miles to stage a play you hadn't yet written? Like so much else where Subject Thomas was concerned, it was all more than a little strange.

I checked the clock on the auditorium wall. The performance was due to start at 20.40. It was now 17.00 meaning there were just over three hours to go. Which was when a messenger did indeed appear from the wings, although the newly-arrived agent wasn't bearing newly-bound copies of a finished drama. He just told the cast that there'd be a final rehearsal at 19.30 and that they could all leave the building for a break before then if they wished.

Not one of them did. They just stayed right where they were, on that stage, still liaising in those same panicked huddles, watching the second hand of that auditorium clock as it ticked down the minutes to curtain-up time.

I went backstage again and could now hear the impatient clicking of two typewriters. Inside the rehearsal room a couple of typists had been drafted in and they were transcribing some largely unintelligible scrawl handed them by Subject Thomas into something resembling half-legible prose. At that stage, according to a hushed conversation between a couple of the stage hands who were being handed the new sheets of paper for copying, the all-important final scenes hadn't yet been written.

One hour later I witnessed what I was to realize was something of a charade. By now the typists were coming in and out of the rehearsal room all the time, no-one even bothering to close the door as they did so. Everything was now in such an advanced state of panic no-one seemed to care who

146

might witness it. Through the press of people – Miss Reitell – the agent from Boston whom I'd now identified as one John Malcolm Brinnin – the lighting guys seeking clarification on this part of the performance – the sound guys checking on that – I could see the bowed head of Subject Thomas, scribbling, then crossing out, then scribbling some more. Then I saw Miss Reitell head across to the agent and tell him, quietly but in a voice that carried all the way across that small room, that it was hopeless, that this wasn't fair on anyone, not on the cast, the audience, even the creator of the show himself and that the performance that night would definitely have to be canceled.

Which was when Subject Thomas cut across. He didn't look in good health at the best of times but now his face was white and he was sweating profusely, at times indeed he seemed to be having trouble even catching his breath. But what he said was clear enough.

There would be no cancelation. The performance that night would go ahead as planned. Then he bent his head back to his scribbled script and I just caught a quick glance exchanged between the agent and the producer which was when I realized she'd just played her last card. She'd just brought him face to face with the possibility of total and complete failure, a prospect he clearly found unthinkable.

The cast were still milling around on the stage. A few minutes before the final rehearsal was due to take place a new script of a sort was handed to them, albeit still without the final few scenes and they took their places on the stage with their still-incomplete scripts in hand. There was obviously to be no pretence that they'd actually learnt their lines, they were just to read from the page. A moment later Subject Thomas joined them and took his place on one of the stools, one actress and two actors to his right, an actor and actress to his left. Miss Reitell stood in front of them all, script in hand and tried to guide them through the new material at the same time as trying to weave it, as best she could, in with the old.

Strangely enough, none of it seemed to affect the attitude of those actors towards him. Despite the fact Subject Thomas was putting them through what had to be just about the most nerve-shredding of experiences, there wasn't a hint of criticism or reproach. They simply fell on the new material, devouring it almost, loving what they were reading it seemed, putting heart and soul into making the words on the page sing.

Again, I didn't get it. To them, he was some sort of a hero. It didn't matter what he'd done – or hadn't done – everything seemed excused by the hastily-typed pages that had just been handed over, yet more evidence in their eyes that the guy was some sort of genius. They looked at him like Iris had looked at him, that star-struck waitress back in Mr Chaplin's party. Until she'd seen him pissing on the plant pot anyway.

On stage, the final read-through limped towards a conclusion but not even the hero worship of the cast could disguise the fact there were still real problems with the piece. In the wings I could see the agent from Boston reading through the two speeches I'd found in his briefcase. The expression on his face said it all. Despite all his fine words a short time before, he really didn't know which one he'd be reading out in just a few minutes' time.

Subject Thomas went away to make some more last-minute changes. Miss Reitell went with him. I patrolled the corridor, could see them in the rehearsal room, he bent over more pieces of paper, she now typing up the new material herself.

I'd no idea what kind of a producer she was. I wasn't exactly qualified to pronounce on that. But she had the same expression on her face as the actors on stage. She loved him. It was obvious. It was also obvious that Subject Thomas was going to get through this because she was determined he would and that was for his sake and not for hers. However embarrassing it might have been for her and the Poetry Center for the play not to be performed, it would be devastating for him and she was clearly determined that would not happen.

The actors were by now in make-up where they were handed more lines of dialogue as they were being fed through, page by page, from the rehearsal room. Outside in the auditorium, the doors had opened and the audience were beginning to stream inside. The sense of occasion was palpable, even I could feel it. Some of those people had traveled hundreds of miles, had purchased their tickets months in advance. They really wanted to be in on something extra-special, the world premiere of a play by a leading poet no less, and it might well prove special but not at all in the way they expected. The next few moments would tell.

The audience settled into their seats. The agent from Boston made his short, nervous, speech of welcome, then he and Miss Reitell took their places at the rear of the auditorium. The actors filed on stage to applause, the most thunderous applause being reserved for the small, podgy figure who took the final seat in the very middle of the stage. A stage hand – as casually as she could – handed some pieces of paper to the cast members as they settled to begin. The actors had finally taken receipt of the ending of the play they were about to perform.

The lights went down in the auditorium, six lights picking out the actors on stage. There was a pause and I could almost feel Miss Reitell tense behind me. Subject Thomas was meant to be the first to speak but for a moment nothing happened. Then, suddenly, a booming voice issued from his unprepossessing and unpromising frame and the play, finally, was up and running.

Which only ushered in the next problem in its wake. Because it felt like we were all in some kind of congregation. The audience was totally quiet, totally still, listening to each and every word as if it was the Sermon on the Mount rather than an evening's entertainment – which was what it sounded like to me anyway.

OK, maybe I had an advantage. It was pretty obvious within the first few moments that Subject Thomas was writing once again about his home town and I'd been there. Even in the first few lines I was starting to recognize, if not actual people, then the type of people I'd encountered among those tall houses and narrow streets.

One actual character did spring to mind though. On my last walk around Subject Thomas's home town, I'd come across a draper standing outside his shop which was tucked in between the local newsagent and butcher. He'd been sporting a panama hat, a bow tie, a butterfly collar and was also wearing immaculately-polished shoes. The moment I heard the description of one of the fictional characters up on that stage – a certain Mog Edwards – I knew, instantly, that I'd seen him before.

But it wouldn't have mattered if every single one of those people and types had suddenly assumed human shape on that very stage. This was the work of a poet, seemed to be the general consensus. A serious guy. And this audience were going to take it ultra-seriously too. The problem being, the piece wasn't serious at all. The whole thing was a comedy but no-one, clearly, had told the audience that.

A couple of times someone had smirked a little at one of the bawdy lines, had giggled even, but had soon been silenced by a glare from another of the night's devotees. Behind, I could hear Miss Reitell mutter an exasperated imprecation to the agent. On stage, a couple of the actors were beginning to falter, wondering if it was their delivery, was that why they weren't getting any sort of response?

I looked round the hushed auditorium, looked at the actors

on stage, all now sweating, their confidence fast dissolving and thought, what the hell? What had I got to lose? So some people were going to think I was a philistine, maybe I was.

One of the actors had started on an extended speech. He was a draper – maybe that actual draper I myself had seen – who was mad with love, who loved his girl more than all the flannelette and calico, candlewick, dimity, crash and merino – although here I started to wander a bit, this guy never believed in using one word when twenty were to hand, that was for sure; and he was telling her to get into his bed where he was going to warm the sheets like an electric toaster and lay by her side like the Sunday roast.

And I laughed. Well, wouldn't you? And yeah, a couple of disciples in the congregation turned round and glared at me but on stage it seemed to give the cast new heart and before long another guy had laughed at the next line and then a girl in the front row had giggled at another and suddenly it was like a giant switch had been thrown as everyone seemed to realize at the same time – hey, it's OK, it's funny.

After that the performance took off. In fact, it flew. Even I sort of enjoyed it. I didn't look at my watch once and, ask Beth, that's a fair old achievement in any kind of theater for me.

And for a moment I forgot all about the play and Subject Thomas. For a moment all I saw was Beth, the absent Beth, the Beth who wouldn't be in the apartment when I returned home that night for reasons I still didn't understand but was still in no frame of mind to probe too deeply.

And then it was over. The lights on stage faded, extinguishing sight of the actors as the final lines sounded. For a moment the whole hall was silent. Then the applause began, bursting through the silence as if through some kind of physical barrier. And it didn't stop. All in all Subject Thomas and his cast took fifteen curtain calls, the last three for himself alone.

Underneath all the applause, all I could hear was Subject Thomas himself saying two words over and over again –

'Thank you – thank you – .'

I wasn't quite sure who he was saying it to.

The cast?

His producer?

His long-suffering agent who looked, from the whey-faced figure he still presented at the rear of the auditorium, as if he really wasn't long for this world and maybe didn't want to be if he had many more experiences like that to endure.

Or just the gods of theatrical good fortune who'd somehow maneuvered that production of his to some sort of safety?

By the side of the stage, I could see the large, kindly-looking actor I'd talked to earlier. He was checking the portable tape recorder making sure he'd preserved the whole thing for posterity, and from the expression on his face it looked as though he had. It was only a home recording of course. Apparently Subject Thomas was going to record the whole thing professionally on his next trip. But it was still going to be good, so he'd told me, to get this first recording preserved in some way and maybe he was right.

I looked at Subject Thomas, moving from cast member to cast member on stage. I looked at his producer who was now joining him and joining in with the general congratulations. They still made an odd couple but they'd done something special that night. I still didn't understand much about his poetry. But even I could understand that.

And as I kept watching him move about on the stage, my mark, my quarry, I began to wonder. Had I been suckered here? Had Con and the readers of his fine magazine been suckered too? Because when he wanted to, this guy could really pull it out of the hat. Just look at tonight.

And all that poetry and stuff he'd written before, that couldn't all be Emperor's Clothes, could it? There had to be something in there even if I still hadn't quite managed to grasp it.

And maybe those antics in Mr Chaplin's party – and all that with Miss Monroe and Miss Winters – maybe that was something everyone just expected somehow and so that's what he did. Maybe that's what all poets did, hell, what did I know?

I kept looking at him, now being embraced by the stagehands as well as the actors.

Maybe we'd all been laughing at him, but the truth was that all the time he'd been laughing along with us.

Maybe even at us.

13

BETH'S FAMILY CAME, originally, from Italy – much as mine, originally, had derived from Nova Scotia. There wasn't too much that was remarkable about that, just about everyone in the States came from somewhere else. Most, along the way, had left their original roots behind and embraced new lives; but some still clung onto the old ways, the older traditions.

Nora had always been fiercely proud of her Mediterranean antecedents. Unlike Beth she'd actually been born there, although having left at the age of two she couldn't exactly remember too much about it. But the land of her birth and the home of her forefathers still exerted a considerable pull for her, and while Beth and myself had made a home for ourselves in the newly-manufactured and purpose-built Stuy Town down by the East River, Nora lived among the Italian émigré population in East Harlem.

Nora's apartment was on 96th Street, not far from the Poetry Center. Local estimates put the Italian population of the area – which stretched all the way from 96th to 125th Street, east of Lexington Avenue – at around a hundred thousand and each street seemed to represent different regions of the old homeland too.

On East 112th there was a settlement from Bari, on East 107th between First Avenue and the East River you'd find émigrés from Sarno, near Naples, on East 100th between First and Second Avenues there were mainly Sicilians from Santiago with some Northern Italians from Piscento and on East 109th a large settlement of Calabrians.

Every year there'd be a festival, the feast of the Madonna of Monte Carmelo. Up to half a million people would crowd the narrow streets of what had become known as Uptown Little

Italy. I'd attended every year myself ever since I'd got together with Beth, always making sure to take in a pizza from Patsy's on First and 117th along the way.

But tonight the streets were quiet. Most of the residents were in bed. Which was where Nora, now eyeing me darkly from her open doorway, quite clearly believed I should be too.

'What do you want, Jimmy?'

I felt an old and familiar bile begin to rise in my throat. Nora always had been over-protective as regards her kid sister, at least in my eyes. The grilling I'd had to endure from her when Beth first introduced me to the family still ranked as one of the most uncomfortable experiences of my life. A laughing Beth told me I should be flattered, it meant her sister was taking me seriously.

Yeah, and some.

I tried to sound calm and reasonable even if inside I was feeling anything but.

'I want to see my wife.'

'Why do you think she's moved out?'

'I don't know why she's moved out, that's the point, that's why I want to see her.'

Nora didn't even seem to hear me, just rode roughshod over all I was saying.

As usual.

'She doesn't want to see you.'

'Why not?'

And now Nora paused. Maybe there was something in my simple appeal. Or maybe I presented just too pathetic a figure right now for her to slide home the ice-pick. Just goes to show that even piranhas can occasionally exhibit some sort of pity at least, because now Nora sounded almost conciliatory.

'Just give her a few days.'

'What for?'

Nora didn't reply, just started to close the door. Old habits –

and the last few years of training – coming to the fore, I swiftly put my foot in the way, prevented it closing completely.

Nora looked down at my foot, then up at me, the expression on her face saying it all. Something was about to get badly hurt and something was telling us both it wasn't going to be the large slab of hardwood in her hand.

Then, just as she was about to demonstrate that all-too obvious statement of fact, a voice cut in from behind.

'It's all right, Nora.'

Beth appeared in the small hallway behind her, the light from the overhead lamp backlighting her hair, imparting to her some kind of golden glow. Then again, maybe anyone would have looked angelic at that moment compared to the glowering Nora.

Nora reluctantly tore her eyes away from me, even more reluctantly tore them away from my oh-so-tempting looking foot and looked at her sister.

'You sure?'

'You're due at the hospital.'

For the first time I realized she was actually wearing her nurse's uniform and had obviously been on the point of leaving for a night shift. Some detective. All I'd had to do was hang around a while until she'd left and then Beth would have been alone in the apartment, no ogre standing guard at the portal.

Nora looked back at me, cast a last, regretful glance down at my foot, a clear opportunity missed. Then she nodded.

'OK.'

Then Nora picked up her bag from a small table in the hall, moved past me and headed out into the night. Beth remained in the doorway looking out at me, but didn't make any move to invite me in.

'I just need to do some thinking, Jimmy.'

I repeated what seemed to be the salient word.

'Thinking?'

'Yes.'

'About?'

Beth didn't reply, just kept looking at me and while she didn't exhibit the same hostility as her sister, it was still a look that chilled me. And I was still a million miles away from even beginning to understand what lay behind it.

'What did I do, Beth?'

Still that same look, still that same, unblinking, undeviating stare.

'What's so awful you had to actually walk out on me? Did I crash a car, drink till I couldn't stand up, hit on every woman I could find?'

And now Beth started to look puzzled.

'What?'

'Pop every pill anyone put in front of me, steal, cheat, lie, piss in plant pots?'

'What are you talking about?'

'Whatever the hell this is all about, did I do anything like that?'

Beth just kept looking at me for a moment. For another long moment I thought she was just going to turn and head back inside, finally closing that large slab of hardwood, foot or no foot in the way. But then she nodded at me instead.

'It's not anything you've done, Jimmy.'

'Then what is it?'

'Look at you.'

'What does that mean?'

'Look what's happening to you.'

I stared at her.

Not all this again.

'You spend your day, every day, and most of your nights too, down in the gutter.'

'That's just my job.'

'All you see, day in, day out, all you deal with are the lowlifes.'

'It doesn't mean anything, not really.'

'And that's all there is for you now.'

'Beth, it's just how I earn my crust.'

'So everywhere you look – with everyone you come across – all you see are the fault lines, the mistakes, the treacheries, the worst in everyone, and I can't stand it Jimmy, what it's doing to you, what it's doing to us.'

'You're over-reacting.'

Beth shook her head, stubborn.

'And you know the worst thing? All the time you're scrabbling round in the cesspool – you're laughing.'

'Just listen to me.'

'You and Con.'

And now I was really starting to get irritated.

'Yeah well, laugh or cry Beth, believe me, sometimes you've just got to do one or the other.'

'I told you before, it's like the whole world's – .'

I cut across again.

'Yeah, I know. One big, sick, joke – well look around Beth, poke your head outside of that nice, safe, warm office where you work sometimes, take a look at some of the people I come across, are you telling me you wouldn't laugh from time to time, that you wouldn't look at what they do and think it's all some kind of joke?'

Beth just nodded at me, cool, level, as ever.

'See what I mean?'

I fell silent, the sounds of the night reverberating behind me but I wasn't hearing them. Maybe I wasn't hearing anything right now.

'Thinking.'

Beth looked at me as I repeated the still-salient phrase.

'What?'

'That's what you said, that you just need to do some thinking, that's why you're not back home, with me, with your husband, that's why you're here, with your sister, you need to do some thinking.'

'That's right.'

'Doesn't sound like you need to do too much thinking to me Beth, sounds to me like you've done plenty of that already, in fact it sounds to me like you've already hung me out to dry.'

Beth's eyes never left my face.

'And when you're not laughing at everyone, you're not believing a single word they say.'

I turned, suddenly sick of it all, sick of trying to defend myself against charges I still didn't really understand.

'Maybe some people don't make it all that easy for me.'

I headed back down the steps, hunting in my pocket for my car keys.

'I'm out of here.'

All I could hear as I headed away was Beth's voice following me along the sidewalk.

'And now you won't even give your own wife the benefit of the doubt.'

I climbed back into my car, keys still in my hand. I looked out through the windscreen but didn't see anything. Maybe I should have stayed and tried to have the whole thing out with her, but something was telling me I could have stood on that doorstep till dawn and still none of this would have been resolved. That thought depressed me more than I dared think about right now.

Reluctant to start the engine, to begin the journey back to

the empty apartment, I flicked on the radio. A music station blared some country hit and I flipped channels, accessing in turn local news, a weather forecast, a transmission from some neighborhood station across in Queens before I came across an educated voice talking about none other than Subject Thomas.

I fine-tuned the station. Had something happened to him after I left, had I missed something? Con really wouldn't appreciate it if I put in my log for the evening and left out something big. I listened for a few more moments, then realized the educated voice was talking about his play that evening, was delivering some kind of review. His tone was warm and supportive too. Something told me Subject Thomas was going to like what he had to say.

Then I became aware of a shape outside the window. I hesitated a moment, then knocked off the radio, wound down the window and looked at Beth.

'What are you doing, Jimmy?'

I just kept looking at her for a moment.

'I've been watching you from the window, why are you just sitting here?'

I still didn't speak and her face tensed as if she thought I was deliberately ignoring her, making some sort of stupid point, which I wasn't.

'Suit yourself.'

She turned away.

'You used to like it.'

Beth stopped, looked at me.

'What?'

'The way I made you laugh.'

She kept looking at me.

'Remember some of the things I used to tell you about, like that guy I was tailing out in the country who got lost and who came up to me, asked me for directions and I ended up escorting the mark I'd been paid to shadow. Or the police officer out in Wisconsin who gave me a description of this guy we wanted to find, telling me everything about him, even telling me all about the mole on his neck, but not actually mentioning he only had one arm.'

It was beginning to sound like special pleading and I knew it.

'It was part of your charm, Jimmy.'

And it sounded like Beth knew it too.

'Playing the clown, the joker and when things didn't matter so much it was fun.'

'What does that mean, when things didn't matter?'

Beth, as before, just rode straight on.

'We were young then, I know.'

Then she paused, as if really not sure what to say next.

'And easy, right?'

Beth struggled some more.

'But we're older now, both of us, things aren't as simple as they used to be.'

I broke in again.

'In the mercy of his means.'

And now Beth stopped.

'What?'

Then Beth kept staring at me as out it came, word perfect, as if I'd memorized it especially, which I hadn't, but something must have sunk in because the lines came out, just like that.

Oh as I was young and easy in the mercy of his means,
Time held me, green and dying
Though I sang in my chains like the sea.

Beth remained outside the car, staring in at me as if I'd just gone mad. I stayed silent, didn't continue. Maybe I had.

'Where did that come from?'

'It was written by this guy I've been tailing. The guy who's been doing all the drinking and crashing cars and popping pills and stealing and lying while his wife –.'

I tailed off, shook my head.

'And he came up with that.'

Beth just kept looking at me.

'Can't get my head round it.'

For a moment I expected another veiled barb but it didn't come. Beth just nodded at me instead.

'People surprise you, Jimmy.'

'Meaning what? Meaning me? You didn't think I was the poetic type?'

I shook my head.

'Just stuck in my mind for some reason.'

'Look around, Jimmy. Properly. There's more than the freak show going on.'

Beth nodded at me one last time as she turned, headed back to her sister's apartment.

'Even with that guy.'

Half an hour later I was heading for home. I'd remained in my car for a few more minutes, but Beth hadn't returned. When the lights went out in the front room I started the engine and began to drive. But I didn't actually go home. I just couldn't take the thought of walking into that still-empty apartment straightaway, so I parked up behind Times Square instead. I made my way over to Grand Central Station, just wanting to be in among a crush of people right now and the terminus was usually buzzing even at that time of night.

A party of businessmen were hollering it up in the Oyster Bar before catching the last train home. A small army of harassed waiters were knocking out portion after portion of Real Maine Lobster Stew, all – as the poster on the wall proclaimed

– 'superbly cooked, delightfully seasoned and just the way YOU LIKE IT BEST!' It smelt every bit as good as it promised but the three-and-a-half dollar price tag didn't seem quite so tasty. I headed back up to Times Square instead and went into the Horn and Hardat Automat.

I fed a coin in one of the slots and turned the chrome-plated knob. A glass window opened granting me access to my macaroni and cheese and a hot cup of coffee. I took it over to a table and looked out over the sidewalk which was still rammed.

Once again I was doing what I always did. Trying to think about all Beth had said without actually thinking about it. Trying to make sense of it by some sort of remote control. Letting my brain see if it could order it all into some kind of coherence while I concentrated on other things like my macaroni and cheese and how to cool my overheated coffee.

14

THE NEXT MORNING I was back in Con's office. My log for the previous evening was on his desk in front of him and the expression on his face was saying it all.

Con didn't like it as much as my previous logs. In fact I had more than a shrewd suspicion that not a great deal in this latest report would find its way into any new profile on Subject Thomas. The birth of his play might have been of all-consuming interest to everyone in that theater that night but Con was looking for something a little juicier than the near-missing of a deadline. So far as anything in the way of sauce went, the previous evening had been somewhat underpowered. A more sober offering in place of the moonshine of previous times. And if Con didn't like all he was reading, he was feeling pretty much the same about everything he was hearing right now too.

'Maybe this isn't about a guy having fun.'

Con looked at me. I may not have been able to think too much about Beth last night – remotely or otherwise, back in the apartment or in that Times Square Automat – but I'd thought plenty about Subject Thomas. For some reason I couldn't stop thinking about him for the rest of that long and still unseasonably hot night.

Con kept eyeing me, dubious.

'What are you talking about, Jimmy?'

'Maybe he's not having fun at all.'

The expression on Con's face said it all too. He wasn't having too much fun listening to me right now either but I pressed on. As I said, I'd done a lot of thinking.

'Maybe this is a love story.'

Con repeated the words, flat and neutral, as if he'd just been handed a terminal prognosis.

'A love story.'

I nodded, hunching forward now all the while.

'Why not? Maybe the guy's tormented.'

Con picked up another of my logs, the one detailing Subject Thomas's activities on his first day in the city.

'Did he look tormented in that diner with Miss Winters and Miss Monroe? When he was sexually assaulting Garbo?'

I ignored that.

'Maybe he's in love with the producer of his, the Girl Friday as you called her, the helpmate.'

Con just eyed me.

'And because he's in love with the producer, the Girl Friday, the helpmate, he's beating himself up about his wife back home.'

Con picked up another of my logs from the desk.

'The wife back home who found all that solace in the arms of twelve Irish laborers?'

'Maybe she's tormented too, maybe that's why she was acting like that, maybe it's the same for her as for him.'

'Jimmy – .'

Con was getting impatient.

'Maybe she's acting like that because she's found out about the producer or maybe she just suspects something, doesn't matter, she's going out of her mind anyway and that's why she's doing all those crazy things, it's a sort of tit for tat, anything he can do she can do better – or do worse – if you see what I mean.'

'Not exactly.'

'Maybe that's what this trip's all about, maybe this isn't some loser plumbing new depths, maybe this is the start of something better for this guy, maybe that's what last night was all about because he sure came close, but Mr Poet did pull it off, he did get that play of his out there, him and that producer of his.'

I nodded at him, starting to become a little encouraged at least as Con stayed silent.

Was some of this actually beginning to strike some kind of chord?

'Maybe what we've got here – and maybe what we've been seeing ever since he arrived – is a guy hitting rock bottom so he can climb all the way back up again. Maybe he had to do all those crazy things to get them out of his system or something.'

Con remained silent, just eyed me all the while. I faltered a little as he kept doing so, now becoming rather more unsure that all this was having the effect I was hoping.

'It's possible that's all I'm saying, it's one way of looking at all this, but if I'm right, if that is what's happening here, then this isn't what we all thought it was, this isn't some rollercoaster ride to hell. This might – might – just be what I said, a love story and if it is, come on Con, think about it, there's still a story here and a damn good one too, you know it and I know it, what we've got so far, OK, that's going to get the juices flowing, but love stories sell too, don't they?'

Con kept staring at me as I finished. For a moment I thought he wasn't going to speak at all.

Then out it came, that same, flat, growl of a voice as before.

'And that's the best you could do?'

'What?'

Con picked up my log.

'You sat in that flea-bitten theater last night, watching him, watching his play, watching his producer, his Girl Friday, his helpmate, you talked to her.'

Con broke off, eyed me keenly.

'You did talk to her, didn't you, Jimmy?'

Con tapped my log as I hesitated.

'Only I've been through this a couple of times now and you don't actually say.'

'I watched her.'

'I'll take that as a no then, shall I?'

'Like I watched him, watched everyone, they all had a lot to do last night.'

'Jimmy?'

'No, I didn't actually talk to her.'

'Not even after the play had finished, once everyone had gone, when they had nothing left to do but go home or go on somewhere.'

Something in his tone began to alert me to something else going on here, something maybe I'd missed.

'I had something to do after the play finished.'

'Obviously.'

What was all this?

And now it was Con's turn to hunch forward over the desk.

'Well, I've been doing a little digging myself into Romeo's little Miss Juliet. To help you out a little here, Jimmy, because I have to be honest, none of us were all that impressed when we read your latest little offering.'

'I just told it like I saw it, just like I always do.'

'So I asked around a little, talked to people who knew people, that sort of thing, the sort of thing that to be honest, Jimmy, I thought you might have done last night rather than daydream into your popcorn.'

'That's not fair, Con.'

'Did you know about the lecture contract?'

I stopped.

'The what?'

'I'll take that as another no, shall I?'

'What lecture contract?'

'The one that producer of his has been fixing for him ever

167

since he got here, maybe from before he even got here, we're none too sure yet but we'll find out, Jimmy, or rather you will once you start doing what we're actually paying you to do and start sniffing around a little, rather than sitting among theatricals and making up fantasies.'

Con snorted.

'Love story? Our man's going on the lecture circuit. He's going to be doing the chat shows, university halls. Maybe that's why she was so desperate last night went well, it's the perfect springboard and there's a not-so-little incentive involved here too.'

Con nodded at me.

'I've seen the contract, Jimmy. Well, a person I know who knows a person in the know has seen it. Mr Poet hasn't actually signed it yet but the word is he's going to and no wonder, I would and you would too and it's going to take him a long way away from scratching a few dumb words on a piece of paper.'

I stared back at him, ever more lost.

'What does that mean?'

'This lecture contract his Girl Friday has been fixing up for him ever since he arrived, maybe even before, is going to net him a thousand bucks a week, Jimmy.'

I stilled, didn't reply as Con repeated that, slowly enunciating each word, rolling each syllable around in his mouth now as if it was a particularly tasty morsel of that Maine lobster from the previous night.

'A thousand bucks.'

He nodded at me, just in case I hadn't heard that right.

'A week.'

Then Con looked at me, almost pityingly.

'This is a love story? Go back to the funny farm, Jimmy, this is a business deal and a hell of a deal, wouldn't you say? Because I would. This is about one thing and one thing only, the good old American greenback and that's why he's been acting like he has and doing all these things he's been doing because he's been celebrating from the moment he landed.'

Con tapped my theater log, destined, I could see already, for the nearest trash.

'Mr Thomas's girlfriend is taking him on the yellow brick road to Wonderland.'

Half an hour later we were down in the French Quarter in the West 20s. Con was treating me to lunch in one of the small cafés that served up the cuisine of its homeland with something of an American twist. Fake in other words.

But the rest of the surroundings were pretty authentic. OK, the place may have lost its original Huguenot character, but the local Church of St Vincent de Paul in West 23rd Street still offered a mass in French. The nearby Cercle Française de l'Harmonie was still a pretty vibrant local social hub and a battalion of the Guards of Lafayette, with its headquarters on West 26th, also kept alive a few national traditions.

French women were catered for too, they could rent rooms in the nearby Jeanne d'Arc Residence, well-known friend to friendless French girls as it described itself. Myself and Beth had been to a concert there once. It had a strange, small-town parish feel inside. The French Benevolent Society, the French Hospital and even a French orphanage had also made their homes in the neighborhood as well.

Con dipped his bread into a steaming bowl of mussels before dunking one of his fries into the same bowl. Then, chewing all the while, he looked up at me.

'Not a problem is there, Jimmy?'

'How do you mean?'

'Just checking.'

'On me?'

'It's not the log, Jimmy. OK, last night was a little short on excitement but that's not your fault, as I told the rest of guys we can't actually invent stuff even if we wanted to, that's not going to do us too much good if any of this ever gets read out in court, right?'

'Right.'

'But all this love story stuff? All this maybe this, maybe that – .'

Con paused.

'I didn't let anyone see that by the way, don't worry, that didn't go upstairs along with that log of yours, the way I saw it that kind of thing was for our eyes only.'

I stayed silent as Con shrugged.

'OK, now and again it happens. We know that. A guy does a tail job and a guy gets involved. He can't help it, he likes a story too, who doesn't? The tail acts in a certain way, doesn't act in a certain way, the guy starts wondering why, from there it's a short step to putting all that in the report because he thinks it's interesting, that it adds something. Only that's not how everyone else sees it. Everyone else just wants to know what happens next.'

Con nodded at me as he held a piece of mussel meat up on his fork for inspection before popping it in his mouth.

'That's all we want. You to tell us that. Starting tonight. He's got a day and a night off. No readings, no performances, no engagements, then he meets the lecture agent to sign the contract. So get out there, Jimmy. Tell me, tell the magazine, tell everyone who's going to read it exactly what happens next.'

Con swallowed, then smiled at me, his smile almost, but not quite, reaching his eyes.

'And nothing else.'

15

HE STILL HAD no idea I was on his tail. As for Miss Reitell, she was too preoccupied with her charge to worry about whomsoever else might be taking an interest in him.

Besides, there was plenty of additional interest to deal with. As ever, Subject Thomas was hardly making himself invisible. The guy was conspicuous everywhere he went and that wasn't just down to the little bow tie and crumpled clothes, not to mention the occasional multi-colored patch he sported on whatever item of clothing he'd grabbed, or been helped into, that day. This guy was noticed because he made sure he was noticed.

Whether that was accident or design, whether it was all part of some act or other intended more to flatter than deceive, I still couldn't decide; but it probably hardly mattered in truth. It was just another stroke of good fortune on a tail job that had already struck pay-dirt in more ways than one. With so many people paying attention to him, I was just another face in the crowd.

Actually I wasn't even that to him. Not because my face was particularly anonymous or because I was especially unremarkable. I'd just been taught by the best that's all.

The tutor in question was another short little fat guy like Subject Thomas although the resemblance very definitely ended there. Frank Wright – no relation to the famous architect either – ran the very first office I worked in. I'd started in the agency as a clerk but I think he'd marked me out for better things from the beginning. He'd been an operative himself for twenty years before swopping life in the field for life behind a desk. But he knew his stuff and – when the right person came along and I seemed to be one such candidate in his eyes – he made sure he communicated as many of those life lessons as he could.

The first lesson of all was the tail job and I still had some of the notes I'd made following one of his briefings. In those days I was nothing but keen.

'You just saunter along – all the time keeping sight of your subject.'

I'd always really liked that word. Saunter. It puts you in mind of going out for a Sunday stroll which was exactly what it should look like according to Frank. Forget all that movie picture stuff about hiding in doorways or peeking out from behind the awnings of shops. Keep it casual, keep it natural, that way who the hell is going to take any notice of you?

Definitely not the mark.

'Barring bad breaks, the only thing that will make you lose him is being over-anxious. So don't force it, don't push the pace. That way even a really clever criminal can be shadowed for weeks without realizing it, although not too many of them are actually that clever anyway.'

Frank had tailed a well-known forger for three whole months without even remotely arousing his suspicions, as the mark himself had grudgingly conceded after his arrest. He rode trains behind him, visited half a dozen small towns in his company just a few steps away from him all the time. He wasn't spotted once.

The other mistake a new operative makes is getting hung up on the subject's face. You worry that unless you memorize every detail then you'll lose him in some crowd somewhere, so again you get too close, show your hand.

Forget faces. They're not necessarily the most memorable part of a body anyway and besides a face can change out of all recognition depending on what's happening at any moment in time – if the mark is happy, sad, in pain, scared beyond belief.

Other things don't change – the general outline of the body as seen from the rear, a mannerism, a way of walking – all those are much more important than actual features. Get that right and you'll pick out the subject in the middle of a baseball crowd while all the while you're just another face in a whole other sea of faces, no-one special, no-one remarkable.

Which was the reason we were now a good few days into the tail job and Subject Thomas hadn't once looked round with any light of suspicion or recognition in his eyes. Which was also the reason his constant companion hadn't done the same. It wasn't just the fact that they were absorbed by other things – he by all he was doing even if he couldn't remember doing it a few moments later – and she by all he was doing too, even if she didn't want to remember it those few moments later either. It was the fact that I knew what I was doing. And Con was right, that was what I should be getting back to right now, my job, my log, sniffing out the hidden and bringing it out into the light.

Maybe it was being around a poet for the first time in my life. Maybe I was getting infected by it all. The flowery prose. The high-blown sentiments. Maybe in some way I'd been trying to compete instead of doing what I was being paid to do, what I'd been trained to do and what I was good at.

Subject Thomas rose in the early afternoon. At least he emerged from the Chelsea just after lunchtime in the company of Miss Reitell, although this time the agent from Boston was with them too. And, just for a moment, as I looked at the dandified figure of the agent walking along with the crumpled poet and the angular producer, I began to wonder if something else was going on here, whether there was some sort of ménage à trois unfolding before my eyes that up to now I'd somehow missed? Along with a few other things it seemed. I made a note of it in the margins of my log but didn't include it in my report. Speculation to be followed up later if required.

Subject Thomas seemed in need of food because from the Chelsea they headed for a diner in the Village. Not Herdt's this time, it didn't seem to have the same appeal now Miss Winters and Miss Monroe weren't in residence. Instead they called into a seafood restaurant on Charles Street. I'd been past a couple of times and had checked out the menu in the window and it didn't look bad. They offered what appeared to be a pretty authentic New England chowder and if I'd been in the mood for something a little more spicy there was a Louisiana gumbo that promised to cook your socks while you were still wearing them.

Beth made a neat gumbo. She threw in chicken, shrimp and crab although, on the grounds of economy, she omitted the oysters. Her secret ingredient was a bottle of something I'd never heard of before but was made, apparently, from dried sassafras leaves which didn't enlighten me a lot as I also didn't know what a sassafras was either, dried or otherwise. But it tasted wonderful. A general opinion that wasn't shared by Subject Thomas as, within moments of his food being placed in front of him – the Louisiana gumbo, his male companion had a sole and Miss Reitell had a crab salad – there seemed to be trouble brewing.

I'd called in to make a reservation for the next night, just another customer at the counter. I'd cancel it in the morning, my subterfuge not extending to booking out a table and then not turning up. Some standards needed to be maintained. There was a mirrored wall behind the counter and I was able to watch the Subject Thomas table behind as the waitress checked through the book in front of me. It took some time as she was also distracted by the unfolding tableau. As were most of the restaurant by now too.

Subject Thomas, it seemed, had taken exception to something in his broth. Only he called it a stew. And he wasn't exactly mollified by the attentions of the returning waiter or by the imprecations of Miss Reitell or the soothing murmurs of the agent from Boston. He also wasn't exactly placated by an interjection from a diner on the next table either, who advised him to, 'Just start eating, buddy'. The way he saw it, their small part of the world would be a much more peaceful place if he did so and an argument then broke out between Subject Thomas and his fellow diner turning that small part of the world into anything but peaceful.

Miss Reitell suggested they leave and that the agent from Boston pay the bill. Subject Thomas seemed to acquiesce to the suggestion, to the considerable relief of the attending waiter as well the waitress who was still checking my booking for the next evening; a relief that was to prove short-lived as Subject Thomas then emptied the contents of his broth – or stew as he kept calling it – over the head of his fellow diner who was quite clearly no buddy of his at all.

All hell broke loose. The diner assaulted Subject Thomas who made no move to defend himself, leaving Miss Reitell to do that on his behalf, a table and several chairs being upturned during the mêlée. The agent from Boston threw a few dollar bills at the waitress and hurriedly escorted Subject Thomas outside. The aggrieved diner threw the sole ordered by the agent from Boston after them and scored a direct hit on the back of Subject Thomas's head just before the door closed, cutting them off from view.

I sauntered outside – that word again – having decided not to make a booking after all. The distracted waitress hardly noticed. On the pavement I almost bumped straight into Subject Thomas but, as he was more than a little distracted by trying to remove traces of cooked sole from his thick, curly hair, there was little chance of his noticing me.

Besides, he was attracting a fair degree of attention right now. New Yorkers are used to all sorts of sights but a man picking fish out of his hair was still going to excite some kind of comment. A couple of guys stopped and made a comment or two. One of them had a girl on his arm and she seemed to find the remarks of her companion pretty amusing. Subject Thomas quite clearly did not and told him so in no uncertain terms. Not content with that, he also passed an opinion on the looks of his girlfriend at the same time. For the second time in as many minutes a fight developed, with the hapless Miss Reitell once again attempting to act as peacemaker and the agent from Boston performing as ineffectual referee.

Subject Thomas, now bleeding from a blow to his nose, stumbled away up the street berating passers-by all the while. Most just looked amused at the sight of the portly figure with fish in his hair and blood streaming down his chin. One didn't look amused at all and started haranguing him back. For the third time in as many minutes another fight developed. Subject Thomas was winded by a blow to his stomach and spent the next few moments retching the contents of his breakfast – his fabled raw eggs and beer by the look of it – up onto the sidewalk.

But some sort of salvation seemed to be at hand in the shape of a young woman who now came up to the retching poet. She obviously recognized him and Subject Thomas seemed to calm under the influence of her gushing praise. With Miss Reitell and the agent from Boston still distracted by the ongoing efforts of Subject Thomas's latest sparring partner to resume hostilities, he stopped a cab for himself and his new companion. Within a block the cab had stopped and his new companion – now in floods of tears – ran away in a state of quite obvious and considerable distress. The driver also climbed out and ejected Subject Thomas himself a moment later.

He landed in the road where he was narrowly missed by another cab. By that time Miss Reitell had caught up with him and she dashed into the street to retrieve her now-wandering charge and steer him back to the relative safety of the sidewalk.

Half an hour later, Subject Thomas was sitting in a nearby Village apartment owned by a sculptor and his wife. I hadn't caught their names, but checked later. David and Rose Slivka. That good old detail, detail, again. Miss Reitell had made a hurried phone call to them as the agent from Boston kept company with Subject Thomas on the sidewalk and tried to dissuade him from eating the fish he was still excavating from his hair.

I was in a phone booth across the street talking to Con who was making notes all the while, having decided this was just too good to wait for the delivery of my latest log. He wanted to get this out there while it was still hot off the street. With these latest antics taking place, first in a busy restaurant and then out on that street itself, there was always the risk some other stringer would pick it up and spook what Con wanted to make sure was our exclusive.

'This I really don't get.'

'Say that last bit again, Jimmy.'

'It just doesn't add up.'

'Jimmy!'

I paused, re-read my notes on the fight out on the sidewalk only for Con to cut across again.

'Not that bit, the other bit about the girl, the cab, what did he do to her exactly?'

'I was outside, Con, I couldn't see.'

'Can you find out?'

'How? She ran away.'

'Ask the driver?'

'He's gone too. Couldn't get away quick enough. Just like the girl.'

'OK, make an educated guess.'

'No.'

'Uneducated'll do.'

'I think that's more your province, Con.'

For a moment there was silence as Con scribbled away on the other end of the line and I tried again.

'I thought Miss Reitell was his passport to the land of milk and honey.'

'How quickly can you get all this over to me, Jimmy?'

'So why's he treating her like this, starting fights, hitting on other women?'

'Jimmy, how quick?'

'You want me to give up shadowing the guy and come over to the office?'

Con got my point.

'No, you stay right where you are, Jimmy, I'll put something together myself.'

I paused again, looking at the closed door of the Village apartment, Subject Thomas and his companions still inside.

'It just doesn't make sense.'

Con came back down the line. He was getting irritated again but I couldn't help it. Maybe all I said to Beth wasn't quite right after all. Maybe deep down some part of me was still interested in, *why*?

'Since when has any of this had to make sense, Jimmy?'

'I told you, Con, this isn't a guy enjoying himself.'

Con cut across again, something in his tone telling me I really was now skating on the thinnest of ice.

'Who cares?'

I could almost see Con now leaning into the phone.

'I'm enjoying it, the magazine's enjoying it and half the

population of this city, hell, half the population of this whole damn country are going to be enjoying it too.'

Con's voice dripped down the phone, his tone now positively fecund with malevolence.

'So keep on his tail, Jimmy, and make sure we all keep on doing that.'

Contrary to popular myth, Harry Houdini didn't die in the infamous Chinese water trick. The reality was much less prosaic and perhaps less fitting too. In real life – or death in this case – he was punched in the stomach by a college student from McGill University who'd heard that the great Harry could withstand any sort of blow without suffering any kind of harm. The great Harry couldn't. The blow ruptured his appendix and Houdini died a short time later of diffuse peritonitis. He was buried in a bronze coffin he'd planned to use in one of his underwater burial illusions.

It wasn't the only inaccuracy in the new movie about him. At one point there was a close-up of the front page of *Variety* showing two photographs of Houdini making an elephant disappear. In the era in which the movie was set, *Variety* never ran photographs except in ads.

At another point in the unfolding action, a newspaper editor looks over the layout for an article investigating what might have happened to Houdini – and then assigns a reporter to go out and do the investigation. Even today that would be the wrong way round. With an article of a speculative nature like that, the story would always be written first, the layout following.

I'd pointed it out to Beth as we'd watched the movie a few weeks before but she'd topped me in the trivia stakes by pointing out that Houdini's real name was Weisz which was the German word for white. In the movie he was being played by

Tony Curtis whose real name was Schwartz, the German word for black.

That was just a week ago. Which felt like it was in another lifetime and maybe it was.

Houdini had died on October 31, 1926. Halloween. From that day onwards the date of his death had also been celebrated as International Magic Day. Today was October 31, 1953. Maybe that's what directed Subject Thomas's steps to that movie theater on 48th to catch the latest hot hit. Maybe there was a strange sense of homage involved. Or maybe by that time it was a case of any old port in what seemed to be an ever more turbulent storm. Subject Thomas had acted out some pretty wild scenarios in his short time in the Big Apple but he seemed to be going for some kind of record today.

He was also playing an increasingly dangerous game as well. To behave badly in front of movie stars was fair game. It was almost expected. As he'd already found to his cost that day, the American public weren't quite so indulgent or forgiving.

Subject Thomas had left the Village apartment about an hour after my call to Con. From the manner of his departure, which was furtive and hurried, I guessed that he hadn't told anyone he was going. He didn't look back as he scurried away up the street, just walked as quickly as those short legs of his would carry him but the effort seemed to exhaust him quite quickly too. He stopped in Washington Square, flopping down on one of the benches. For a while he watched some of the chess players bent over their games. One of them inclined a silent invitation his way but he didn't even seem to see him. The chess player, having elicited no response, moved onto another of the huddled spectators.

Subject Thomas remained in that semi-catatonic state for a few more moments, then brought a letter out of his pocket. He seemed to hesitate over opening it, but then slid his finger under the flap. As he turned it over I could see it had arrived via airmail.

Subject Thomas paused again, then read. His expression didn't seem to change the whole time. But when he lifted his head back up again he looked as if he'd aged a hundred lifetimes in just the last few moments.

He stood, rolled the letter into a ball and threw it into a nearby trash can, then headed away again up the street. Pausing to recover it, I followed. Whatever was in that letter seemed to be pretty incendiary stuff if the effect on the visiting poet was anything to go by, but there was no time to immediately probe any further.

By now Subject Thomas was barging into more passers-by. He didn't seem to even see them. He was also stepping out into the road causing traffic to brake violently as it tried to avoid him. Once again he scarcely seemed to notice. Then he dived into a liquor store and bought some whiskey. Back out on the street he started drinking it from the bottle. A street bum held out his hand as Subject Thomas walked past and he handed him the bottle. It was less than a minute since he'd picked it up from the liquor store and it was empty, which earned him a volley of abuse.

By now he also seemed to be having more trouble breathing. It was another unseasonably hot day and the smog was bad. It hung over the whole city like a shroud. Maybe that's why he'd decided to dive into the movie theater, maybe he just wanted to get out of the stifling air.

Or maybe that was something to do with the girl.

She was waiting in the queue for the screening. She was about twenty, maybe a couple of years older and her cheeks were painted to resemble bright red geraniums. She'd already attracted the attention of several of the guys in the same queue but had ignored them all. Then Subject Thomas made his approach and, like other women before her, she seemed to instantly recognize him and – equally instantly – melt as she did so.

OK, now I didn't suspect him of some gigantic confidence trick anymore. I still couldn't make head or tail of his poetry – the odd memorable verse aside – but I had watched his play and had quite enjoyed bits of it too. But I'd still never – in a million lifetimes – understand the hero worship those confusing and sometimes confused barrage of words piled high on the page seemed to provoke in his admirers.

Subject Thomas took her by the hand and she followed him inside the theater as if she was being escorted along by a doting parent. Little else about the subsequent encounter was to raise images of that innocent kind.

I bought a ticket and followed them inside, seating myself about three rows behind. I still had his letter in my pocket but hadn't yet looked at it and I wasn't going to get a chance for the next couple of hours either as the movie had started by then.

For some reason Subject Thomas seemed quite genuinely spellbound by the events unfolding on the screen but his companion seemed rather more engrossed with him. She tried leaning over and whispering in his ear a couple of times but he didn't seem to even realize she was there. He certainly didn't answer or even turn to look in her direction. She tried a couple more times again and received the same lack of response. So then she decided on something a little more attention-grabbing instead.

For a moment I didn't realize what she was doing. But then it became what you might call only too obvious as she moved her head down his body and began unbuttoning his trousers. A moment later, Subject Thomas – his eyes still fixed on the screen – gave a small gasp.

It was as if I could see Con before me. It was as if I could hear his voice inside my head from that very first briefing when

I thought a surname was a Christian name and I'd never even heard of any sort of wood let alone one that had anything to do with milk.

'Oh – and Jimmy – .'

Once again I was by his office door, that so-called portable tape recorder in my hand, looking back at him.

'Any chance you get to – .'

Once again Con hesitated.

' – you know – .'

And once again I finished it for him.

'Help the guy hang himself?'

'Hey.'

And once again I could see Con, as if he was up on that screen now too, spreading those arms of his wide in injured innocence.

'Would I say that?'

I still thought he was too good a lawyer to have let the magazine he represented print anything like that original profile. But now it seemed pretty tame stuff compared to everything else that was going on. Like right in front of my eyes. And I also knew what else Con – if he really was there right now – would have said to me too, because in certain cases even a brave lawyer likes to hedge his bets a little, not rely solely on a single log from one its star detectives.

Sometimes a little corroboration came in handy also.

I nudged the guy sitting next to me.

'Look at that.'

His eyes never left the screen.

'I'm watching the movie.'

We'd just got to the bit where Harry and Bess were at the magicians' dinner and another magician, Fante, was offering a prize to anyone who could free himself from a straitjacket. Harry had just accepted the challenge and the guy sitting next to me clearly wanted to see if he managed it even though, to be frank, it wouldn't have been much of a movie and Harry wouldn't have been much of an escapologist if he couldn't.

Or maybe he thought I was coming onto him. This was, after all, 48th Street.

'You can see a movie any day of the week.'

'Beat it, mister.'

'Don't see that every day. Well, not outside one of those booths they're working down the street anyhow.'

Reluctantly he tore his eyes away. I'd piqued his interest at last. A moment later and his full attention was on something other than that silver screen. Mr Curtis and his dubious dice with historical fact had now been well and truly supplanted.

'Is she doing what I think she's doing?'

All credit to Subject Thomas. His eyes were still glued on the screen despite the bobbing head in his lap. Either this guy was a serious movie fan, a genuine Houdini freak, or he was so canned that he was almost literally on some other planet right now, because in my book only an alien could have failed to respond to all that was happening to him at present.

'Looks like it to me.'

The guy nudged his companion, a longshoreman from the look of his jacket. This time it was easier to divert him from the screen. Harry had extricated himself from the straitjacket, impressing Fante but also provoking advice from the old magician to the younger practitioner that he should get out now, at the clear height of his powers. Fante was citing the example of Johann Von Schweger who'd retired in that way, also after such a demonstration of his extraordinary powers. But Harry wasn't listening and neither, now, was the longshoreman.

'Well, take a look at that.'

His companion nodded back.

'I have been. For the last five minutes.'

'And you didn't tell me?'

'I'm telling you now.'

I cut in.

'And do you know who that guy is?'

'I don't care about the guy, mister – who's the girl?'

His companion nodded again.

'Yeah. That's what I'd like to know too.'

By now the commotion was attracting interest up and down the row and from the rows behind and in front as well.

'Hey, buddy.'

'Forget the popcorn for a minute, take a look over there.'

'That beats ice-cream in the intermission, right?'

'Go, baby, go.'

And then it started. From a growing cacophony of shouts and exhortations came a stamping of feet and a bout of sustained cheering, the whole theater now urging the girl and Subject Thomas on, much as his wife – initially at least – had been urged on by a similar small army of onlookers at that carnival back home.

On screen Bess had just persuaded Harry to give her his prize, a single, round-trip boat ticket to Europe. She was telling him they could cash it in for a down-payment on a house, but no-one was paying the slightest attention to that anymore.

The girl didn't even pause. Subject Thomas didn't even seem to hear the cheers and catcalls. He just kept watching the movie as everyone in that movie theater watched him.

Half an hour later and the management had thrown him out. He was bundled from the foyer into the arms of Miss Reitell who'd heard about some commotion in a fleapit and had, presumably, put two and two together. Subject Thomas

– unprotesting as ever – was bundled in turn into a taxi by his protector and the driver was told to get them to the Chelsea.

I didn't bother following. What was the point? How was he going to top that even if he did manage to extricate himself from Miss Reitell's clutches, which I doubted? There was a determination in her manner that I wouldn't have cared to brook.

Instead I went into a small diner a couple of doors down from the movie theater and smoothed out the letter he'd screwed up earlier and thrown into the trash.

The letter, as I'd already suspected, was from his wife. She must have posted it either before or immediately after her carnival exploits but there was no mention of them. The only thing she seemed to be interested in was her husband, although from the tone I wouldn't have laid odds on their remaining wedded too much longer. This was one little lady back home who seemed to have well and truly reached the end of the road.

… there is, without exception, no wife in the whole of creation treated like I am…

See what I mean?

She also delivered a pretty devastating character assassination too, calling Subject Thomas along the way –

… weak, drunken, unfaithful and a congenital liar…

Which was a touch hypocritical given all I'd witnessed outside that bar in their home town, but again it was only Subject Thomas's exploits that were the matter of the moment, she didn't waste any time on hers –

… after this dose of concentrated humiliating ignominy I am, once and for all, finished…

It actually went on like that for pages. I must have read the whole thing at least five or six times. But I'd probably only have needed to read it the once for those bile-filled phrases to lodge themselves in my mind and probably in his too.

But – and presumably just in case her husband hadn't got the message – she saved the best for last –

... whatever you do or say, however foul, always goes down, fuck you...

But there was something else in there too, something aside from the litany of abuse; and that was the major gripe she seemed to have with her husband, the principal reason for that dose of concentrated humiliating ignominy, as she termed it.

I read that particular passage as I read the rest, over and over, not really understanding it the first time and no more enlightened on any subsequent reading either. Because now we really did seem to be in some sort of parallel universe where nothing ever seemed to be as it was, and even less made sense. Now I really had absolutely no handle on him, on her, on anything he did or anything she said.

I put down the letter again, looked out through the steamed-up windows of the diner onto the street. Couples were strolling past, checking out the movie posters, taking a look at menus pasted up on the doors of small restaurants nearby. Behind me another couple were debating the relative merits of a cheeseburger over a calzone, only to decide to order both on the agreement they'd each share the other's. I looked down again at the letter Subject Thomas, female, had written to her husband, then I screwed it up myself and dropped it into the nearest trash can. That wouldn't be going into the report which I wasn't going to write till later anyway.

For now I was going to see Beth.

16

UP IN LITTLE Italy, there was some sort of street festival going on with some saint or other being celebrated. Then again, there was always some saint or other being celebrated in that neighborhood or so it seemed to me and, if there wasn't, they'd invent one. At least that's what I'd told Beth. Once. Until she repeated it to Nora at a family meal that same evening. Nora's subsequent verbal assault didn't quite reach the heights that Subject Thomas, female, had managed in her letter to her spouse, but it was still pretty impressive stuff.

I dodged yelling kids, vendors selling pizza, life-size statues being carried along on floats and rang the bell of Nora's apartment hoping against hope that it would be Beth who'd answer the door.

'Jimmy.'

The greeting was as level as the Missouri flats. Delivered in a tone of voice that told me more eloquently than mere words could have managed that I really wasn't welcome. Accompanied by a pair of eyes that stared at me more coldly than any creature from the deepest ocean. And neither the voice nor the eyes belonged to Beth. For not the first time in the last few days a wish on my part had proven to be just that little bit too hopeful.

'I want to see Beth.'

The owner of that cold and level voice and those even colder eyes just kept staring at me and for not the first time again I wondered how on earth it was that I could face down some pretty tough individuals in the course of my work, but always managed to feel like an awkward schoolboy when faced with my wife's big sister.

'It's not convenient, Jimmy.'

'Look. Nora. Please – just five minutes. Less – two minutes – whatever. I'm here because it's important.'

She didn't reply.

'I should be working – right now – in fact, especially right now.'

She still didn't reply.

'Tonight's the best so far – if you knew.'

I broke off. What the hell was I doing talking about work? Nora's attitude to work, to any kind of work, was simple. It was either useful, like hers in the hospital. Or it provided a service like Beth did with the hospital records. Or it was a waste of time like mine. A trifle, not even to be discussed, so why was I even mentioning it?

But in truth I knew exactly why. I was talking just to fill the silence. The world had spiraled out of balance in a way I couldn't even begin to understand and all I wanted to do was get at least some small part of that world, my world, mine and Beth's world, back under some kind of control.

'But I'm not working, because I don't want to work, I only want to see my wife, so please, Nora, will you just tell her I'm here, ask her to come out and see me, I won't even come in, not if you don't want, I'll just stay right here the whole time.'

For a moment she eyed me again and for a moment I thought she might weaken. Then she shook her head, said it again.

'It's not convenient, Jimmy.'

And then she did it. Then she did the one thing I'd never have expected her to do in a million lifetimes, would indeed have scorned any suggestion she might do if anyone had been crazy enough to suggest it, because it was impossible, unthinkable. But she did it, out on that doorstep with me standing before her, with the carnival going on behind, she did it and it might have been just the one simple word, but it blew my world apart.

'Please.'

I stared at her for a moment unable to believe the evidence of my ears. Had I actually heard that? Or was that my over-active imagination making it up? But as I kept staring the door behind her didn't change shape and the pavement didn't melt beneath my feet either. I really was standing outside her apartment and I had just heard my sister-in-law actually say – and now I repeated it –

'Please?'

Nora hesitated.

'What?'

I just kept looking at her.

'How long have we known each other, Nora?'

'What are you talking about?'

'How long?'

'What's that got to do with anything?'

'I must have met you the week after I met Beth, so how many years is that?'

I think she knew. From the hunted way she was looking at me I think she realized only too clearly that she'd just made something of a mistake.

'And in those years, in all that time Nora, in all the time I've known you, that has to be the first time you have ever – ever – said that to me.'

I nodded at her again, repeated it once more.

'Please.'

'Just go home, Jimmy.'

I looked beyond her. It wasn't the uncharacteristically tentative plea that was really interesting me now. It wasn't even the uncharacteristically tentative tone. It was what lay behind it.

What, exactly, wasn't convenient about my seeing Beth that evening? And why had Nora abandoned her lifetime's quest to act the ultimate hardnosed ball-breaker and utter the one word I'd never thought I'd hear from her lips, at least not addressed to me, the no-good husband of her darling little sister, a man who had always been a perpetual disappointment in her eyes?

'I said, go home.'

I looked back at her, my old fears fading fast. It was truly amazing what one little word could do. The power it could bestow. Maybe that explained the appeal of Subject Thomas. When his many and varied followers looked at him they didn't see a fat, crumpled figure in a patched and ill-fitting suit. They didn't see the drunk or the clown. They saw the words he'd somehow managed to produce and somehow everything else didn't matter anymore.

'Know what Beth'd say?'

'It's late, Jimmy.'

I just rolled straight on.

'She'd say I'm doing it again, I'm looking at you and I'm thinking, there's something she's not telling me, something she doesn't want me to know, but that's me, right? That's what happens when you spend all your time down in the gutter, you start thinking that's where everyone else lives too, you start thinking that everyone's got something to hide just like the lowlifes and losers I tail every day and then you start looking for things that aren't there, reading things into even the smallest words people say, like – .'

I nodded at her. Nora's eyes hadn't left mine once.

'Please.'

Nora held eye contact for a few moments longer, then nodded back.

'Right.'

And, suddenly, I'd had enough. Tonight was proving to be

a first in more ways than one because now I did something I thought I'd never do. I moved past her, ignoring the upturned palm raised in warning, just moved on into that small hallway, still empty aside from Nora and on towards Beth who was, presumably, in the small sitting room.

'I want to see my wife.'

'Jimmy.'

She called after me, but now there was more resignation than anything else in her voice. She knew this particular battle was lost. One way or another, through persuasion or sheer brute force, I was going to have the encounter I wanted.

As I opened the door to the sitting room I heard Nora's voice once again behind me.

'It's not what you think.'

Half an hour later and I'm standing by one of the rain-washed exits leading off Times Square. Taxis are passing within inches of me as I stand on the edge of the sidewalk looking at the lights, at trippers heading in and out of shows, at the bars, the hotels, the movie theaters. No-one's standing still as I seem to be standing still right now, trying to remember how I got there.

Did I walk, take a cab, ride the subway, did I see anyone on that journey, did I talk to anyone?

All the time trying to remember every detail of the last half-hour, perhaps in some vain hope I might forget all that immediately preceded it back in that apartment.

But I remembered it all of course. I remembered pushing against that door and I remembered first seeing Beth standing, rising up from the sofa that Nora had bought from a dime store back in the Village and had then spent weekends refurbishing and restoring.

Next to her on that sofa was a man, about my age, maybe a

little stockier in the frame, maybe not quite as tall, but my sort of age and build nonetheless. Quite a regular-looking guy too – he had a pleasant enough smile – even if at the moment he was looking a little nervous and that smile seemed more than a little forced.

'Jimmy.'

Beth hesitated, then looked back at her companion, almost as if she was seeking permission to speak. I didn't say anything, just waited for her, that old detective's trick again, why do the mark's work for them, if they're going to convict themselves let them do it out of their own mouth, right?

From behind me, Nora broke in, eyes only for Beth, which made two of us in that room. Aside from a quick glance at her companion, I just kept my eyes fixed on my wife. It was another old trick. Never let the mark out of your sight. And, in any confrontation, always stare straight at them, don't break eye contact, let them break it instead, let them duck their eyes and turn away, always a sure sign they've something tasty to hide.

Beth looked beyond me at her sister.

'It's OK.'

Nora shrugged, seemingly helpless, which must have been another new sensation for her that evening.

'He just – .'

'I said it's OK.'

Then Beth looked back at me and to be fair to her she held my gaze, steady now too. Maybe I shouldn't have spent all that time telling her the tricks of the trade when we first met.

'Just leave me alone, Jimmy.'

'I have left you alone, Beth, for the last week I've left you alone, I've given you time, that's what you asked for, wasn't it? Time to think, isn't that what you said? So what are you saying now, that you need more time to think, is that it?'

Beth just kept looking at me.

'So how much more time do you want? Why don't you tell me and then we'll both know, rather than just you being the one who knows? Another week, a month, a year, can you hazard a guess, give me some kind of likely timescale, it's not that much of a schlep from Stuy Town, but why waste all that effort, right?'

Then I nodded to her side, feeling if not actually seeing her companion tensing all the time as he realized he was now moving into the very center of the frame, which meant he not only had decent looks and a pleasant smile but brains as well.

A combination Beth had always gone for in the past, or so she claimed, and one she might just have gone for again.

'And while you're updating me on all that maybe you could also let me know how he's helping you do all this thinking you say you've got to do, this young man you've got here in this room with you, this handsome young man you're sitting with, all alone, in this room while your sister tries to stall your husband out on the doorstep?'

Beth just ignored that.

'Nora's right, Jimmy. This really isn't what you think.'

'Well actually Beth, I don't want to *think* anything and if someone actually *told* me something I could understand then I wouldn't need to think anything at all would I, then I'd *know*.'

Beth just looked at me, her face stiffening all the while and now I'm thinking, incredible. I walk in to find my wife – my wife – who decided she wanted to be alone for a while – in a cozy little twosome with some guy and she's the one who's beginning to look seriously pissed.

But then there was a distraction in the shape of her companion – the pleasant-faced young man with the slightly nervous smile – rising ever more nervously now to his feet.

'Look – maybe I should leave.'

'Why?'

He stared at me, didn't reply as Beth cut across.

194

'Jimmy.'

And now it was my turn to ignore her.

'It's a simple enough question, why do you think you should leave?'

The man looked across at Beth and now he was the one who looked as if he was seeking guidance. What the hell had been going on here? These two seemed to have plenty to hide if the constant looks they were exchanging were anything to go by. This all looked horribly – unendurably – intimate.

I nodded at Beth again, including Nora in the gesture, keeping my eyes on the pleasant-faced young man all the time even if he really didn't seem to be finding this all that pleasant.

'This isn't what I think – I've got it all wrong – I'm so wide of the bull's-eye I might as well be tilting at windmills – so why should you leave?'

Beth stood between us as if she now feared some kind of physical assault and maybe she was right. Maybe that had been in my mind from the moment I pushed open that door and I was only now beginning to realize it.

'Jimmy, stop this.'

'Stop what, Beth? What is there to stop? If you'll just tell me that, maybe at the same time as you tell me what I'm thinking, we can wrap this up right now and I can do what you obviously want me to do and that's go, leave you to your sister and your friend.'

Then I broke off, staring at that friend, my eyes now never leaving his.

'See, in my world and this may not be a world you understand, I don't know, my wife probably does because she seems to know you quite well but I don't so I'll explain. In my world people leave when they've done something wrong, when they've been caught doing something they shouldn't, but that can't be what's happening here, because this isn't my world, this is my wife's world and bad things don't happen in her world, only in mine, isn't that right, Beth?'

The question was to her, but my eyes were still fixed on just his face.

'My life's full of all sorts of liars and cheats and moochers, in fact I've just been on the tail of one of the very worst and maybe Beth's right, maybe after a while it does start to affect you, does make you look at people in a whole new way, maybe sometimes there's a trick of the light and all you see are shadows where there aren't any.'

He glanced at Beth again and she half-raised her hand as if to say, it's OK, don't worry, he'll be out of here before long and then we can get back to what we were doing before.

But not without my getting the answer to a very simple question.

'Who the hell is this, Beth?'

No-one answered.

'I said – .'

'I heard you, Jimmy.'

'So?'

The guy turned, picked up his coat.

'I'll see you tomorrow, Beth.'

'So you two work together, well, it's a reasonable deduction if you're going to see her tomorrow, that's where you probably met, down among the filing cabinets, who'd have thought life among all those hospital records could be such fun.'

'Bye, Beth.'

He hadn't even looked at me as he started to move towards the door.

Bad move.

'I'm talking to you.'

'He's not talking to you, Jimmy.'

That was Nora.

'No-one is.'

Nora again.

'Then I'll just have to talk a little louder.'

I stepped close, too close, to the pleasant-faced young man and now there wasn't even the ghost of a smile on his face.

'Because you're not leaving until I get some answers.'

Things were a bit of a blur after that. I remember some shouting and some pushing and shoving – you couldn't say it ever developed into what you might call a fight – in fact the pushing and shoving mainly involved myself and Nora and if I'd enjoyed a brief advantage outside her apartment it was an advantage she well and truly claimed back inside.

But most of all I remember Beth's face as Nora escorted me back towards the door. There was a wounded quality on display that I'd never seen before. Some deep sense, again, of a sadness I couldn't divine. As if she was looking at something that could never now be reclaimed, at a world once familiar – still recognizable indeed – but now cast forever in some alien form.

Was that what we'd come to without my even realizing it – and definitely without understanding it? For Subject Thomas, male and female, it was easy to understand. They behaved like monsters, to each other as well as to everyone else, they deserved everything that came their way, right?

Were we to go the same way simply because one boyhood dream – of college – a law course somehow never taken up – had tempered into something else?

I turned into a bar seeking solace, Subject Thomas style, in the comfort of bourbon. As nursemaids went it had few equals as I began to discover just a short time later. Maybe the great man knew a thing or two after all.

17

I WAS OUT in the city into the early hours, doing all the things guys do when they say they're enjoying themselves – visiting bars, then more bars and, just to vary it a little, a few more again.

Companions came and went, almost exclusively male. At least I think so. Faces tended to merge after a while. Some journeyed with me for a few moments, some for longer. With some I talked about sport. The recent single-point victory of the Lions over the Cleveland Browns merited some dissection at one point, I recall. On a more serious note an extended discussion began at another stage in the evening on the fate of the Rosenbergs.

Some of those companions became confidants, although what exactly I confided in them I can't now remember. I know I didn't talk about Beth to anyone. But I knew the conversation I wanted to have with her because it was running through my head all the time, over and over, repeated as if on a loop, refinements and amendments being added all the while, but the essence remained the same and it was ugly and it was raw and it was mean, which was exactly how I was feeling. And, all the time, fresh impetus if it were needed, was provided by that expression on her face, the way she looked at me as I was finally bundled out of the door.

As if *I* was the one who'd done something wrong. As if *I* was the one who'd transgressed in some way.

As if all this, in short, was my fault.

It was an inner exchange that went something like this:

'So all I see are the fault lines –

– all I look for are the mistakes people make –

– all I imagine is the worst in everyone –

– all I do is laugh at them all the time –

– never believe a single thing they say – '

I walked on, through the night, not now hitting the bars anymore.

'And now you know why, right Beth?'

Just moving with no direction and less purpose, that same inner exchange reverberating all the while.

'At least that way I'm never disappointed.'

And then I saw him. Subject Thomas, up ahead, his unmistakable, shambling figure being poured from a taxi in through the front door of the Algonquin. Unlike most of the neighborhood bars – with the Algonquin being a hotel – that bar wouldn't have closed even at that time of night so long as you were a resident and Subject Thomas was in the company of several other revelers who, from the proprietary manner in which they strode through the door, looked to be just that, or at least were giving a pretty good impression of being the same.

I hesitated for a moment, then followed, aware I was crossing some kind of Rubicon, but way past caring. I didn't even know why I was following him inside, but that didn't stop me either.

Maybe it was the night for it. Forcing everything to some sort of head. Or maybe, like Subject Thomas himself, I was now well and truly into self-destruct mode, pushing each and every button I could find.

I strode through the doors a few moments after the Subject Thomas party swept inside. Even at that time it was surprisingly busy, although being the Algonquin maybe I shouldn't actually have been that surprised. In the boho stakes it didn't rival the Chelsea where a party was probably going on in the lobby right there and then, but it was still pretty louche, as I'd heard it described on some radio show sometime. I'd meant to look up what that meant but then hadn't bothered. I'd sort of got the drift anyway.

Partly that was due to the hotel policy of giving impoverished writers a free room for the night in exchange for an autographed copy of one of their books.

Partly it was the regular attendees at the monthly salons whose members had always included all sorts of luminaries from the worlds of literature and entertainment.

Partly it was the resident cat, called Hamlet, who was even now looking at me from the chaise longue in the lobby with a wary expression on his face as if he'd just spotted trouble, which maybe he had.

And partly it was due to the raucous cacophony of yells, whoops and hollers I could hear from the bar on the other side of the lobby which told me only too eloquently that Subject Thomas was very definitely in residence and hadn't hightailed it up to some room or other for a deep and meaningful discussion about iambic pentameters or whatever the hell literary types are supposed to talk about when they got together.

A harassed duty manager came out of the bar and had a word with an equally wary concierge. They too looked as if they'd just spotted trouble which was fortunate because that meant no-one – Hamlet aside – was taking too much notice of me.

I moved closer to the bar. Now I was in earshot of all that was being said, as opposed to the white wall noise of incoherent ranting and raving I could hear from across the lobby, Subject Thomas was sounding loud and clear, above the rest of the voices.

Had this guy been in the war? From the little I'd read up on him I didn't think so, he'd spent most of those years writing propaganda movies from what I'd understood. But now he was raving about machine guns and grenades and bullets ripping through walls and ceilings and bodies being ripped to shreds by round after round of sniper fire, of those bodies then being turned into carcasses and of skin being obliterated by geysers of blood erupting from inside.

His companions seemed to regard all this as a highly individual form of cabaret – and maybe it was, although Subject Thomas seemed genuinely agitated as he plunged on. It had all sounded like fantasy at first but was now beginning to sound increasingly less so as he piled detail on top of more detail, as he fulminated on to the increasing roars and cheers of his companions, most of whom didn't seem to be taking too much of it in but most of whom didn't seem to be caring too much anyway.

Two, quite beautiful, black girls came out from the bar looking bored. From their exchange it was pretty clear they were hookers who'd been swept along in the party and had come back to the Algonquin on the understanding that business matters would be concluded in the usual manner. It had dawned on them in the last few moments that few among the party were capable of concluding any sort of business at present and they were now debating their chances of getting past the bellhops in the Waldorf where, it seemed, a large delegation were just in from the UN.

'Have you business here, sir?'

I tore my eyes away from the two girls to see a large doorman who'd now approached from the other side of the lobby. The manager had returned to the bar where I could hear him attempting to calm the commotion. The walls of the Algonquin were thick and most of the bedrooms were several stories above the bar, but the racket Subject Thomas and his cohorts were making could have awakened the dead.

I looked at the doorman as he eyed me, taking in my sodden coat, my wringing wet shoes, categorizing me instantly as an unlikely hotel guest but not wanting to alienate me completely. I might be a late straggler making up the rear of the party in the bar which included, as he'd no doubt been told, some famous poet or other, although there didn't seem anything particularly poetic about all that was taking place through there right now.

The girls sashayed past us. Behind the doorman, another woman eyed me. She had to be in her seventies but was decked out like a mannequin with a quilted black and white jacket, several ropes of pearls and white chalk make-up. You couldn't tell if her look was ironic or deadly serious. Maybe she couldn't either.

'Yeah. I've business here.'

'Could you tell me who with?'

He was good. Practiced and smooth. He couldn't have been more than forty, around the same age as Subject Thomas, but he looked like he'd had several lifetimes experience in dealing with all manner and types of guests and situations.

The doorman nodded over at a phone in the lobby, just behind the chaise longue and the reclining Hamlet.

'I'll page them for you.'

The doorman took a couple of steps across the lobby intending that I follow. Most would, it would have been an instinctive reaction. Maybe I would have done too but right at that moment a fresh burst of raucous laughter and cheering broke through from the bar as the Subject Thomas party told the hapless manager, in no uncertain terms, what he could do with his attempt to put a lid on their enjoyment of their evening, which was now very much the early morning in truth, but who the hell was clock-watching? Because they certainly weren't.

I nodded towards the bar instead.

'I'll just follow the noise.'

The bar of the Algonquin was dark with leather booths. It was the kind of place you'd need a mini flashlight to inspect the bill which was perhaps fortunate given the rumored size of some of those checks. The walls were the deepest of deep blue. The entrance was actually a little draughty, so most people crossing that threshold made sure they kept moving on towards whatever entertainment they'd planned for themselves inside.

Waiters patrolled the booths making sure the guests didn't have to do anything so vulgar as stand at the bar and order drinks themselves. But when I walked in I couldn't see the bar because of the Subject Thomas party crowding around it. Apparently it was the way drinking was done back in England. Or wherever. The usual tradition was to stand in front of the bar blocking access for anyone else, waiters included, and it was a tradition Subject Thomas was clearly determined to maintain.

I knew I only had a few moments. The doorman would definitely be coming in sometime soon just to check that the interloper in the lobby who'd now gravitated into the bar really did have business with one of their honored guests and wasn't just some bum on the lam, looking to score some free drink and entertainment.

And now I knew what I wanted to do with those few moments as well. A short while before, following the Subject Thomas party into the lobby, I didn't really know. Now, suddenly, everything was crystal clear.

'Hey, Mr Thomas.'

I called across the bar, advancing all the while. I couldn't actually see the man himself. He was buried in a press of acolytes and admirers.

'Mr Thomas.'

A large gentleman detached himself from the group and looked at me as I continued to approach. He was heavily-built, had probably been delegated to handle any trouble earlier in the evening and was obviously intending to execute a similar duty now. The problem being he was having difficulty focusing and his speech was slurred and he didn't look as if he could handle a highball right now, let alone any sort of disturbance.

'Leave us alone, pal.'

'This'll only take a minute.'

'Mr Thomas is indisposed.'

He had trouble over that last word but I wasn't listening anyway. Because now I saw him. Briefly, the press of people at the bar had parted and Subject Thomas was now just a few feet away from me, his face even more bloated than normal, his hair matted, looking as if this was the last place he should be right now but looking, also, as if it was the very last place he was going to leave right now too. But that's what the demon drink did to you, right? Maybe the Temperance crowd had it right after all.

'And why would that be?'

The heavy gentleman just blinked.

'What?'

I raised my voice, intending to pitch this to Subject Thomas himself, over the heads of his companions.

'All that drinking, cheating, lying and whoring.'

What the hell?

'Hey.'

That was my heavily-built companion now starting to stare at me as if I'd just landed from some other planet somewhere. Subject Thomas himself didn't look round. Not a tousled hair on that head of his moved one jot. He might as well have been back in that movie theater staring at Harry's antics on screen.

'Don't say it's finally grinding our famous wordsmith down.'

My voice was carrying all right and now I was starting to attract all the wrong sort of attention too as waiters started to look over, as waitresses glanced towards the lobby, as some more of Subject Thomas's new friends started to register the discordant note, the spectre at what had been, up to then anyway, a doubtless munificent feast.

'What's happened, has Charlie slapped a writ on him?'

'Who the hell's Charlie?'

'Damage to his begonias? Or whatever else he pissed on in those pots of his?'

By now I was talking at full volume and the whole bar was starting to quieten which was quite something given that a few moments before it was resembling a definition of bedlam.

'Or was it that little cutie who ran out of that taxi, has she made some sort of scene, is that why the main man's feeling a few degrees under right now?'

The heavily-built companion made a quick mental calculation, factoring in how much he'd drunk, the current speed of his reflexes and the chances of coming off second-best in an encounter with a clear madman, and then made a decision that was surprisingly lucid and clear-headed in the circumstances.

'I'm calling Security.'

He'd actually just been beaten to it by a waitress who'd been dispatched by the barman to the lobby to do just that, but I didn't tell him. I wasn't finished yet and didn't want to waste any time with distractions.

'Hey, don't get me wrong, I'm a fan.'

'Doesn't sound much like it to me.'

We were joined by another of Subject Thomas's night-time companions and this one was from the same sort of production line, stocky build, low forehead, large stomach, blinking eyes.

I shook my head in vehement disagreement.

'He's a genius.'

The men paused, wary, looked at each other. Had they got this wrong, was this just an eccentric fan making some in-joke references they hadn't understood?

'You know his work?'

'Everyone else pretends. Puts on a face. Not this guy.'

The men were starting to relax as I nodded away before them, dredging a poetic phrase – or so I hoped – from some distant memory.

'He's out there, red in tooth and claw, whatever he wants to do he just does it, what we'd all do given half a chance, right?'

One of the guys turned, yelled across the bar.

'Hey, is this guy one of your poets? You should hear him.'

I rolled on, hardly pausing.

'Take what you want, when you want it, who cares who's watching and who the hell – who the *hell* – cares what anyone thinks, screw them, right?'

Now the faces were tensing again and out of the corner of my eye I saw the doorman who'd approached me in the lobby arriving with a couple of resident goons. The waitress who'd exited a few moments before was also with them and she was pointing across at me although you'd have to be pretty slow on the uptake not to spot the source of the new commotion right now.

'I'm telling you, this guy is so far ahead of his time he's practically in orbit.'

I sensed rather than felt the tap on the shoulder. They trained them well in the Algonquin and the gesture was light. But I wasn't fooled. Like the Stuy Town security outfit, they also paid top dollar and usually secured the best kind of muscle for that dollar too – muscle with brains, but not afraid to use a little brawn if the occasion arose.

'Why don't we leave these gentlemen to their drinks, sir?'

I nodded, immediately. Another lesson from the days in the agency. Never provoke confrontation unless it's absolutely necessary. Disarm. Reassure. Then, when everyone's defences are down, make your move.

'Sure thing, no problem.'

I turned away from the companions who glanced back at Subject Thomas. He was still facing the bar. Whether he'd heard me or not I'd no idea.

It didn't matter. He soon would.

'Neat bar by the way.'

I made for the door, the doorman falling in step with me.

'Thank you.'

'Maybe I'll come back one day, spend a little longer.'

For a moment he kept walking, unaware I'd doubled back. The two goons who'd been keeping pace with us also kept walking for that all-important moment too. Either the Algonquin wasn't quite paying the top dollar for its staff it used to do or these guys needed a serious refresher course.

I only needed a second or so to cross the bar and move to the side of Subject Thomas.

And now he saw me. And now he heard me too. And his bulbous lips moved as well although nothing came out. But that didn't bother me. It wasn't conversation I was after. He was used to homage and I wanted to pay my own and maybe he was used to homage of the more literary variety, but what the hell? A fan's a fan, right?

'Mr Thomas, sir, let me shake your hand.'

I reached out and took it in mine. His hand flopped limply as I pumped it vigorously up and down. The doorman and the security goons were now back at my shoulder again and I knew there'd be no light, cajoling, invitation to leave this time. Something was telling me I was now in trouble.

One second later I was proved right.

One hour later again and I was back on the small balcony of the apartment looking down on the walkways winding through the neat, ornamental gardens, at the benches where families would sit and watch their children playing and where old-timers would take in the final rays of the evening sun.

On the guardrail was the bird who'd looked at me, a little balefully I thought, as I rolled back the door and stepped outside. His – or her – expression said it all. It didn't know what had been happening with me lately but it had been getting more than a little hungry. I went some way to putting that right at least by taking nearly a whole loaf of stale bread from the basket – we were clean out of fresh anyway – and then stood and watched it as it gorged on the belated feast as if it was some kind of Last Supper.

Maybe it was. Maybe we wouldn't actually be living here too much longer. With two wages coming in we could just about cover the bills. But one person living alone would never be able to keep it going on their own. If that was my status right now – a single person living alone – then the writing was on the wall in the accommodation stakes as well, perhaps, as in every other.

Dawn was breaking by now. It was still too early for the first of the commuters to begin the trek over to the subway but a few other birds were now out and about, circling the balcony, looking at the chosen one tucking into breakfast, wondering how he – or she – had been proffered a banquet like that while the rest of them had to forage around among trash bins for scraps. The bird on the balcony didn't take any notice of them, just kept dipping down into the pieces of bread, shaking large crumbs loose and swallowing them before moving onto the next.

It had been too huge a night on all fronts. I knew the fine detail of Subject Thomas's antics in the movie theater should really now be in a log winging its way to Con for his arrival at work in an hour or so's time, but I hadn't dragged out the Smith Corona yet to even begin committing all that to print.

I also knew I was going to have to confront my antics in the Algonquin sometime too. I could only dimly recall what I'd said, what kind of a scene I'd created in there, although more and more of it, unwanted and unbidden once again, was coming back all the while.

But it was the final act in what might prosaically be called the night's three-act tragedy that was really pounding through my head right now of course, the encounter with Beth in her sister's apartment, the encounter with Beth and the pleasant-faced young man who'd decided he really should leave even though he'd done nothing wrong.

It was all too much to take in, to absorb, but given the way these things usually pan out, it wasn't over yet either.

From behind, a voice broke in.

'Jimmy.'

I turned to see Beth standing in our small kitchen looking out at me. For a moment I didn't move, didn't speak, didn't do anything. By my side the bird took one last peck at the piece of stale bread, then flew away, trailing a small line of crumbs as it did so. Maybe my feathered friend had now its fill. Or maybe it was the sensitive type who really didn't want to intrude on private grief.

I reached out, pushed the remaining bread off the guardrail. Some of the other hovering birds dived after it.

Then I looked back at Beth.

'What's the matter?'

I moved back into the kitchen, closing the sliding door behind me.

'Your fancy man busy right now so you thought you'd call in on your husband?'

'Don't be ridiculous.'

How neat was this? She was the one shacked up in some apartment uptown with some strange guy and I was the one who was being ridiculous. That out-of-balance world again, I guess.

'You wanted time alone, time to think, that's what you said.'

'That was true.'

I nodded. Now we might be getting somewhere. It's what I wanted after all, just some simple, plain, honest truth.

'So was he helping you do that?'

'I'd have explained if you'd given me a chance.'

'I gave you plenty of chances.'

'If you hadn't just badgered me like you're badgering me now.'

Beth eyed me, looking as baleful now as the bird out on the balcony just a few moments before.

'There was no need to take a swipe at him.'

Dimly, as she spoke, more memories returned.

'And if you hadn't just stormed off like that I'd have told you he's a friend of Nora's, not mine, well, a colleague anyway, he's a doctor, she's a nurse on his ward and she asked him to call in on me.'

Suddenly I stilled, a dull fear beginning to settle on my stomach again.

'What did you want to see a doctor for?'

Was Beth ill, was that what this was all about, had I got this whole thing horribly, unforgivably, wrong?

She didn't answer for a moment and I felt the panic beginning to rise in my voice.

'Beth?'

Still, she didn't reply.

'Why do you need to see a doctor?'

And then, finally, she looked at me.

'Because, Jimmy, I'm pregnant.'

I just stared at her for a long, long moment.

'You're what?'

Beth didn't bother answering a question she knew was more a reflex response than anything else.

'You're pregnant?'

I was floundering big-time.

Beth nodded.

'And I don't know if I want to be. Not with how things are right now.'

'I'm not hearing this.'

'I don't know if we're ready for it – no – correction.'

Beth shook her head.

'I don't know if *you're* ready for it.'

But I was still about thirty seconds behind and not catching up all that fast either.

'You're pregnant and you never told me?'

'I'm telling you now.'

'I don't believe you, Beth, how could you keep something like that from me?'

'I wasn't going to keep it from you. For Christ's sake, Jimmy, just listen to what I'm saying for once will you? I was just going to think a few things over, that's all.'

I cut across, more angry now than I could ever remember.

'Beth, you think over a fight, you think over a move to another apartment, you think over a vacation, you don't think over a baby.'

But Beth hit back hard. She seemed pretty angry right now too.

'Ask me why, Jimmy?'

'What?'

'Ask me why I needed to think things over, ask me why I didn't tell you straightaway?'

'OK, why?'

And every word came out strong and clear, as if they'd been rehearsed over and over which maybe they had.

'Because I don't know how a baby, Jimmy, fits into a world that's a big, sick joke.'

Beth nodded at me as I stared back at her.

'Do you?'

I just kept staring at her.

18

FOR THE REST of that day I walked.

Again.

Anywhere and everywhere.

Again.

I knew the phone back in the apartment would be ringing almost non-stop by now as Con tried to get hold of me. In a rare demonstration of neighborly sensitivity I took the receiver off the hook so the occupants of the apartments next to ours wouldn't be disturbed. Then I made sure I wouldn't be similarly disturbed by walking the island, then the whole island again and then walking it some more.

I cut up FDR initially before taking a left on 57th and then into Central Park. When I tired of all that greenery and kids playing baseball I headed down to the Battery, cutting through the Village, not even looking at the Chelsea or the White Horse or Herdt's and just stood on the dock looking out at the Statue of Liberty. Needless to say, I had no real clue where I was going. And, suddenly, out of nowhere, a few stray sentences floated in front of my eyes.

I'd picked up another of Subject Thomas's books the day before, just after leaving the small diner and before I'd made my journey uptown to see Beth. I'd passed a bookstore and had seen it in the window. It was a new work by my guy – well, new-ish. And it wasn't poetry this time, but prose – a collection that had first appeared in an earlier form a decade or so before, but which had just been reprinted in the US.

I'd only managed to get through the first chapter so far but, from what I could see and from a quick scan of the rest, it seemed to set the tone.

The chapter was called 'A Fine Beginning' even if the events it detailed – so far as the main protagonist was concerned – promised anything but.

The story involved the adventures of a young guy called Bennet, Sam Bennet, who'd left his home to travel to London. He's seeking something but he doesn't know what. He's supposed to be getting a job on some newspaper but on the train ride he destroys a list of all his former contacts in that field. Then he sits in a train station waiting room where he comes across an acquaintance, a certain Mr Allingham, who questions him about his plans.

But Sam, it seems, doesn't have any plans. He doesn't, in fact, see the point in making any, because he sees the world as meaningless and just intends to let things happen.

What's the point of trying to make sense of anything, Sam wants to know, when there is none?

But Allingham can't accept that. There's sense in everything, he tells his young companion, otherwise no-one would be able to carry on. People must know where they're going, otherwise the streets would be full of people just wandering about and having useless arguments.

No prizes for guessing why those stray sentences were floating through my head, right?

Was that what he was doing?

Subject Thomas?

Right here, right now, in NYC?

Was his story some sort of prophecy – or prediction – on his part?

And was it what I was doing now too? Had my quarry's actions somehow started to infect me also?

Beth had left a few moments after her final, parting crack. I hadn't offered too much by the way of a response and she seemed to have run out of too many other things to say too and no wonder. How do you top that, right? So she just left. I remained seated in the kitchen for a moment, ignoring the tapping on the window from the bird who'd returned in the hope of seconds. Then I'd taken the phone off the hook and begun my walk.

Oddly enough it wasn't the baby I was actually thinking about. That was all still too abstract I guess, too unreal. Most men I knew couldn't really get their heads round the reality of being a father until a squalling bundle was actually deposited in their arms, so I was probably no exception there. All that was on my mind were two of the unlikeliest bedfellows you could ever yoke together, two people indeed who'd never met and who probably never would; Beth and Subject Thomas.

Beth hadn't been as viciously damning in her condemnation of myself and my life as Subject Thomas, female, had been of her husband's adventures and activities. She hadn't descended to the language of the gutter either in her description of my faults and failings. But there was still some sort of connection there and part of the reason I was walking – anywhere and for apparently no purpose – was to try and work it out, to try and find that connection as if that might provide some sort of route map, some way back to something that might already not exist anymore.

I couldn't rely on any help from Beth. She'd said all she'd had to say and she certainly wouldn't speak to me anymore about it. I had tried calling her from a phone booth as I came onto the Battery but Nora had intercepted the call. She informed me that Beth was in but didn't want to speak to me and that I could either accept that or go throw myself in the Hudson and that if I ever came round there again and made a scene such as the one I'd made the previous night then she'd throw me in the Hudson herself. I told her I believed her and hung up.

I thought of contacting Beth some other way, by letter or even by making some sort of recording on that portable tape recorder that Con had given me and which I still had back in the apartment, but then decided against that too. I couldn't see that going down too well. It smacked too much of the tools of the trade, the trade she hated so much, the trade she believed had infected everything we'd previously shared together even if I still really couldn't see it.

I was still just a detective. A simple reporter of facts. Does a war reporter suddenly turn into a killing machine? Does a court reporter suddenly turn into a lawyer? But I couldn't say that to her of course. I couldn't say anything. She was just leaving me alone to think things over. Leaving me to think about what we were and what we'd become which was an old tussle and one I was still those million miles from resolving.

I knew what Beth would say. Maybe that was because I didn't want to resolve it. Maybe I was just some junkie strung out on it all. Maybe the sad truth was that after too long getting high on the sort of stuff I dealt with day in, day out, I now needed the hit.

Was he the same? Subject Thomas? I still knew nothing about him. How he started – how do you start being a poet anyway? I still didn't know what dreams he carried around back in that home town of his when he looked out on the world and thought, I know what I want to do. I want to pick up a pen and write.

Did he start off back then thinking he had his pen and his paper and all those words that were floating around in his head and everything would be simple? That he'd just sit there and write them all down? Only things didn't turn out quite so simple, did they? So what went wrong for him and how?

The dream for Beth and myself was pretty simple of course. The college course, the law degree, Beth becoming a teacher. All a bit more conventional than the path chosen by Subject Thomas but we'd still been pretty excited by it all.

Was it extending the job with the agency by that one more

year, was that when the rot set in? Beth had listened to all the arguments I'd put forward and had nodded in all the right places too. When times were good it made sense to grab the dollar, a year wouldn't make much difference in the grand scheme of things and it did mean I'd start on the college course with the two of us on a more financially viable footing.

But there was still something in her eyes. There was still a hesitation in her voice as she relayed the change of plans to her sister later that night as we met up in a diner on 42nd Street before taking in a show, *A Tree Grows In Brooklyn*, as I recall. It was a hot ticket at the time but thanks to the agency we could afford it.

And a year later, when I started talking about education like that, wondering what it really was when you actually got down to it, whether it was something you found in the pages of some dusty book somewhere, at the knee of some out-of-touch professor, or something you found out on the streets, among the people who actually break and make the law as opposed to those who just study it; that was when something started to die and I knew it.

Maybe the truth was, I was scared. Maybe I'd found something I could do, something I was good at and I didn't want to risk failure in another field by giving it up. I'd found a world I could live in and if Beth didn't want to live in it she didn't have to. I was making good money, enough for both of us, enough to consider accelerating her own college course ahead of mine.

And if any of the guys back in the agency asked me about my change of plan, the fact I was still there, months after I'd told them I'd be finishing, it was easy, just shrug the shoulders, put on the face. Hey, what do you expect feller, in this world, what the hell ever works out?

Maybe it was the same for him. For Subject Thomas. If anyone asks, Why aren't you back there, in that little shack? – or garage as Maddox called it, although I still couldn't imagine the sort of car that might squeeze in there, nothing produced out of Motor City that was for sure. But if anyone says, shouldn't you be back there, cranking out some more of those words, would he put on the act as well? Don't even think about the disappointments, the hopes that don't work out, the dreams that don't come true.

Just play the fool.

The clown.

That letter. The one written by Subject Thomas, female. The part that caught my eye as I was about to put it down. The part I'd missed on my first scanned reading, the major gripe she seemed to have with her husband, the principal reason for what she called that dose of concentrated humiliating ignominy, the reason I felt as if I really was in some sort of parallel universe where nothing ever seemed as it was and even less made sense.

It wasn't the girls he was hitting on. And it wasn't the drinking. It wasn't even being away from home and leaving her to bring up their kids on her own in that strange, beat-up, broke-down backwater of a place as my original guide had so pithily described it.

It was the lecture contract. The one he'd been carrying around in his pocket ever since he'd arrived, according to Con. The one that would take him on the lecture circuit, the chat shows, the university halls, the one that would take him from the relative obscurity of the poetry presses to something approaching superstardom, the one that was going to guarantee him a thousand bucks a week.

The yellow brick road to Wonderland.

That's what had done it for his wife. That's why she'd poured all that bile into that hate-filled letter.

In her eyes it was simple. She'd married a poet, not a pantomime clown. She'd married a man she believed in, only to find he didn't believe in himself. That letter probably wasn't a goodbye despite everything she may have said which was plenty. It was probably some sort of wake-up call if he still had the ears to hear it which, to be honest, I doubted. Subject Thomas female wasn't to know it but her husband looked way past all that now to me.

Or maybe she did know. Maybe that's what was also behind that extended howl of anger and pain masquerading as a letter from the land of herons and strange shaped houses and narrow little streets. Anguish for a life that had been lost, a world destroyed.

A short distance away a gang of kids were playing hopscotch. I watched them for a while trying to clear my mind of Subject Thomas, male and female, and of Beth, trying to lose myself in the mechanical repetition of the game.

Then I looked up as a shadow fell across me.

19

CON CAUGHT UP with me the next morning and I'd never seen him so angry.

Con immediately steered the pair of us into an unusually up-market location for one of our meetings, Theatercaféen; although maybe I was going to find out that this was one of Con's regular haunts. Maybe I'd got that wrong along with so much else.

The famous café that, up to that point, I'd passed but not visited, had undergone something of a makeover in the last couple of years but the rumors were that the new owner – a third-generation descendant of the original owner, Ellen Brochmann – was unhappy with the look and was going to reverse what she saw as an unnecessary modernization process. How and where I'd picked up that piece of NYC gossip I had no idea. Maybe it had become second nature over the last few years, a magpie storing away titbits that might become useful. But I didn't mention any of that to Con. Right now, interior décor seemed to be the last thing on his mind.

'What the hell did you think you were doing, Jimmy?'

I hadn't been in touch with him since my confrontation with Subject Thomas in the Algonquin, but it was pretty obvious from fairly early on in our exchange that he'd been comprehensively updated on it all anyway. There were always a few stringers hanging around the lobbies of places like that. Photographers, freelancers on the lookout for some little piece of the action, something they could hawk around the newspapers for a buck or two. I hadn't actually made it to print but my exploits had made it to the ears of my erstwhile employer representing one of the biggest magazines in the city. And, much like Subject Thomas when he first became acquainted with the profile run by that same magazine, Con didn't like it.

Not one little bit.

'OK, Con.'

'OK!'

Con stared at me in disbelief. From the walls, portraits of Norwegian luminaries stared down at me too. It was one of the traditions of the café that portraits of visiting dignitaries should be hung there. Right now I wished they'd opted for a different sort of tradition. It was bad enough having one pair of bulging eyes staring at me from across the table. With the rest of them staring down too, I felt like I was in the middle of some kind of gigantic peep show.

Con leant forward, speaking very deliberately, making sure each word sounded loud and clear, which it did.

All too loud.

And all too clear.

'This was going to be one of the best stories you've ever done for us, Jimmy.'

Con clicked his fingers, a loud cracking noise reverberating round the restaurant causing a waitress on the other side of the room to look over, wondering if she was being summoned.

'And you blew it. Just like that.'

I didn't reply. What, after all, could I say? I just kept my head down as Con leant closer. Across the room the waitress relaxed. She could see we weren't exactly interested in refills right now. We seemed to have other things on our mind.

'You didn't only break the golden rule – actually got face to face with the guy – even shook his hand from what I heard.'

Con paused, maybe waiting for me to contradict him, even at this late stage hoping that the nightmare presumably spelt out to him by some stringer would turn out to be a figment of his overheated imagination.

I stayed silent.

'And I heard what you said to him too, Jimmy, you gave him his greatest hits of the last few days, as good as told him who you were, that you'd been tailing him.'

In front of us the coffee was untouched. Something told me it was destined to stay that way.

Con shook his head in disbelief.

'For Christ's sake, Mr Poet may be canned twenty-three hours out of twenty-four but even he can sniff a tail when it's staring him straight in the eyeballs. And even if he can't, the joint was packed and not just with his friends either, with waitresses, bellhops, security, do you think they didn't hear you too?'

Con was over-reacting. The vast majority of the waitresses and bellhops in there that night would hardly have heard me, let alone taken any notice.

As for his friends, they probably wouldn't even remember their own names the next morning let alone a troublesome drunk. Subject Thomas would have been the same. He could have been with us at that very table and he wouldn't have remembered or recognized me.

But I didn't point that out. Because I didn't care. After the sort of night I'd had, Subject Thomas didn't seem so important anymore.

Not that Con saw it that way.

'This isn't just you Jimmy, it's the magazine too. Even Mr Dipso's probably got enough brain cells left to work out who might be behind it all.'

Once again he was over-reacting.

Once again I didn't point that out.

Because, once again, I didn't care.

Con looked at me for a long, long moment, then he nodded.

He'd said what he'd come to say. Now it was time to do what he'd come to do.

'You're fired, Jimmy. I've put someone else on the story.'

I nodded back. I'd sort of worked that out for myself.

'I can't keep the lid on this one and right now I'm not sure I want to. You've done a lot of good work for us over the years, but this – .'

Con didn't finish. He didn't need to.

I nodded again, picked up my hat and stood. As I turned for the door Con cut across again.

'You need to straighten yourself out, my friend.'

I left it a couple of days. For the whole of that time I didn't leave the apartment. I just wrote my log instead. Not the log for Con. That bridge was well and truly burnt into cinders now. A different kind of log instead. All the weird stuff that had been going through my mind on that walk through Central Park, down through the Village, past the Chelsea, past the White Horse and all the way down to the Battery.

I didn't know how much of it made sense. Most of it would have been completely incomprehensible to Con. More evidence if he needed it, which he probably didn't, that his number one gumshoe had well and truly careered off the rails. But would Beth find it incomprehensible? Would she take it as yet more evidence that her husband had well and truly come unstuck? Or would she see something else in it all? I mailed it to her a day later, waited another day, then made another trek up to Little Italy to find out.

I hesitated as I came up to the front door, memories of my last visit swimming round inside my head. For a moment I didn't do anything, didn't approach, didn't ring the buzzer or use the ornamental doorknocker that Nora had found in some jumble sale in a local church bazaar. Nora always had been a great one for taking in other people's unwanted goods.

Rugs.

Bedspreads.

Doorknockers.

Wives.

I took a deep breath. I'd tailed some tough customers in my time. I'd reminded myself of that immediately before previous encounters with my redoubtable sister-in-law and now I was doing it again. Some things never seemed to change. Hoping against hope that I was wrong about that, I raised my hand to press the entry buzzer.

The door opened before my finger made contact. A pair of eyes stared out at me from the open doorway. I swallowed hard, nodded at the apparition.

'Nora.'

She kept staring.

'Look – about last time – what I said – how I was.'

Nora kept staring. She really wasn't going to make this easy for me, was she?

'I'm – .'

I shrugged, a gesture of apology, sincerely meant.

'You're what, Jimmy?'

See what I mean about not making it easy? Spell it out, Jimmy, don't hide behind shrugs and half-sentences and half-smiles you might think are boyishly rueful because they look like so much hogwash to me.

'I'm sorry.'

She looked at me for another long moment. I wondered, briefly, if she wanted me to go down on my bended knees or something, or if I was to be banished to that local church of hers to don sackcloth and start intoning laments.

'OK.'

Nora nodded, quickly, back but she seemed to mean it. Then she swung open the door to reveal Beth standing in the hallway. Maybe she'd been summoned by the sound of our voices or maybe she'd been there all the time, waiting – like her sister – for the apology.

'I'm going to the bookstore. I'll be half an hour. You'll be OK?'

That was to Beth who just nodded. Nora nodded back and made to move past me.

'Picking up anything good?'

Nora paused, eyed me again.

'Yeah. I'm starting on a self-help course. Evening class. Care to guess what that might be?'

'How to deal with schmucks?'

I got it in before her. And I seemed to get some credit for it too. For a moment a smile briefly illuminated her lips, but only briefly.

Then she was gone.

I looked back at Beth who inclined her head towards the sitting room. It seemed I wasn't to be left standing on the doorstep this time at least. I followed her in and Beth took a seat. There was no offer of something to drink, no invitation to take off my coat. Beth didn't seem to think I'd be staying too long. Or maybe that's what she was trying to decide.

Beth didn't speak either, she just folded her hands in her lap, let the silence continue, clearly waiting for me to break it. In the past I'd have looked round the room and made some crack about Nora's latest addition to the furnishings quotient but something told me that wouldn't go down too well right now.

'I sent you something.'

Beth nodded, her eyes flicking almost involuntarily to a thin pile of papers on an old sideboard Nora had sourced from an antiques market in New London when she'd gone through what she'd described as her colonial phase. Around that time she'd also found an original Shaker bedstead on the same trip along with a pew from a Providence meeting house, not to mention a genuine Boston whaler footlocker. No trips down to Macy's to pick up some leatherette Williamsburg wing chairs for her. Nora set high standards in her fixtures and fittings, as in everything else.

It was a family trait she once told me, fixing me with those steel grey eyes and a certain look on her face and Beth was looking at me with much the same look on her face right now too.

At the same time, she just let the silence gather pace.

'I know it probably didn't make a lot of sense.'

I hesitated, but she didn't contradict me and I ploughed on.

'And I don't really know why I said all that about the guy I'm tailing.'

I paused, in the interests of historical accuracy, corrected myself.

'Have been tailing.'

Beth stayed silent, still made no comment.

'I know you're not going to be all that interested in him or what he's been doing, I was just – I don't know – trying to work through some things, I suppose, trying to make some sort of sense of it all.'

I paused, not really sure what else to say. I'd said it all in my log or so I'd hoped. But I was beginning to get an all-too familiar feeling that maybe I'd not done that quite as successfully as I'd hoped.

'Oh, they were fine words, Jimmy.'

'They weren't meant to be fine.'

I tailed off, angry suddenly, choking it back. What the hell did she mean by that, did she think I was trying to score marks for composition or something?

'But you always have been good when it comes to things like that.'

Beth nodded across again at the pile of papers and now I looked at them again too, just laid out there like that and I began to get uneasy. They were for her eyes only, had Beth shown them to Nora, was that what this was all about, had they been forensically dissected by the predator of Paradise Heights and I was now about to suffer the same treatment?

'Con always said your reports should get a Pulitzer.'

'That wasn't one of my reports either.'

I broke off again.

'Beth, come on, give me a break here.'

She just kept looking at me, not unkindly, but still not in the mood to give me any kind of break either.

'It's not true though, is it? Any of it?'

'What the hell does that mean? You think all that's lies, that I've been sitting in that apartment for the last few days, not going anywhere, not seeing anyone, just writing all that down for you and you think it's just – ?'

I tailed off, genuinely bewildered and not a little hurt right now too. What had I written in there to give her that impression? How could all this have gone so wrong?

'Oh, it's accurate Jimmy. I'm not saying that. Everything you're telling me about this guy you've been following – and what he's been doing – and his wife and what she's been doing too – all that happened, I'm not saying it didn't. You don't make anything up, I know that. One of the reasons Con trusts you so much I guess.'

'Trusted me.'

I cut across, in the interests of historical accuracy once again. Or maybe I was trying to tell her something but Beth just rolled on.

227

'But they're still not true and you know why? Because you're not interested in truth, Jimmy, not really.'

I stared at her.

'And that's what I want now, that's what I want from you, the truth, about you, about us and I'm not going to get that from a few words on some pieces of paper about some guy you've been following for the last couple of weeks.'

'So how am I going to do that? How am I going to tell you the truth, what am I supposed to do?'

Beth just kept looking at me and there it was again, that sadness behind the eyes, the same sadness etched in the new lines I could now see on her face.

'I don't know, Jimmy. That's the trouble.'

Beth held my stare, steady as they come.

'I don't know if you can anymore.'

20

THE LOST WEEKEND was a movie released in 1945, starring Ray Milland and Jane Wyman. It was directed by Billy Wilder and based on a novel by Charles R. Jackson about a writer who drinks.

I wasn't a writer. I didn't create fictional characters and pitch them into imaginary battles in the way the hero of that movie did. But myself and Don Birman – the hero of the book and of the movie, played in the latter by Mr Milland – did share one thing in common; we drank.

That night became my equivalent of *The Lost Weekend*, I guess, which made the setting pretty appropriate too. For some reason and don't ask me how, I ended up on the Bowery, well-known haunt of bums and losers of each and every description; including, that night, myself.

The Bowery hadn't always been that sort of neighborhood. At one time it had been a much more respectable place to live in and frequent. No less a famous personage than the last Dutch governor of New Amsterdam, the old name for the present-day New York, had retired to a farm there and was buried in its private chapel.

It was the theater trade that signaled its decline. Not that the early shows weren't anything but grand spectacles – the original Bowery Theater was founded on a site purchased by John Astor no less – but it dragged in its wake a whole raft of low-brow concert halls attracting in turn brothels, beer gardens, pawn shops and flophouses. Soon the whole area had become a magnet for prostitutes and their clients, a center rivalling even the Tenderloin, mainly grouped around The Slide on Bleecker Street and Paresis Hall on Fifth.

These days the key word was 'cheap'. Everywhere you looked there were cheap clothing and cheap nick-nack stores, cheap movie theaters, cheap lodging houses, cheap eating houses, cheap bars. Sailors home on shore leave flocked to the area. And, tonight, an out-of-work private eye.

But those movie echoes didn't end there. Because something else was happening that night too. In among the neon and the sirens and the shouted conversations and the smashed glasses and the peroxide blondes and the Bowery bums that floated in and out of vision as I stumbled from one bar to the other, thoughts were forming, reforming and connecting all the while. Decisions were being debated. Actions contemplated. Anger was fueling most of those decisions and contemplated actions and I knew it. A desire to hit back and hit back hard. I'd laid myself on the line and seemed to have had it all thrown back in my face, so maybe it was now time to throw a few missiles myself.

And so – and as the night went on and as I drank more and more – I actually started to drink myself sober. The fog that had enveloped everything at the start of the night finally began to clear as the first rays of sun began to illuminate the still-packed streets. I finally began to see what I wanted to do and should do. Like Don in the movie, I actually began to see some sense in it all.

And so I made my choice. I put down my last drink, went back to the apartment. I showered and changed, left out some bread on the guardrail for the bird.

And then cut across town to see Con.

Con's office was on the first floor of the walk-up but the ground floor was guarded by the usual gatekeepers. Secretaries, receptionists, even a bored-looking security guard recruited from another of the old detective agencies. In truth, his presence was there to reassure the gatekeepers more than anything else. There had been the odd occasional threat of retaliatory violence from some baseball or football star irritated at some article or report or other, although they'd usually turn out to be so much hot air in the end. The threats either fizzled out or were lost in the arcane workings of the legal system to re-emerge some years later with some small compensation paid to the complainant and a tiny retraction on some obscure page of its latest issue by the magazine.

It was also good PR. To hire a protector meant you had something to protect. It made Con and the rest of his employees feel as if they were precious cargo in some way, fueling their sense of self-importance.

It also made for one more obstacle I had to circumvent along with the rest of the gatekeepers. I had to wait for my moment for a couple of hours but finally it came as I knew it would. I didn't want to announce my arrival in the usual way as I knew what would happen. Con would flatly refuse to see me. So far as I was concerned he'd made his position clear: I was history. A face from the past he had no wish to see again in the present or the future. I'd had my chance and that was that.

But I wanted to see Con. And I wanted an opportunity to plead for a second chance too. And the only way I was going to achieve either was by adopting a bit of good old-fashioned subterfuge. A practical demonstration, if you like, that the old skills were still none too rusty.

I'd been keeping watch on the offices from a diner across the street. Con had appeared once to take personal delivery of some package or other, possibly from my successor on the Subject Thomas tail job or possibly from some other operative altogether. He ran that kind of operation. Always more than one wheel spinning in the air.

A truck pulled up and a couple of delivery guys emerged from inside. It was moving towards lunchtime and a busy place like that never did anything so desultory as actually stopping for a break. Food was delivered instead and distributed via a checklist that had been filled in by each of the employees that morning.

I'd seen the checklist once myself while I was waiting to see Con. There was a mouthwatering selection on offer, from ham and cheese stromboli to grilled Reubens with coleslaw, po boys to sloppy joes, philly cheesesteak or – if you've had a really heavy time of it the previous night – just a plain and simple chicken salad on rye. The arrival of the goodies each lunchtime always provided something of a welcome distraction. So I just picked up one of the trays from the several left behind in the truck. Then I followed the delivery guys inside, strolled past the gatekeepers and security guard trying to identify their current choice of the day and headed up the stairs to the first floor.

I paused outside Con's office and put my tray down on a low table with back issues of the magazine stacked on top. The delivery guys would find it once they started making their trawl of the different floors. I'd no wish to add the theft of a tray of takeaway snacks to my current and myriad list of misdemeanors which, now, included impersonating delivery drivers. As well as falling down spectacularly in Con's eyes, of course.

I could hear the man himself on the phone as I approached his office door. Through the frosted glass I could see him pacing up and down on the small patch of carpet in front of his outsize desk. He sounded pissed and, as I opened the door without knocking, the expression on his face confirmed it.

Con was half-turned away from me as I entered meaning I was treated to a good few moments of his ranting down the phone before he saw his new visitor.

'He was on the corner of 48th and Fifth, that's the last time he was seen anyway.'

Con broke off, listened for a moment.

'How the hell do I know? He lost him after that.'

Con listened some more.

'I don't know, he could be back in the Village by now, hell, he could be anywhere so try all the usual haunts, begin with the Chelsea, try and get a line on that producer if you can or see if that agent of his is back in town.'

Then Con all but exploded.

'For Christ's sake, what do you want me to do, come down there and start looking for him myself, what am I paying you for?'

Con slammed the phone down so hard it was in danger, once again, of needing urgent surgery. Then he turned and saw me standing in the doorway looking at him. The expression on his face – already dark – darkened some more. Maybe it wasn't only the phone that was going to need some medical assistance here.

Then Con spoke.

'Jimmy.'

Flat. Hostile. The same tone Nora had adopted a few nights before as she too stared out at an unwelcome presence before her. But I'd survived Nora, so maybe I could survive Con. Hell, I'd survived Nora, I could survive a pack of rabid hyenas.

'I want to come back on the story.'

Con just eyed me for a moment. I didn't elaborate. There didn't seem to be much else to say.

But Con didn't seem to agree. He seemed to think there was plenty more to say.

'Is there something wrong with your hearing as well as your brain these days, Jimmy?'

'My hearing's fine. My brain's fine too.'

'Your memory then? You don't recall the fact or circumstances of our last meeting? In that nice little café down near the Battery? All those pictures on the walls? That attentive waitress? The half-decent coffee? The bawling out I gave you?'

'I remember all that.'

'But you thought I was just joshing you? That it was all some kind of joke? Good old Con, right? He really had me going there for a minute.'

I stayed silent again and Con nodded at me.

'You're busted, Jimmy.'

And now it was Con's turn to stay silent. Now Con seemed to have decided there was little else to say.

'I've been doing a lot of thinking.'

'Shame you didn't do too much of that before.'

'I can do what you said. I can straighten myself out. Just give me a chance.'

Silence once again. From down the corridor I could hear the sound of the delivery guys doing their rounds and I really didn't want any interruptions right now. I knew I was drowning and fast. All Con needed was one diversion in the form of his regular salt beef and egg over easy on rye and that would be that. I'd be heading back down to the gatekeepers on reception either at my own volition or in the company of the security guard who'd be doing some actual work for a change.

'You know me, Con.'

'I thought I did.'

'You still do. I've not changed, I promise. OK, I tied a couple on. OK, I got sloppy, I know that, but I'm clean now, really clean and you know what I'm like when I am clean, when I'm really on a case, we could be locked together in a padded cell for a month, when I'm on his tail the guy won't even know I'm in the same city.'

Con stayed silent. Whether that was because he was thinking this over or whether he was granting a dying man his last speech to a judge and jury, I couldn't tell.

But that's what he was right now, at least so far as I was concerned.

Judge and jury.

I hunched forward over the desk, Con-style. Behind me, on the other side of the door, the delivery guys had found the tray I'd brought up with me and were bending over it, wondering how the hell it had wafted its way up those stairs like that, all by itself.

'And you need me, Con. I heard you when I came in. This new guy's screwing up right now, yeah?'

Con just eyed me sourly.

'Story of my life.'

'Losing the mark, letting the tail get away, I wouldn't do that, you know I wouldn't and here – .'

I handed Con a sheaf of papers.

'A gesture of goodwill. My log from that movie theater. You heard about that Con, hell, the whole city heard about that and OK, you can't run it now, old news and all that, but it's still good background, isn't it? An eye-witness account from a man who was actually there, who saw the whole thing in good old glorious technicolor?'

For the first time since I walked in there was just the hint of amusement creeping across Con's face. I hunched even closer, pressed home what I hoped would be the beginning, just the beginning anyway, of an advantage.

'Trust me.'

He eyed me.

'Please.'

That word again.

Con kept looking at me.

'Can I?'

'Yes.'

'I'd like to, Jimmy.'

'You can.'

'Because this is the best yet.'

'Yeah?'

Con nodded as I stared at him, really not seeing how that could be possible.

'Better than all the stuff he's been getting up to before?'

'And getting better all the time.'

I couldn't help it. I grinned, a grin that just kept getting wider and wider.

'Now that I want to see.'

Con had started to grin just a little wider too.

'Mr Poet's two days into the bender to end all benders and yeah, this new guy's screwing up, missing him in bars, going to the john when he's going out of the door, heading after him down one street when he's already getting in a taxi and going down another.'

'Amateur night in Dixie.'

'So yeah, I need you, Jimmy. But I need the old Jimmy, not the Jimmy who nearly screwed everything up for us in the Algonquin, the Jimmy who nearly blew this whole thing so high up into the sky we might all have been surfing on the clouds, I need the real Jimmy, the Jimmy who floats behind a mark so soft and quiet it's like you're a shadow or something, not a person at all.'

A tap sounded on the door.

The delivery guys.

Con ignored it.

'I need the old Jimmy back, firing on all cylinders. Alive and kicking.'

The door pushed open and one of the delivery guys entered cautiously, a wrapped sandwich in hand. He glanced at the two of us facing each other across the desk, *High Noon* style. He didn't know what the hell was going on here and the expression on his face said it all; he really didn't want to.

I nodded back at him.

'He's back, Con. Firing on all cylinders.'

The delivery driver returned outside to his companion who was still scratching his head over the tray of sandwiches that had mysteriously levitated themselves from the back of their truck and deposited themselves one floor up on that low table.

Back in his office, I kept eye contact with Con, straight and steady, not blinking once.

'Alive and kicking.'

Con just kept staring back at me.

21

THAT SHADOW?

The shadow that suddenly fell across me the night before my Theatercaféen meeting with Con?

I hadn't mentioned anything about that to Con. And what happened shortly after that apparition materialized hadn't found its way into any of my logs either. Something told me it probably never would.

That same night, I was in a room only it wasn't like any room I'd ever been in before. If I had to try and describe it, it was more like being inside some kind of consecrated space, the atmosphere was that hushed, that respectful. It was a little like the atmosphere in the first few moments of the premiere of Subject Thomas's play those few nights before. Which, in a sense, was all quite appropriate as the focus of all attention inside, the cynosure of all eyes to coin a rather more high-blown phrase, was the main man himself.

The cynosure of all eyes, eh?

Maybe this stuff really was rubbing off after all.

I'd seen the flyer earlier in the day. A few had been left in the lobby of the Chelsea and a few others had been tacked up on small billboards, mainly in and around the Village, discreet hoardings dedicated to similar artistic evenings and endeavors. Meetings of local writers' groups, symposiums devoted to all-matters cinematic, the latest gathering of some literary salon or other and, on this occasion, a poetry reading by a visiting poet.

Subject Thomas hadn't been hosting too many of those sort of events in the time I'd been tailing him. A couple had been mooted I knew that much, but in between movie stars and plant pots they seemed to have taken something of a back seat. But he had undertaken a few similar engagements on his previous trips and had more or less fulfilled each and every one of them too.

From somewhere he'd gained a reputation as an unreliable attendee, which was actually unjustified. Whatever else he may or may not have done, when Subject Thomas had a prior engagement the guy committed to it. Look at that play of his. He'd rather have torn that theater down brick by brick than not put on a performance that night. This guy knew when he had to work and, when he had to, he did. It was when he wasn't working that the problems usually arose.

From all I'd read of those previous and similar evenings, they tended to be strictly solo affairs – just Subject Thomas, a book and a lectern. So even if any had actually been arranged on this latest trip of his, I probably wouldn't have attended anyway as they wouldn't have promised too much in the way of interest and intrigue for the likes of Con. In the normal course of events there wasn't too much likelihood of anything taking place within those hallowed walls that might find its way into the pages of any magazine or, later, into some courtroom.

But then again, these weren't the normal course of events.

That shadow for one thing.

I arrived with just a few minutes to go before the evening's event was due to commence and it was clear, pretty well right from the start, that this audience was different to the audiences I'd been more used to seeing around him up to that point. Ever since he'd landed in New York, Subject Thomas hadn't exactly been unused to attention, but the attention on display that evening was of a very different character and hue. No roaring boys from the Algonquin. No roistering revelers from the White Horse either. These were different types with different concerns and the man himself seemed different that night too.

I took my usual place at the rear of the room within sight of the exit, covering my tracks, old habits dictating my actions as ever; all primed and ready for a quick getaway should circumstances so dictate.

At the head of the room and across a sea of politely listening heads, Subject Thomas then appeared on a small stage to a smattering of applause which he hardly acknowledged before his talk – and subsequent reading – started. It took me a few moments to get up to speed on it all, but it soon became clear that Subject Thomas was beginning the evening by talking about his father, a man who'd recently passed away so we were all now being told.

That was news to me, a biographical nugget that hadn't been in any of Con's copious logs, although there was no particular reason it should have been, I guess. Con's sphere of interest was strictly defined by one thing and one thing only; the land of the living.

And, much like his audience, Subject Thomas's tone was different now too. He was quiet, concentrated, as if he was trying to work something out, something that had been gnawing away at him for a while.

To be honest, all he was saying at first didn't seem all that coherent and as I listened in, unseen and unheralded at the back of the room, I was thinking, terrific, here we go, this guy's obviously been on the sauce again. Because his father, so Subject Thomas was averring – and I'm quoting directly – was a militant atheist, a statement greeted initially with some small, spluttering laughter as the audience at the reading clearly took that as some kind of educated joke of some description.

But I knew my mark by this time and I didn't join in. Because I also knew this guy was far from joking about anything right now.

Subject Thomas's father, it seemed, was an angry man and the figure he was most angry about was one he couldn't even decide existed; and that was God. But if God did exist then all

Subject Thomas's father knew was that he hated him. As a boy, his small son would come down into the kitchen of his boyhood home to find his father looking out of the window at the sky, his eyes bloodshot and bitter, his voice a low rasp as he'd curse that it was raining that day, before spitting bile at the unseen deity seemingly responsible for it all.

At school – Subject Thomas's father was a schoolteacher so I next learnt – he'd physically assault any misbehaving pupil, on one occasion actually kicking a particularly recalcitrant miscreant right out of the room. And as he grew older so his morose moods clearly worsened. In one of the more memorable phrases of that evening, the world had always been the color of black tar to his father, so Subject Thomas further averred, but as the old man grew older it grew ever darker.

But then something happened. Then some strange change crept over Subject Thomas's aged parent, a process that took place side by side with his increasing infirmity; and which crept up on them all so slowly that Subject Thomas didn't realize it was happening at the start. And when he did realize it was happening, it took him some time to work out exactly what it was, possibly because the nature of that change was so unexpected.

Because the inescapable fact was that his formerly-irascible father was growing mellow, was becoming softer somehow as his various ailments multiplied and became more serious. It was almost as if some personality change was happening side by side with his physical decline.

Subject Thomas, as he himself confessed, didn't really know what he felt about it and so he tried working it out in his own time-honored way. He wrote a poem about it. And even though he wrote it some time before his father died he'd decided, from the start, never to show the poem to him. But he was going to share it with the assembled audience before him at present because now he opened a slim volume and began to read and the first few lines immediately set the tone.

Do not go gentle into that good night,
Old age should burn and rave at close of day;
Rage, rage against the dying of the light.

And at first I'm thinking – along with most the audience at that reading if the appreciative nods around the room were anything to go by – that this was actually all quite simple and sweet, quite touching even. Subject Thomas's old man was dying and his son doesn't want him to go, so he's telling him to fight, to not give in, to not give up, although that did raise something of a question its wake.

Why hadn't he shown the verse to his father in that case? If this was some imprecation to a beloved father to not simply fade away, then why not share that appeal with its subject? It seemed a curious and strange omission. At the start of it all, anyway.

Then came the second verse and the first line didn't quite seem to carry on where the first three had finished – something about wise men knowing, at their end, that dark is right – but maybe I had that wrong, I still wasn't exactly up to speed on all matters poetic, despite these last couple of weeks shadowing one of the undoubted masters of the craft.

But then came the next couple of lines and now the wise men didn't seem to be getting such a good press –

Because their words had forked no lightning they
Do not go gentle into that good night.

Which made me pause a little again and that wasn't just because of the new tone – of anger almost – that was now starting to creep into our host's voice. Because wise men they might be, but they still seemed pretty bitter too at the end if the last lines of that verse were anything to go by and Subject Thomas was starting to sound pretty bitter now too.

I looked round the audience as Subject Thomas continued in that booming voice of his and as he now moved on to different kinds of men – first, to good men who were obviously different types to the wise ones; but they didn't seem to fare any better and nor, a verse or so later, did another type, the wild men, those men who –

– caught and sang the sun in flight,
And learn, too late, they grieved it on its way,
Do not go gentle into that good night.

And on it went. So what was he saying here? Who was he talking about? Just about anyone and everyone from the way all this was sounding. Admittedly, I was still only just about hanging onto it all, catching meaning where I could and I certainly wouldn't have been able to able to give any sort of class on it all, but to me it still seemed pretty clear what was on his mind and the next verse, now focusing on a different sort of men again, seemed to make it even clearer too.

Grave men, near death, who see with blinding sight
Blind eyes could blaze like meteors and be gay,
Rage, rage against the dying of the light.

And by now I think the whole room had worked it out. Hell, even the dumb gumshoe at the back of the room was beginning to work it out, so all those Ivy League souls had to have done, right?

This was no paean of supplication to a dying father. This was something much more primeval and it was the tone our man was now employing as well as the words he was intoning that was making that all too clear.

All this seemed like an anguished howl of regret – and it didn't matter if you were a wise man or a fool, a saint or a sinner – it didn't matter what your life amounted to in the eyes of others – what reputation you might have garnered for yourself, in your own imagination or otherwise; what did it mean to you as you looked out through your eyes and your eyes only and looked out on a bay where no lightning had ever forked?

What if you only discovered your eyes could have truly blazed at the moment the light in them was extinguished?

And so the message seemed simple, at least to me. Only one emotion would see a tortured soul wailing at the moon as their end came and it was pure and it was simple; and that was regret. Regret at a life not lived, at chances not taken, at shadows mistaken for substance and maybe that was why Subject Thomas had never shown those verses to his father, maybe because the old man would realize, only too acutely, that in his son's eyes he was among that number and so could take no comfort from it?

Or was that just what I was taking from all this? That gumshoe at the back of the hall? Maybe because that was something I was more than wrestling with myself right now?

Regret.

At all sorts of things. But mainly, of course, at Beth and myself.

But then came the last verse and now this seemed to be another sort of game changer all by itself. OK, hands up again, I had just about hung on to the last few verses and I still wasn't going to claim for my reading of them any sort of definitive insight either. Maybe everything I was taking from it all really was just so much hogwash.

But now, and all of a sudden, there seemed to be a direct appeal to the man he'd decided would never read those words. A direct address to a man debarred from hearing them, which didn't seem to make too much sense at first.

And you, my father, there on the sad height

Which was when an image flashed through my mind, the image of my own father, a man I'd always elevated to some sort of distant height as well, a man who – in my mind – had always looked down on me also.

Curse, bless, me now with your fierce tears, I pray –

And then the poem veered back into what the guys in Tin Pan Alley would call the chorus as he – and maybe all of us too – were urged not to go gentle into any good nights once more.

And there was applause but it was muted, not because the audience wasn't appreciative but because they all seemed to be trying to work it out as well and Subject Thomas didn't speak for a few moments either, as if he was aware of that and he was allowing us all the space to do that. Or maybe because he was trying to do the same himself.

I just kept looking at him some more. What was he saying in that last verse of his to his dying father? It was as if he was pleading for some sort of response from him, any sort of response at all, it didn't matter, whether that be a blessing or a curse.

So was that what was behind all those expressions of regret, was it actually directed not at deeds that had or hadn't been done, at a life – or lives – that hadn't been properly lived? Was it regret for something else instead? Regret for a relationship that he could only write about, not speak of directly? A relationship, gone wrong somehow, that he couldn't put right? A relationship he could share that night with others – and which he did; but which he just couldn't share with the other figure in that actual relationship, the father up there on that sad height?

It didn't sound like he was seeking approval as such, but it did sound as if he was searching for some kind of recognition at least. And, in the continuing and silent space that followed that reading, there she was again, swimming through my mind once more, not my father or Subject Thomas or his father either, but Beth.

And for that moment, once again, it was as if he was writing about us. Which was crazy, he didn't know us, but it was as if he did. Because what else did I really want, at that exact moment, but to right a relationship with the most important figure in my life? To gain her approval, yes – but hell, even to just provoke some sort of response would be something. Her blessing, her curse – anything had to be better than the not-so-slow decline that seemed to have stricken us both right now. Anything would be preferable to the silent sadness which was all I'd seen lately in my wife's disappointed eyes.

Or, yet again, was that just me? Was I just taking out of it all something that was resonating with all that was happening in my life right now? Was that not really there at all?

But once again also – and from the continuing silence currently filling that room – if I was, then it really didn't seem as if I was the only one.

And now I'm thinking something else. Now I'm thinking, maybe that's what poets do. Maybe that's why everyone gets so dreamy about them. Maybe that's what was behind Iris's hero-worship and that reflection from that air stewardess that the meaning of the words didn't matter, that you just had to feel them. Maybe I was actually starting to feel them now too. And maybe that's when they actually started to make sense.

Maybe that's the trick they all somehow manage to pull off. I thought it was the Emperor's Clothes but maybe it isn't. Maybe these guys just come up with the sort of words that mean a hundred different things to a hundred different people and out of those hundred different meanings not a single one is wrong.

At which point Subject Thomas's eyes seemed to sweep round the room, almost as if for the first time he realized where he was. And then something else happened. Because then I realized that Subject Thomas was now looking straight at me and for once – on this trip anyway – this wasn't the face of the clown, or the buffoon or the performer looking out from above that ill-patched suit and bow tie. This was a quite different face with some sort of message in those eyes that seemed to be directed solely at myself.

But then I realized I was wrong about that too. Because he wasn't looking at me. Or at least not just at me. He wasn't looking at anyone, he was looking at everyone.

Did that make any sort of sense? Con wouldn't have thought it made any sense at all. But I was starting to do so.

And there was something else that didn't make sense, at least not to the likes of Con. That shadow that had fallen across me as I watched those young kids playing hopscotch? The shadow that had led me from there to here, to this room, this reading? There had never, of course, actually been one. And Con wouldn't have made any sort of sense of that either but – and once again – maybe I was just starting to do so too.

22

EVERYTHING I'D BEEN told was right. This was the best yet. Meaning Subject Thomas was at his very worst. Life, all-too sweet before for Con, was fast becoming a whole lot sweeter.

I caught up with the new tail in Washington Square. He'd left an agency in the Midwest to try his luck in the big city and the way things were panning out he'd be heading back West again pretty soon. You either had it or you were so far out of the ballpark the gates were locked behind you. You could either merge, chameleon-like, into your surroundings or you stood on the fringe, as conspicuous as if you were a bad smell.

As categories went, the Algonquin aside, I usually managed the former. My unhappy companion seemed to inhabit the latter no matter what he did or how hard he tried. He updated me, somewhat gloomily, on the patchy surveillance he'd managed to conduct so far. He was still being paid so, and despite his gloomy demeanour, he had no choice. Then he headed back to the office where he suspected, with some justification, that he was about to be canned.

He had come across something interesting though. Not interesting in terms of anything that might make it into any magazine profile. Just interesting I guess.

On one of his recent and ever-more drunken perambulations, Subject Thomas had spilled the contents of his wallet on the sidewalk. With the help of some well-disposed passers-by he'd managed to scoop most of those contents up again but he'd left a piece of paper behind. The hapless tail had picked it up and now handed it to me, in turn, along with the rest of his report.

It was an old and yellowing newspaper clipping. It comprised a few lines of text and a photograph, dim and hazy, of a thin little boy dressed in what looked like a droopy sort of gymkhana costume. The caption below the photograph made it clear that the little boy was the twelve-year-old Subject Thomas. He was the son of a local couple, Mr and Mrs D. J. Thomas, so the clipping stated, which also went on to report that he had been the victor in a short dash at the annual games of some local school competition.

The young and hapless tail thought it was weird. Subject Thomas had obviously carried that old clipping around with him for more than twenty years. I looked at the yellowing piece of paper and had to admit I found it pretty strange too.

Within a few moments of getting back on his tail, I managed to track Subject Thomas down to the Chelsea. After the spilled wallet incident Miss Reitell had escorted him home but not before he'd stumbled down Fifth Avenue making gargoyle faces again at more passers-by. As before, most took it as yet another eccentric out on the street. Some wondered if it was some sort of performance art. Others wondered if it was a set-up of some kind, there'd been rumors flying around the city for days about a new TV show being launched where unsuspecting members of the public would be exposed to the actions of seeming lunatics and their reactions filmed for the later enjoyment of a wider audience.

Others simply didn't like it. And told Subject Thomas so in no uncertain terms. Subject Thomas, as always, seemed to view that as a personal affront and it only served to redouble his efforts to needle them. One such encounter had ended with Subject Thomas flat on his back outside the Empire State bellowing like a beached whale at the clouds above. Miss Reitell, somewhat wearily now according to my new contact, the exile from the Midwest, had scooped him up and deposited him in a taxi before the driver could pretend he hadn't seen her outraised hand. They'd been back in the Chelsea ever since.

I took up residence in the lobby and picked up a selection of the day's papers. The year was now approaching its end and one of them had listed the highlights so far.

Top song, apparently, was Dean Martin with 'That's Amore' although 'Stranger in Paradise' by Tony Bennett, a favorite of mine and Beth's, had run it a close second. The top movie was *From Here To Eternity* although I had to admit I preferred *Shane*. The top book was something called *Go Tell It On the Mountain* by a new writer, James Baldwin. I hadn't got round to reading it although Beth had bought it, I seemed to recall. She always devoured the books' pages in the Sunday supplements, marking out that week's hot picks. I had read the year's other favored read though, *Casino Royale*, by Ian Fleming. In other news, as the readers were wont to say on the radio, Ernest Hemingway had won the Pulitzer Prize and some British guy had made history by climbing Mount Everest.

The mountaineer in question was called Hillary, first name Edmund, and was actually a New Zealander, but that was probably close enough for that particular newspaper. A bit like Con and his original assertion that Subject Thomas came from England, well, near.

Then, suddenly, there was a commotion across the lobby and I looked over to see an all-too familiar spectacle playing out.

Miss Reitell was once again attempting to shuffle her charge across to the front door. She was carrying a large bag at the same time, so it wasn't easy. Presumably, given the bag she was carrying, she was hoping they could both get out of the city for a short time at least which would have been a considerable relief to her in the nursemaid stakes and something of a relief for the city now too.

Miss Reitell managed to get Subject Thomas, complete with bag, outside although only with the help of a bellhop who looked as if the antics of this particular guest were beginning to lose their appeal for him now too. Or maybe the tips were beginning to dry up a little as his stay went on. Or maybe the bellhop just had that kind of face. Miss Reitell shepherded Subject Thomas into the back of the cab while she stowed the bag in the trunk. Then she got back into the cab itself at which point all hell broke loose.

I'd watched him do a fair few crazy things in the last couple of weeks but even I couldn't believe this one. I think I may even have blinked a few times just to clear my vision, just to make absolutely sure; but there was little doubt about all that was happening now.

Subject Thomas had taken a handkerchief out of his pocket. For a moment he looked at it as if unsure just what it was. Then he took a box of matches out of his pocket and set it alight.

What the hell was he thinking of? Miss Reitell certainly wanted to know and so did the driver as smoke now began to billow through his cab. Did he think he was lighting a cigar or something? In truth it didn't really matter what he was thinking, all that mattered was what he'd done and all that mattered, in turn, was that something be done about it and quick.

The driver bellowed, a little like Subject Thomas had bellowed a short time before I imagined on the sidewalk of Fifth, although there was definitely more panic in his extended demand that someone do something about this guy! Which meant, for all practical purposes, Miss Reitell once again. For a couple of moments she just beat at her charge with her bag in a fairly ineffectual attempt to extinguish the flames. All the while the handkerchief burned in front of Subject Thomas's staring and seemingly-fascinated eyes.

Then she took off a scarf she was wearing and attempted to wrap it round the burning cloth. The net effect was that now there was a scarf and a handkerchief on fire in the back of that cab and now the driver was protesting ever more loudly. For a moment I wondered if, in the interests of simple humanity, I was going to have to break my cover for the second time in a week and approach the mark directly, this time to render some assistance. Something told me Con wouldn't be too delighted about that no matter the circumstances but what was I supposed to do, watch the cab go up in flames taking Subject Thomas and his companions with it?

Salvation came from the bellhop. Or, rather, salvation came from the bar of the Chelsea via the bellhop who rushed out from the lobby with a soda siphon in his hand. One extended blast from the nozzle and Subject Thomas was now soaked from head to waist but so was the handkerchief he was holding, not to mention the scarf that was wrapped somewhat inexpertly around it. Steam billowed out from the inside of the cab in place of the naked flames that were dancing inside there a few moments before.

The driver remonstrated with Miss Reitell. He seemed to realize there was little point in berating the actual culprit. A shaken Miss Reitell hit back and she hit back hard too, which was pretty impressive in the circumstances. As I'd already seen back in the Poetry Center she seemed to be quite some lady. But my attention was only partly on the developing altercation out on the sidewalk. I was rather more occupied with Subject Thomas who'd now opened the far rear door, the one furthest away from his helpmate, and was slipping out of the cab and heading down the street.

In terms of a spectacle the confrontation between his erstwhile producer and the cab driver promised richer pickings, but duty was calling and I followed the departing Subject Thomas instead.

The first stop was Lord and Taylor on Fifth. Always a cut above the likes of Macy's, this was one seriously up-market department store. Beth had taken me in there a couple of times before the prices had driven us out. Subject Thomas cut a strange figure as he wandered among the frock-suited sales staff, ignoring all polite offers of assistance as those same sales staff tried, and largely failed, to ignore the small puddles of water he seemed to be trailing in his wake.

Then he assessed a mannequin for shape and size. In truth the mannequin was considerably taller and a hell of a lot slimmer but Subject Thomas obviously seemed to think they were a pretty good match. Before anyone realized what he was doing and certainly before anyone had chance to intervene, Subject Thomas had removed the shirt and jacket from the mannequin and exchanged it for his own. Then he strolled out of the shop.

I kept following.

The next stop was Sutton Place. Again it was a fair old walk but Subject Thomas didn't even look at any passing cabs. Maybe, having already risked immolation in one, he really didn't want to push his luck in another. Or maybe he just wanted fresh air.

I'd noticed it before, but he really did seem to have trouble breathing at times. Maybe it was the smog or maybe he was asthmatic or something. But time and again he'd pause to catch his breath, sometimes raising his face to the heavens as if seeking something purer to inhale, before looking back down at the sidewalk and moving on.

At Sutton Place, Subject Thomas announced to the

receptionist manning the desk – a receptionist clearly alarmed by his curious appearance – that he was here for the party being thrown by one of their residents, William Faulkner. I'd heard of him but hadn't read any of his novels. I had dipped into one, *As I Lay Dying* I think it was called, while marking time in a second-hand bookstore in the Village but had abandoned it after a page or two. *Casino Royale* it sure wasn't.

The receptionist had also heard of Mr Faulkner but she quite clearly didn't know anything about any party. She buzzed up to his apartment by which time Subject Thomas had moved away from the desk. By the time she'd finally made contact with Mr Faulkner – who was working at the time and also didn't know anything about any party – Subject Thomas had removed all his clothes and was standing as naked as the day he was born in the lobby.

For not the first time where Subject Thomas was concerned, all hell broke loose. The receptionist screamed, a concierge bolted from his booth at the far end of the lobby and began throwing his clothes back at Subject Thomas who, reluctantly and with no undue haste it had to be said, began to put them back on. He didn't appear to have put on any underclothes before he came out so he didn't put any back on now. But within a few moments and with a now near-hysterical receptionist insisting over and again that there was no party taking place in Mr Faulkner's apartment, Subject Thomas was back out on the street.

I called Con from a phone booth on 47th. I'd arranged to call in at least a couple of times that day. Partly that was so Con didn't have to wait for my log for his next update. Partly – and we both knew this – it was so he could keep a check on my movements at the same time as I was keeping a check on my quarry.

I understood that. I'd damaged something by my antics in the Algonquin. There was a serious case of breached trust to repair and it was going to take me some time to regain my former status of golden boy so far as he was concerned. But from the awed tone in his voice as I recounted Subject Thomas's adventures thus far – all the while keeping the man himself in sight as he now stood outside a peep show blinking at the photographs of the delights on offer inside – I was quite clearly now going some way at least to doing that.

The rest of the afternoon passed in a similar vein and, in truth, it was all beginning to get a little familiar. Subject Thomas would wander into a bar and then be thrown out again within a few moments either for non-payment or because he took exception to someone inside doing something he didn't like, such as breathing.

Sometimes it was worse if he was made welcome rather than cast out. In one particularly riotous bar down on the Lower East Side his accent quite clearly made him an object of considerable curiosity – and his drunken confession that he was a poet only fanned those flames. He was commanded to produce a poem on the spot by way of proof of his profession and for a moment I feared things might turn a little hostile if he refused or otherwise failed in his allotted task. His drinking companions were in a good mood right now, laughing along with him and with each other, but you could still sniff danger in the air. At any moment the mood could turn and a crowd of cheering companions could suddenly turn into something more sinister.

Subject Thomas blinked a few times, took out a pen, took out a piece of paper and then he did it. He actually wrote a few lines down on a piece of paper. From across the bar I watched, rapt, as one of his new companions picked it up and started to read it out loud. If this was a few lines from one of his published poems it was going to go way over the head of everyone in there.

But it wasn't. It was some sort of limerick instead. Later, after the new companion had recited the offering and after the laughter had died down I retrieved it from under a table where it had fallen and put it in my pocket. I kept it as a souvenir although I never showed it to Con. So far as poetry was concerned it might have been a little on the simplistic side and it certainly didn't scale the heights of his sad tribute to his soon-to-be deceased father, but as a piece of entertainment it read pretty OK to me.

There was an old bugger called God,

It began.

Who got a young virgin in pod.
This disgraceful behavior
begot Christ our Savior,
Who was nailed to a cross, poor old sod.

Which, like I said, was not bad, especially in the circumstances. But only a short time later my fears about the deteriorating atmosphere proved only too prescient. His drinking companions soon moved on from demands for more verse to a different kind of entertainment. They began cramming lighted cigarettes into his mouth and Subject Thomas stumbled towards the door. If he'd been having trouble breathing before he seemed to be having even more trouble now.

Outside he was stopping strangers again, asking them if they could see what he was seeing – or what he claimed to be seeing anyway, it was always difficult to tell with him, was this real or some kind of game? A game that sometimes even he, the instigator, seemed to be having trouble controlling?

What he was seeing – or claimed to be seeing – were abstract shapes of some description. But as he couldn't describe those shapes in any sort of detail, that wasn't of too much use to his more or less unwilling audience. Pretty well all of them moved on, most without listening all that politely. He may not have been dressed like it but he was quite clearly a drunken, rambling, bum. Another of life's not-so-little casualties as seen day in, day out, on the streets of the good old Big A.

And, once again, I began to wonder. I'd debated with myself before whether his antics were all part of some strange act, some self-fulfilling prophecy perhaps, a desire to live up to a hard-earned reputation in some way.

Now I was wondering again. Maybe the reputation had taken over. Like an actor reluctant – or unable – to slough a part once they'd left the stage, Subject Thomas just didn't know anymore how to say goodbye to the clown.

He'd written about it. All that stuff with Sam Bennet and his fine beginning, that wasn't any sort of beginning at all. Maybe now he'd become the character he'd created. Maybe it had taken over, taken him over.

But suddenly he seemed to pull himself together. Maybe it was the sight of a passing cab that had galvanized him or maybe he'd remembered some appointment or other. But all of a sudden he shot out his hand, the cab stopped by his side and he told the driver, more or less coherently, to take him to the White Horse. Then he settled back on the rear seat.

I called in and made another of my regular reports to Con. I was in no rush to follow. I knew where he was going to be for the next few hours and had a pretty shrewd idea what he'd be getting up to as well. Just more of the same. Subject Thomas seemed to be turning ever faster in the same small circle, like a rat on a wheel, unable to stop himself or break free.

Con was now beginning to sound a little bored with it all too and the phone call didn't last too long. I think even he was now beginning to suspect that, in the entertainment stakes, Subject Thomas was fast approaching the worst sort of state so far as a magazine man was concerned: old news.

He was coming to believe in me more and more though, was becoming increasingly assured that I was all I claimed to be.

The old Jimmy.

Alive and kicking.

Back in the very center of the action and firing on all cylinders.

I put down the phone and dialed Nora's apartment. For once, Nora herself didn't answer. Beth's voice wafted down the phone instead. I hesitated. I didn't know why I'd called and didn't know what to say. I just wanted to hear her voice. Beth paused too, but then she was the first to speak.

'Leave me alone, Jimmy.'

Then the line went dead.

I arrived at the White Horse twenty minutes later. From the raucous laughter coming from inside it seemed I'd been right about Subject Thomas remaining there for the next few hours at least. I went inside to be greeted by a caricature of the man I'd last seen just a short time previously.

He was coming to look more and more like some sort of monstrous puppet. His face was now chalk-white and his lips seemed to be made of rubber. He was recounting what I recognized as the Sutton Place incident without making too much sense of it all, but that didn't seem to matter too much to his companions. The state they were in he could have recited the Old Testament backwards and they'd still have greeted it with the same chorus of barracking approval.

More and more drinks were being placed in front of the favored son, more and more exhortations issued from the ever-swelling audience that Subject Thomas drink and drink fast so those glasses might be refilled. Subject Thomas duly obliged and more drinks were duly proffered. More and more pictures were taken of the various attendees in there at the time with the famous poet, while the famous poet in question blinked and drank and grew ever more puppet-like. At one point he asked, in a quiet voice, for some ginger beer and was greeted with the kind of extended laughter that would have gladdened the heart of Sammy D.

Ginger beer?

One of the greatest drinkers in the city wants some ginger beer?

Get out of here and have another bourbon.

And he did.

After another half-hour, Subject Thomas stood and announced he wanted some fresh air. Several of his companions mimicked a bout of vomiting, having a shrewd idea just what he'd be doing out in that not-so-fresh air. A new round of drinks were ordered from the bar for his return once he'd made a little space for them.

A couple of the guys went with him in case he needed helping up including, I now noticed, the first of his heavy, thick-set companions from the Algonquin. Not that he spotted me. It was as much as he could do at the moment to spot the door. At one point in the unsteady procession towards it, he seemed to be making straight for one of the windows instead.

I followed them out onto the sidewalk. In the daylight and with the sun now beating down on his face, Subject Thomas looked even more grotesquely puppet-like than before and a couple of passers-by stepped round him as if afraid they'd be contaminated or something. It was still unseasonably warm. And the smog was getting worse by the day. There were more and more reports of people falling seriously ill in different parts of the city with the combination of the heat and the ever-deteriorating atmosphere and it didn't seem to be doing Subject Thomas much good either. Then again, neither was the bourbon, not to mention whatever else he was ingesting right now. A few of his new friends seemed to have brought other substances along with them that afternoon too.

With Subject Thomas taking in great gulps of air – which

mainly involved inhaling exhaust fumes from various passing motor vehicles – I hailed a cab. As it drew to a halt I held up a hand, one finger upraised, a signal that the driver give me just one minute. The driver nodded back and I turned, for the second time in all the weeks I'd been shadowing him, to my tail.

'Mr Thomas – hey – Mr Thomas.'

Subject Thomas once again didn't move, just kept concentrating on forcing more and more air into those lungs of his. But his heavy-set companion turned and for a moment, somewhere deep down in Neanderthal land, some dim connection was made as I took Subject Thomas by his unprotesting arm.

'Hey, steady pal.'

'I just want to talk to Mr Thomas.'

Through a miasma of drink the heavy-set companion blinked at me.

'You're not going to get much conversation out of him right now.'

Then he stopped, more and more of that dim connection now slowly forming.

'Don't I know you from somewhere?'

By now I was steering Subject Thomas, step by step, towards the cab and he still wasn't making any move to resist the onward momentum. It was like guiding a child towards a candy store.

'It's OK, it's OK, I've got you.'

The companion from the Algonquin was raising more of an objection though.

'What the hell are you doing?'

Which was a good question and it would certainly have been a question an apoplectic Con would have been asking right now too if he could have seen us. But Con couldn't see us. And Subject Thomas's companion was too befuddled to do anything other than rant incoherently after us as I folded his charge, now my charge, into the back of the cab and told the driver to drive.

Just drive.

Anywhere so long as it was far away from here.

Then I looked back at my new companion. He still hadn't uttered a word and for a moment I marveled. What kind of world did he inhabit these days that a total stranger could accost him in the street, could virtually kidnap him off the sidewalk and he'd not utter so much as a single word of protest or complaint? What the hell was going on inside that head of his right now?

But that was only a passing thought, dismissed as soon as it was raised. I had other things on my mind instead, things I wanted to say to him, things I wanted to tell him right now.

I wanted to talk about that shack of his set into that cliff and about those strange little houses and winding streets.

I wanted to talk about that play of his and how I got it, how I really got it, how I knew it was a comedy, that you weren't supposed to sit in silence as if you were attending a funeral or something, that it was funny and it was alive and that all those people he'd put on stage, they were all the people from that town of the strange little houses and the winding streets and I knew that because I'd been there. I'd seen it, I'd seen them, I'd talked to them, I'd talked to one of them in particular, Maddox, who was probably in that play of his somewhere and he'd given me one of his books.

And I wanted to tell him about the stewardess who seemed to understand what at least some of the words in those books meant even if she couldn't actually explain them.

And I wanted to tell him about sitting in that poetry reading of his and understanding something at least of all he had to say about that most exquisite of tortured emotions – regret.

And I wanted to tell him about Beth and about her college plans and about this dream we both had to do our courses and how it hadn't quite worked out and how we now seemed to have stumbled at some fork on that road which could be some kind of cul-de-sac only I wasn't sure about that, not yet. But maybe that's what this was all about, these last few weeks, this tail job, maybe it was all part of my finding out, maybe that's what I was doing right now in the back of that cab with him and maybe I wasn't the only one who could do that too.

Maybe he could do that as well. Maybe we could both do that together. We were as far apart and as little alike as anyone could imagine – a poet from a town far away across the sea where no-one ever seemed to have heard of straight lines and had definitely never seen a straight wall if those houses were anything to go by – and a gumshoe from Long Island who'd never met a poet and had never read a single line of poetry until he'd come along. And some of it now sounded pretty OK too even if, like the stewardess, I still wouldn't have liked to give any kind of lecture on it all. But we'd been thrown together these last few weeks – the poet and the private eye – and the strangest thing was that now I felt I knew him, even if I still didn't as yet understand too much about him, so maybe it was time to try and do that and maybe if I could do that, he could do the same. If he could get to know me, get to understand why I did the things I did as well then maybe something might come out of all this, something that would be good for both of us.

All that I intended to say.

And more.

Then I looked at him again.

And had second thoughts.

23

TEN MINUTES LATER and the cab, myself and Subject Thomas were uptown in Little Italy. The cab was parked by the sidewalk, Subject Thomas was inside. I was outside Nora's apartment banging on the door again. Beth was alone inside and I knew that for a fact. Because on the way up there I'd stopped at a phone booth and had phoned my sister-in-law in work and asked her to meet me back at the apartment. And that was as in right now. If not sooner.

The door opened and Beth looked out at me with something of a world-weary expression on her face. This wasn't easy for her. She had a lot of thinking to do as she'd already told me and, apparitions on the doorstep, hot on the heels of phone calls in which that same apparition didn't even speak, weren't helping.

As she was about to tell me.

'Jimmy – .'

But I didn't let her.

'He's in the cab.'

Beth stopped.

'What?'

'I thought maybe I could bring him in, well I did until – .'

I broke off, didn't pursue that for now, didn't want to pursue it. That could wait for Nora.

Beth looked behind me at the idling cab, at the figure slumped in the back.

'Who's in the cab?'

'The guy, the guy I've been tailing.'

She kept staring at me.

'He was drinking down in the Village, I picked him up from the bar, got him in the cab.'

'The poet guy?'

'The poet guy, the young and easy guy, only he's really not looking all that young and easy right now.'

'Jimmy, what is this?'

'I don't know what it is, not exactly, but I know what it isn't, this isn't about the freak show, not anymore, this is different, this is about me trying to do some good for a change.'

A voice cut in behind us. Nora had been as good as her word and had come up from the hospital as quickly as she could. My sister-in-law might have been something of a harridan in all other matters but she always had been the first to respond when someone sounded in genuine trouble.

'Jimmy, what's so urgent?'

Nora looked at her sister.

'Beth?'

But Beth just looked back at her, as lost as Nora right now.

I gestured towards my companion in the cab.

'He's probably OK, probably just needs to sleep it off or something but I don't know, I just don't think something's right, his breathing's not right, I'm sure it isn't.'

Beth nodded behind Nora.

'The guy in the cab, Nora, the guy Jimmy's been tailing.'

I nodded too.

'He's been hitting it solid now for forty-eight hours, maybe longer, I don't know the last time he ate, the last time he slept and maybe that's it, one good meal, a decent night's sleep – .'

I stopped, turned back to Beth.

'I'm not going to do it anymore, Beth – stand back and watch this guy go to hell and back – .'

Then I turned back to Nora, aware I was babbling, knowing that this was all sounding pretty incoherent right now.

'Please Nora, just take a look at him, check him out, yeah? I really don't think he's in a great way.'

'OK, OK.'

Then Nora turned and was gone. For once she hadn't tried to challenge or divert me. For once she hadn't tried to interfere between Beth and myself either, although she'd probably have called it protecting her little sister. For once she seemed to take everything I said at face value, as if for once in my life I might just be playing it straight and meaning every word. Meaning, in turn, that somewhere, somehow, there may be such a thing, even in an imperfect world, as miracles. Or maybe Nora, as usual, had just got this right.

'I've been doing some thinking about what you said – no, wrong, I haven't actually been thinking about anything else. I've been thinking about that log I sent you, all those words and I've been thinking about all the other things I could say to you as well, I even wrote some of them down.'

'I didn't get anything.'

'I didn't send anything. Because you're right. What's the point? All that, it's just words, cheap and easy.'

Beth was struggling herself now.

'It's not I think you didn't mean all that, Jimmy.'

Then Beth paused, failing herself to put all she was thinking and feeling into words now too.

'But you want something more. Something different.'

'Maybe. I don't know.'

'And so do I.'

Beth looked at me.

'And so I thought, what do I do, how do I convince you, about you and me, about our baby, about the future?'

Beth looked across at Nora in the cab. I looked too. She was talking to Subject Thomas and he seemed to be talking back, she actually seemed to be getting through to him.

Amazing. I hadn't managed to extract a single syllable. Give it another five minutes and he'd be sitting in her small kitchen drinking her home-made chicken soup and she'd be looking at me with that all-too familiar expression on her face – the guy just needed a little bit of TLC, Jimmy. What's wrong with you, why's everything always got to be such a big deal all the time?

Beth looked from the cab back to me.

'And you thought a bit of old-fashioned abduction, kidnapping might do the trick?'

It was rubbing off. I always knew it would. Living with her big sister. She was already starting to mimic Nora's somewhat special way with words. Even Subject Thomas could learn a thing or two from that one. Back at the cab, the woman herself now had her new charge half-in and half-out of the door. He could probably already smell the soup.

'He's in trouble, Beth. Him and that wife of his. You were right from the start, this isn't a guy having the time of his life, living it up while the cat's away and all that, this is a guy, I don't know – .'

I clicked my fingers, Con-style, at the same time as I became dimly aware of Nora now pausing at the cab door, looking over at us.

'This is a guy *that* far away from ending it and that's what this is really all about, it has to be, the way he's acting, the things he's doing, he might as well hang a sign round his neck. Hell, maybe he is hanging a sign round his neck only nobody's reading what it says and there's no-one who's going to do that either because he's a million miles away from home and even if he was back there right now, back home in that strange little town with all those winding streets and crooked little houses, back with his wife, I don't know if even then – .'

I tailed off, not really sure what I was saying, pretty sure that only about half of what I was saying was even halfway coherent right now, but Beth seemed to be getting it.

'He hasn't got anyone, Beth. Anyone to make him see some

266

sort of sense, so I thought if he had me, if I could make him see that – .'

Beth just kept looking at me.

'It's not too late for him and it's not too late for us, he might think he's grieved the sun on its way but he hasn't and we haven't either.'

But then, suddenly, before Beth could even start to ask what the hell all that about the sun was supposed to mean, Nora was at my elbow. Subject Thomas was still back by the cab, still half-in, half-out of the rear door and now I could see the driver eyeing him, dubious, wondering about his fare probably, the meter was still ticking so he shouldn't be out of pocket but this guy did look sort of unreliable.

Nora clearly had some doubts about him too, but they were nothing to do with any ability on his part to pay any fare.

'Jimmy, your passenger.'

'Thomas, that's his name.'

'We have got to get him to hospital.'

I looked back at her. This really was a night for new experiences. Nora almost looked scared right now.

'Fast.'

I kept looking at her, then back at Subject Thomas. He was still half-in, half-out of the cab. His face was even more bloated now, his breathing coming in ever more ragged gasps. For a moment as I looked at him, he looked back at me and for the first time something approaching recognition illuminated his eyes. For the very first time in all the weeks I'd been tailing him he looked straight at me; and for that moment too there was the ghost of a smile.

Fast was the word. One minute later that cab was moving again. I was in the front seat, Nora and Beth were in the rear, Subject

Thomas was between them. Nora was administering some basic first aid, doing whatever she could to assist his erratic breathing. All the time the driver piloted us towards the emergency room at St Vincent's, housed in the Seton Building, ironically just a few blocks from the Chelsea on the corner of 11th and Seventh. For all his extended excursions around New York, Subject Thomas, it seemed, was finally returning home.

His lips were now blue and his breathing seemed to be getting shallower. He also seemed to be having small seizures. I didn't ask Nora what was happening and she wouldn't have answered if I had. All her efforts were focused on her unexpected patient.

We pulled up outside St Vincent's a few moments later. Nora headed inside and came back out with two doctors. Beth's companion from the other evening wasn't among them. These were young guys, second-year residents from the university I was to later discover, each with less than three years' experience since qualifying. That wasn't evidence of any sort of neglect on the part of St Vincent's, it was just par for the course in any hospital in the city at that time of the evening.

At that stage Nora really didn't know too much about this new admission. She knew he was a famous poet and she told the attending doctors that. She also knew he'd been drinking heavily before what was quite clearly some sort of major collapse and she told them that too.

We followed the two doctors and Subject Thomas inside. A nurse had now come to assist and the first thing they did was administer something called Dilantin to calm the seizures I'd witnessed in the cab. That was all tied in to his breathing difficulties apparently and for the next hour they worked to try and restore that breathing to something approximating normal.

With his breathing then more or less stabilized, the doctors next attached a saline and sugar drip. Body fluid samples were taken away for testing. All the time an ongoing physical examination was taking place and I heard short snatches of their conclusions, most of which meant little to me although one phrase did stand out.

Both sides of his brain, apparently, were malfunctioning. I'd no idea what that meant exactly but – and not for the first time that night – I felt a chill settle over me. Beth must have felt the same because she took my hand in hers, the first physical contact we'd had since she'd left our apartment to go and live with her sister. The doctors also then found evidence of bronchitis on both sides of his chest and Subject Thomas was dispatched for an X-ray.

By this time Miss Reitell had arrived in the company of some friends. A short time later the agent from Boston arrived. Miss Reitell and the agent milled around the corridor outside X-ray and I withdrew to a quieter part of the hospital and took out my log.

My job wasn't finished yet.

24

A SHORT TIME later, Subject Thomas was wheeled out of X-ray. He was now wearing an oxygen mask and his hair was limp and wet. His face was scarred with large blotches and he seemed to be in the grip of a constant fever. I heard his agent from Boston moan to Miss Reitell that this was the worst day of his life. It didn't look such a hot one for Subject Thomas either.

He was wheeled past us and taken on to a public ward which was standard procedure. If you had money or an insurance scheme a private room was arranged. As this patient had come in with no money in his pockets and no insurance documentation either, he was taken in an elevator to St Joseph's East, a public men's medical ward on the third floor. Aside from Subject Thomas the ward housed about thirty patients in all.

A lot of the patients in there with him were quite obviously desperately ill. There were stroke victims, patients recovering from heart attacks as well as from operations ranging from stomach ailments to cancer. A constant stream of nurses moved from bed to bed, handing out medication, changing dressings, irrigating bladders, managing IVs, on and on in a seemingly-never ending loop.

Immediately – and despite the constant attentions of the harassed nurses – the agent from Boston and Miss Reitell set about trying to secure some extra help for their joint charge and, with no disrespect to St Vincent's, Subject Thomas needed it too. If you were on a public ward then you were largely in the hands of the less experienced house staff, usually interns straight out of medical school or junior residents such as the ones who'd first met him on admission. Nurses on a public ward did their best admittedly, but they didn't normally average many more than three per shift. I knew that because I'd heard Nora complain long and loud in the past about her workload. Up to then I hadn't taken much notice. Now, as with everything else, it all went into the log.

More friends and companions began arriving and immediately began chipping in for Subject Thomas's care and for a transfer to somewhere a little more private. At one point that night a donation arrived from the White Horse which struck me as ironic. All that money he'd poured into that tavern's till. Now some of it at least was coming back to its donor.

The same junior doctors who'd escorted him into the hospital were in attendance most of that night. There was a visit from an older guy – a neurological specialist from the little I could glean from Nora – but he didn't stay long. Another guy arrived too, one whom Miss Reitell greeted as if he was an angel who could answer all their prayers. I'd seen him once before in the Poetry Center and recognized him as the doctor Miss Reitell had summoned on the night of the premiere of Subject Thomas's play to treat her oft-troublesome charge.

The doctor, I'd already established, was called Feltenstein. I hadn't taken to him back in the Poetry Center and didn't see too much that was endearing about him right now either. Now I was studying him a little more clearly, it was obvious he worked out and pretty regularly too. He also looked like the kind of guy who didn't take any prisoners and he obviously wasn't about to start doing so that night. The junior doctors attending Subject Thomas were told in no uncertain terms that their patient's problems were simple and they began and ended with one word.

Drink.

It was difficult to argue with that given that his clothes were stashed in a box under his bed and, even with a lid on that box, the smell of booze was still pretty strong. But there was still something odd in the burly physician's insistence on the correctness of his diagnosis. It was almost as if he was forbidding the younger men from exploring any other cause behind their patient's collapse and I began to wonder why.

Up to that point I'd gone along with the liquor angle myself. Given the evidence I'd collated myself over the last few weeks it was a pretty easy conclusion to reach. But was there something else? Was that why this particular doctor seemed so edgy and aggressive right now?

By now Beth had joined me. She could have gone home. There wasn't all that much reason for her to stay, Nora was working and so was I, in a sense anyway. Con might not be actually paying me for any of this – in fact I had a shrewd suspicion that Con wouldn't be paying me for anything ever again – but I still wanted to complete my log.

But Beth seemed to sense that my log – the note-taking – wasn't for the magazine anymore, but was for me as well. It was to complete something somehow, even if I didn't know exactly what that was. And maybe that's why she stayed, so she too could find out.

A tense Nora came to see us after another hour or so. She told us that the doctors had found evidence that Subject Thomas had been injected with morphine a short time before his collapse. She didn't know if that had any bearing on his current condition but she did witness a blazing row between the older guy who'd briefly looked in on him and the barrel-chested Dr Feltenstein summoned by Miss Reitell. The hospital seemed to think they'd been misled in some way by him, or at least not given all the relevant information. The combative Dr Feltenstein clearly disagreed.

All the time Subject Thomas lay in his hospital bed as his charts were checked and his blood and oxygen levels monitored, his breathing still coming in great rasping gasps. All the time too, more friends, companions and hangers-on arrived. They were prevented from entering the ward itself by the nurses, Nora included, but that didn't stop them standing outside the glass partition that separated the ward from the corridor and feasting their eyes on the fallen hero on the other side.

It was probably one of the most uncomfortable aspects of the whole thing. Subject Thomas was virtually on public display and that public were now beginning to assemble, first in their dozens and then in their hundreds. But, at this stage at least, and despite the ever-swelling fund to pay for his treatment, it was considered too dangerous to move him and so there he remained.

For the next couple of days I remained too as I melted, invisible, into the background, old habits and skills once again still clearly extant. Beth came and went with sandwiches – full grinders for the most part – and coffee. We didn't say too much to each other. Partly that was so we'd draw little attention to my constant, if inconspicuous, presence. Partly that was because there was no need. I knew I had her support in this even if she still didn't totally understand what either of us were really doing right now. Once it was all over, one way or the other, maybe we'd work out what it was all about.

It wasn't difficult to blend into the background anyway. More and more of those friends, companions and hangers-on were arriving all the time, meaning I became even more of a shadow on a wall. From the little I could glean from conversations I overheard, mainly conducted by the agent from Boston, a telegram had been sent to Subject Thomas, female, in her home in the town of the winding streets and the crooked houses. The telegram hadn't gone into too much detail. She'd just been told that Subject Thomas had been hospitalized. But it would still have been enough to set alarm bells ringing loud and clear and there was a clear expectation she'd be making an appearance herself in the next few days.

If all I'd witnessed back in their home town had been anything to go by that appearance should be worth recording, particularly if the producer was still maintaining her watch over her unconscious lover and charge. More than one visitor had already been quite clearly offended by the way she'd taken up the role of the wracked and grieving partner. One of the visitors indeed had also already chided her – and none too gently – that more hadn't been done so far to bring his actual wife to his bedside, but Miss Reitell didn't even seem to hear. She didn't seem to be hearing anything right now.

Other telegrams were fired off to old friends of Subject Thomas seeking information about any past health issues. A major bust-up took place between Feltenstein and the two junior doctors still attending to Subject Thomas, with the older doctor openly threatening to wreck the careers of his younger colleagues if they continued to question his simple diagnosis that the problems of their patient began and ended with just that one simple word. Or maybe that one simple word repeated over and over again.

The bust-up was resolved by the appearance of the senior neurologist who summoned Feltenstein to his office. I never discovered exactly what took place in there but a short time later the combative, barrel-chested doctor – now looking not quite so combative or barrel-chested, more than a little deflated in fact – left the hospital and didn't return.

Nora came to see Beth and myself at regular intervals. There wasn't a lot to report at this stage, the doctors were simply aiming to maintain Subject Thomas's breathing by keeping his airways clear of mucus and administering anti-convulsants.

Early the next morning, Subject Thomas was given a tracheotomy to remove any stray matter that may have been obstructing that breathing and he was then, finally, transferred to a private room where he was put in an oxygen tent. Meanwhile all his personal effects and belongings were cleared from his hotel room in the Chelsea and delivered to the hospital by the manager, a Mr Gross; an appropriate sort of name for that den of high-living and excess I'd always thought. Mr Gross clearly believed his latest – and perhaps most colorful guest right now – wouldn't be returning anytime soon.

Soon after he was put in that oxygen tent another friend, or maybe companion, or maybe hanger-on, arrived. It was difficult to tell, there were so many by now they tended to merge. This particular example was a painter and she arrived at the hospital with a large bag which contained the prayer books of every major faith, so she revealed. It was called covering all bases, I guess.

I had received a couple of messages from Con during that time. Like the rest of the city he'd been caught up in the story of our visiting poet's somewhat spectacular collapse. Like the rest of the city he wanted updates and had guessed, accurately, that I'd be in the best position to supply them. But I didn't return any of his calls or answer any of his telegram messages. Later, when there was something to say, maybe. For now I just kept in the background, watching and recording, taking notes.

I caught a brief glimpse of Subject Thomas inside the oxygen tent as the door to his room swung open later that day. He clearly still had a high fever and his breathing didn't sound all that improved to me, despite the tracheotomy. And his face seemed to be changing color virtually all the time, one moment red and perspiring, the next blue and pallid.

The agent from Boston left the hospital briefly to travel to a reading that had been scheduled for that evening to offer apologies for Subject Thomas's unavoidable absence. He wasn't going to elaborate on the reasons as he made clear to Miss Reitell because he simply didn't know what to say.

On his return he started a fund to help assist with the growing hospital expenses. As he made clear to anyone who might listen, the medical fees were going to be totally beyond their means because one thing was pretty certain already. Subject Thomas wasn't going to be coming out of that private room and that hospital anytime soon.

That evening, word came through that his wife had boarded a Stateside flight some hours previously and had now just landed. A couple of friends, companions, hangers-on, immediately left the hospital to meet her. They were beaten to it by a doctor from St Vincent's who reasoned, rightly, that she deserved some sort of sensible update rather than any hysterical resumé from little more than ever-more distraught fans. As Subject Thomas's wife was brought back to the hospital, Miss Reitell left for a nearby apartment, a tactical retreat that was to prove a wise precaution.

Subject Thomas, female, blew in like a whirlwind. She'd clearly been drinking on the way over and after standing by Subject Thomas's bedside for a few moments, scarcely able to take in what she was seeing right now it seemed, she saw the agent from Boston. Within moments her hands were round his neck as she attacked him with, first, her fists, and then her feet. One of the companions who'd met her at the airport clearly approved of the assault, exhorting her all the while to go for the jugular.

Security arrived and Subject Thomas, female, was taken into a waiting room where she next attacked a nurse and pulled a crucifix from the wall. More goons from Security arrived, including one carrying a straitjacket. Within moments of arriving at her husband's bedside, Subject Thomas, female, was dispatched to River Crest, a nearby, private, psychiatric clinic. As she was led, struggling and yelling, into a waiting ambulance, another of the friends, companions or hangers-on alerted Miss Reitell and she duly returned to the hospital.

I slipped, briefly, into his room while all the mayhem was

going on outside in the corridor. Nora was in there with him and she just gave a slight shake of the head as she saw me. The message was clear enough. This really wasn't looking good. Subject Thomas's fever seemed to have subsided, for which small relief much thanks I guess, but his breathing had become almost inaudible now, just a succession of small gasps followed by long breathless intervals that seemed to last forever.

I left the room and went back into the corridor and waited, as we all seemed to be waiting right now even if no-one actually wanted to put into words just what we were all waiting for. But maybe no-one needed to.

In the event Subject Thomas died alone. A nurse – not Nora – had just bathed him and she left the room to dispose of the soiled sheets. He was only alone for a few moments. Then a man I took at the time to be another friend, companion or hanger-on – but who was a fellow-poet I later established, called John Berryman – went in to see him. But it was too late.

Suddenly there was a loud commotion and the now-anguished Mr Berryman dashed back outside, immediately berating the agent from Boston as he did so, fairly yelling into his face, telling the agent that his charge was gone, he was gone and where the hell was he? As if his being there would have made some difference somehow.

So that was that. Now there were no more small gasps. Just a long breathless interval that was, all of a sudden, no interval at all.

Did she know? It was all I could think at that moment. Struggling in her straitjacket, a few miles away, did some realization dawn, was some connection made? I couldn't know of course, and never would.

But for some reason I now saw her, his wife, not actually

with him in that room as the nurses returned and began doing their final, routine, checks; I just saw her in my mind's eye.

I saw two pictures, one real and right there before my eyes, the other imaginary, but just as real somehow. Subject Thomas immobile in his bed, destined never to move again, at least not in this life; and Subject Thomas, female, by his side, railing not only against the actual straitjacket that was currently restraining her, but a much more insidious one now too.

The junior doctors returned, as did the senior neurologist. The agent from Boston was approached and was told someone had to perform an official identification. The agent from Boston tossed a coin with another friend, companion or hanger-on and the friend, companion or hanger-on clearly lost because he disappeared into the small private room to perform the necessary procedure.

Across the city the news of his death had already begun to spread. Note after note was handed to me by a succession of nurses with a request that I contact my caller who, apparently, was from some magazine or other. Each note went into the bin.

Beth returned and seated herself by me as I completed my log. Then I did something I hadn't done before on completion of any assignment. I wrote two words at the bottom of the report.

'The End.'

Beth looked at me, quizzical. Lifting my head I became aware of her stare and looked back at the two words, somewhat quizzically – and a little amused now – myself.

What was happening here? And what was that, some sort of literary flourish? Had I suddenly become caught up in this somehow, had I suddenly imagined I'd become some sort of writer myself, as opposed to a gumshoe setting down an official record of observed events? Maybe I should go the whole hog and begin with, Once Upon A Time...

I made to cross it out, but Beth reached out, stopped me.

Behind her, more and more faces were now haunting the corridors as yet more friends, companions and hangers-on arrived to pay their own respects and bear testimony to their own small part in the unfolding story.

And, suddenly, looking at them, I realized I hadn't written any sort of conclusion at all. What I'd written was actually more of a question. Because this wasn't an end at all, in a sense it was much more of a beginning. Subject Thomas might have achieved some sort of renown in his life, courtesy of the sometimes strange combination of words he labored over in that small shack set into the hill on the fringe of that odd little town of winding streets and crooked houses, but that was nothing compared to the life he was going to have now.

And, for a moment, as I kept looking at the swelling cacophony of mourners and even though they weren't actually there right now, I saw once again Subject Thomas's agent from Boston and I saw his lover and I saw his wife, still in her straitjacket, all mixed in somehow with all the assorted, hovering, poets and painters; and they all looked the same, they all looked trapped now. As if all that was happening had enmeshed them in some way and from that point on they'd never be free from it all.

Behind the hovering mourners I could now see the nurses through the half-open door of his room, preparing Subject Thomas for the morgue. But then I became aware of Beth's eyes still on me and I could see that she was actually asking me a very different question right now.

I followed her eyes back to my log once more.

Those same two words again.

'The End.'

So was it? The end of something for the two of us as well? And if that was true, if it really was the end of something, was it also the beginning of something else? And was that why Beth had stayed with me, in that hospital, for the whole of that time, because somehow she'd begun to realize that too?

I looked back at Beth again. She held my stare, level and steady as ever while all around us milled stray souls, trapped in time.

I held Beth's stare myself. Now it was time to find out if that was going to be as true for us as it would prove for them.

CON WAS, ONCE again, like a coiled spring. He hadn't even said a word about my not returning his calls. All he could see, all he was looking at indeed, was the state-of-the-art portable tape recorder I'd placed back down on his desk as I arrived.

The news of Subject Thomas's death had dominated all news bulletins for the last couple of days and, as Con had told the powers-that-be time and again, the magazine had the inside track on the whole thing.

And, as he also made clear, that was something of a major deal. None of them could have imagined that a simple tail job would turn out this way. The only thing the magazine had in mind at the start of it all was a possible, if improbable, appearance in a law court at some time in the distant future. As it happened they'd bought a grandstand seat at one of the biggest shows in town before anyone else even realized there was a show in the first place.

No wonder Con couldn't stop pacing the office. The events of the last few days of Subject Thomas's life were going to send the circulation of one of Con's major clients into orbit.

'OK, so we can't run it like we wanted, not a lot of point now, right? That libel case isn't taking place anymore, that's for sure – .'

Con's face broke once again into the widest grin I'd seen this side of a split watermelon. I had the impression he'd only have needed the very slightest encouragement to break into a jig right there and then on his stained office floor watched, all the while, by all those faces from all those covers from all those years. I made a mental note to myself not to do or say anything that might be mistaken for that encouragement, slight or otherwise. I'd seen some unsavory sights the last few weeks and had no wish to round it all off by having to witness something like that.

'But we've still got one hell of a story – one *hell* of a story and it's all down to you Jimmy, you got the whole caboodle, every single little detail from the moment he landed right to that final drum roll.'

Con feasted his eyes on the tape machine, postponing the gratification, savoring once again the moment.

'Always had faith in you, Jimmy, did I say that?'

'Something like it, Con.'

'And I meant it. Every single word.'

Con depressed the play button on the recorder and was rewarded by an extended hiss. Con knocked it off and hit the fast forward button instead. Then he paced the floor some more, clearly unable to keep still right now.

'We'll just make it a human interest story instead.'

'A modern morality tale.'

Con grinned, more than a hint of the wolf in the smiling rictus. He depressed the play button on the recorder again.

'Morality tale, you crease me sometimes, Jimmy.'

Once again an extended hiss played out across the office. Con looked down at the machine to make sure it was actually working, that the spools were turning, that he hadn't been pressing the wrong button or something. But everything seemed to be in order.

'So where's this log of yours start, Jimmy?'

I didn't reply, just let him work it out for himself. Con was a clever guy. He'd get there sooner or later.

Con pressed the fast-forward button again.

'Do you think they're all like that over there? All those poet guys, do you think they're all like him?'

Con grinned again, a new thought striking him.

'Hey, if they're not yet they soon will be right, once they start reading the series we've got planned, we might have just kick-started a neat little cottage industry here, Jimmy. Just imagine, a whole line of them, all like that guy, this could be our pension, my friend.'

For the third time Con hit the play button and for the third time was rewarded with the same extended hiss playing out across the office – and now Con was slowing, his tapping foot beginning to still.

Con looked at me.

'I'm not hearing anything, Jimmy.'

I didn't reply. Con kept looking at me and now he was starting to work it out. Maybe it was the expression on my face. Or maybe it was something else. But Con kept looking, all the while decoding all I was telling him without saying a word.

'Because there's nothing here, right?'

Once again, silence.

'So what's the idea, Jimmy?'

A new – and clearly awful – thought struck him.

'One of the other guys hasn't got to you, have they? Because if they have, we're not unreasonable, you know that, we can negotiate.'

I stood, casting a last look back at the portable recorder, at the office, at all those magazine covers looking down from those walls, at the still-staring Con. Despite everything I was going to miss all this – and him as well – in a curious kind of way.

I half-expected some last appeal from Con as I opened the door. I almost expected him to call the security guy to physically prevent my leaving until I'd been searched or something in the hope that I'd brought at least some of my hospital log in with me. The conclusion of the modern morality tale. The final page in the story.

But I hadn't. Because it wasn't the final page.

Beth was right about that.

It wasn't The End.

A memorial service was held a couple of days later. I went along. Beth came too, as did Nora. I guess by now we'd all come to feel some kind of connection. Con didn't attend or if he did I didn't see him. I could have missed him – there was a real crush of people packed into the church that day – but somehow I doubted it. Whatever connection I'd come to feel with Subject Thomas, I doubted Con would have felt the same. And the magazine world had probably moved on by then anyway. Another week, another face, another cover.

The service was held at St Luke's Chapel which, despite its name, was more of a grand, old-style, church. Some four hundred people packed inside. Two ecclesiastical gentlemen, the Reverends Weed and Leach – according to the printed order of service we were handed on arrival – were to conduct a Protestant Episcopal Service with readings from Chapter 15 of St Paul's Epistle to the Corinthians. A musical ensemble, Noah Greenberg and his Pro Musica Antiqua, were to sing two motets by Thomas Morley, 'Agnus Dei' and 'Primavera'.

I'd no idea what a motet might be. Neither Beth nor Nora had heard of it either. I checked up on it after the service ended and discovered that it was a piece of music in several parts with words. The same dictionary definition noted that it was – and here I'm quoting exactly – 'not intended for the vulgar who wouldn't understand its finer points and so would derive no pleasure from hearing it'. Which was sort of telling me, I guess.

It had been quite a few days. Money matters had raged above Subject Thomas's dead body with bills to pay and fees to settle. But one bill that didn't have to be settled was St Vincent's.

Extraordinarily for a private hospital, it announced that it would waive all fees for his treatment.

I'd once tailed a famous baseball player. Whatever restaurant he went into no-one would ever let him settle the bill. Maybe this was that kind of gesture. Or maybe it was something else. Already rumors were beginning to circulate about some possible medical malpractice, seemingly involving the fiery Dr Feltenstein. Maybe St Vincent's had an early eye on the moral high ground in all this. Like Caesar's wife, and perhaps mindful of any potential future lawsuits, they wanted to appear, from the very beginning, to be above reproach.

Someone had sought permission to make a death mask and, incredible as it sounded to me – almost as incredible as an NYC hospital offering free treatment to a patient – permission had been granted and the somewhat macabre procedure had been carried out.

A decision had also been made to transport Subject Thomas's body back to that strange little town with the winding streets and crooked houses for burial, which seemed fitting. He'd never looked at home in the big city to me, but then I hadn't seen him back in his adopted home either. Something was already telling me he didn't exactly merge in with the scenery there either.

There'd been a hundred and one other things to attend to as well, the usual sort of stuff following any sudden death, particularly the sudden death of a celebrity and it all seemed to have taken its toll on the remaining players in the rollercoaster ride that had been our visiting poet's last few weeks on earth.

His wife, Subject Thomas, female, was at the front of the church although, mercifully, not now strapped in any straitjacket. That had been removed within a few hours of her husband's death. She didn't actually seem to want to be at the service and didn't seem to approve of the readings or the choice of music. Maybe she didn't understand its finer points. Or maybe she didn't understand anything right now. Maybe, in her position, no-one would.

The agent from Boston had chosen not to attend. That seemed curious to me, but maybe he had compassion fatigue or something. But Miss Reitell snuck in at the back just as the service was starting. Despite all her previous behavior back in the hospital, she clearly didn't feel it her place to assume any sort of prominent position here and now. Several people who'd been in that hospital shot her severe glances as she came through the door, but I actually felt sorry for her. She looked like the loneliest person in the world as she stood there, seemingly unwanted and very definitely alone, but then a companion came to her side to offer some kind of support at least. Beth recognized him from the reviews in the more up-market supplements. He wasn't a poet but a novelist from the Deep South, William Faulkner, the man who hadn't hosted the party for his fellow-writer and who, now, never would.

The service drew to a ragged close and from there Subject Thomas's body was taken up to the Hudson where it was loaded onto an ocean-going liner, the *SS United States* bound for Southampton in England. Subject Thomas, female, followed the coffin on board in the company of a last straggle of onlookers and had an immediate altercation with the captain about the cabin she was offered. Some unconscious echo of her late husband's arrival in the city a few weeks previously, I guess. Then she gave a final interview to one of the remaining flock of hovering journalists where she made clear her determination to take her husband home, averring that the Americans should never have any reason to claim him as one of their own.

I watched that liner pull away from the quayside and pull downriver before heading out to sea. I stood while the journalists and photographers and friends and companions and hangers-on all drifted away, the show over, the spectacle concluded.

All the time Beth stood by my side, both of us just silent, watching. And all the time I wondered.

Why did he do it? That's the one thing I'd never understood and maybe never would.

Why start on all this in the first place? Why seek out that small-time lawyer back home and tell him he wanted to take out court proceedings against one of the biggest magazines in the world?

And forget the David and Goliath aspect to it all. Forget the fact this was a lawyer more used to concluding local house deals than frequenting the corridors of any libel court; and how long did Subject Thomas think he was going to survive swimming in those shark-infested waters? Forget all that and look at what they'd actually written about him.

It wasn't that bad. OK, a few of the descriptions were perhaps a little racy and maybe some of the epithets more than a little pithy but if you read it properly, in the spirit it was intended, then the tone was affectionate enough.

And OK, if it went out of its way to detail his deficiencies as a family man, it more than made up for that by praising to the skies his abilities as a poet of undisputed renown. He was a complicated figure, in other words. A man of many sides and numerous contradictions.

Welcome to the human race.

The fact was he could just have ignored the whole thing. Hell, he could have framed it and put it on the wall of that small shack of his back on that almost vertical cliff-face and worn it as some sort of badge of pride. I just didn't get why, of all the things that must have been said about him over the years – and by people a hell of a lot closer to him than some Stateside magazine too – he chose to take that kind of offence?

Was it the money? Was he dazzled by the possible bounty on offer? He may have had only an extraordinarily remote possibility of winning, but had he read about some of the pay-outs some stars had managed to cleave out of an adoring judge and decided to throw his own grasping hand into the ring?

Again, I didn't buy it. OK, it was a matter of common knowledge that he was always on the rocks when it came to cash, but he had salvation literally at hand. This was the guy who carried round a lecture contract in his pocket for the whole of his last trip, a lecture contract guaranteeing him a thousand bucks a week. Just one week of that kind of money and Beth and I would be living rent-free for years.

But he never signed it. With one stroke of that pen of his he could have accessed the kind of money the rest of us could only dream of, only he never brought out that pen of his and he never signed on the dotted line either. Meaning, I guess, that he didn't want the magazine's money even if he had ever imagined they'd just meekly roll over and pay out.

By now the liner was a distant shape on the horizon and soon wouldn't even be that. Soon it would have disappeared from view along with its cargo but I had a feeling the questions that cargo had dragged along in its wake would take a little longer to fade from view, certainly so far as I was concerned.

Maybe that was my professional training. Maybe it was something else. Maybe all of us had been changed in all sorts of ways by the last few weeks because I just couldn't help myself, the questions kept on multiplying and the next one was simple, perhaps like them all, but the answer promised – and perhaps like them all again – to be rather more complicated.

Why take on the biggest magazine in the country, if not the world? Why tell the biggest magazine in the country, if not the world, you've got me wrong, what you've written isn't true, that's not me? Why do all that and then spend every waking moment proving them right? Why dedicate every one of those waking moments to proving to the whole wide world, never mind the magazine, that they couldn't put a piece of the finest paper between all they wrote about you and all you do?

From the moment he arrived in New York it was as if he'd dedicated himself, single-mindedly, to blowing his own case. And he knew he was being followed. He had to. OK, I'd been good up to then but, looking back, I had to have blown it in the Algonquin and even if he didn't actually spot me after that he must have known I was still on his tail. It should have been the biggest of all wake-up calls. But everything he did after that was worse, if that were possible, than anything that had gone before. The exchange in the Algonquin didn't seem to act as any sort of brake on him. It just seemed to spur him on instead.

Was he so far gone by then he didn't care? Was he so ground down by the situation at home that he'd simply gone beyond even trying to put anything right? If that letter from his wife was anything to go by things on the domestic front sure looked pretty terminal. So had he just given up?

Or was there something else going on, something else behind the relentless piling up of excess on excess? Beth certainly seemed to think so. To the casual eye he might have looked like that classic kid in the candy store. Anything he wanted he just reached out and he took. The whole wide world was just one big open door to him, certainly once he arrived in the States. But – as Beth believed and as Nora was later to concur and who was ever going to argue with her – in the end was he just hoping that someone, maybe for once in his life, would close that door?

That someone would just say no?

Or was it – a fitting thought for a poet maybe – all down to words in the end? Or at least one word. Because this was a guy who must have written millions of them. Hell, I knew he'd written millions of them. It wasn't just the books – and I'd still got the one Maddox had given me – look at that desk in that shack of his, all those words on all those pieces of paper, all tumbling over each other, written down, crossed-out, amended, revised, discarded, picked up again. He spent his whole life among words, seemed to spend every waking hour indeed trying to pin down just the right word for that particular line.

But out of all those words on all those pages, out of all those words rushing all the time through his head, did everything come down to just the one simple word in the end?

Help.

The liner disappeared, finally, from view. There was no-one left now on the quayside, just Beth and myself. So we left too, hailed a cab and headed back to Stuy Town which now felt like home again.

Beth had moved back in a few days before. The bird was in its usual place on the guardrail on the small balcony waiting, more or less patiently, for food. Families still played in the gardens below. Bored security guards patrolled the walkways. Excited couples took possession of their brand-new apartments, other couples moved out. The world was slowly returning to normal.

Everything was as it had been just a few weeks before apart from the hot snap which had now given way to snow, the first of the winter. Already Christmas was in the air. The first of the stores had even decorated their windows. Old-timers shook their heads and made disapproving noises about Yuletide dawning earlier and earlier as the years rolled by. Pretty soon, so they claimed, they'd be running Santa Claus jingles before the fall.

I stood on the small balcony looking down on it all and feeding my bird. I still hadn't come close to cracking the mystery that was Subject Thomas and suspected I never would.

But on our way back from that quayside something else had come out of all those thoughts and questions, one piling on top of another.

Beth had listened as I'd rehearsed the latest as she'd listened to each and every one of its predecessors, which was when I saw a small smile playing on her lips. When I pressed her, wanting to know what it was all about, that small smile grew wider and I soon found out exactly what it was all about. Because, and as she now pointed out, for a man who wasn't interested in little matters like *why*? I was certainly taking a keen interest in probing the many and varied causes of this guy's behavior, which I think is what they call another little word.

Touché.

Only now, it seemed, wasn't the time for words. Because Beth took my hand, steered me back inside our apartment and closed the door on my bird. For once, he – or she – didn't protest its exclusion. Maybe he – or she – had already had its fill that day. Or maybe my feathered friend realized this really wasn't the time or place.

THE TRAIN PULLED round the headland as the sun came out from behind the castle on the opposite hillside. For a moment the whole estuary was painted brilliant blue. Even regular travelers looked up from their books and papers as the train clattered slowly along the beach. Non-regular travelers – and there were at least two on that train that day – stared out of the window, transfixed.

This time there was no fruitless search at a station for a train that would never run to a town that boasted no halt. I took our bags, crossed the few steps from the platform to a waiting taxi – not Maddox this time – and didn't, this time also, mispronounce the name of our destination.

I hadn't been back for a while but in a curious way it felt like I'd never been away. Maybe it was the kind of place that had that sort of hold on you. Or maybe it was something else. Maybe that was all due to those words I'd been reading almost daily lately. Words that immediately conjured up pictures of a strange little town with winding lanes and crooked houses. So the moment the taxi drove down into that town, past the church where Subject Thomas was now buried, it felt as familiar as if I was driving along FDR.

The funeral had taken place the previous November, a couple of weeks after the ship containing Subject Thomas's coffin had set sail from New York. Odd stories filtered back about the funeral, some true, some best described as nearly true. But they were all published nonetheless. Jimmy Stewart said it once and he had it right. If it ever came to a choice between facts and legend, always print the legend.

The local ferryman – the somewhat exotically named Booda – had apparently appointed himself the Master of Ceremonies as the people of the town filed past the open coffin in the house belonging to Subject Thomas's mother. Most hardly recognized the rouged and lipsticked face that stared back at them. A local reverend was quoted in one of the NYC newspapers wondering what the hell the Yanks had done to him? Had they brainwashed him, doped him or inoculated in some way? I didn't quite get the last bit but still knew what he meant. It was all part of the general feeling that they'd seen him off to the States a hale, hearty and untroubled man, and he had returned to them a fallen angel. That may be more nearly true than true, but it was that old adage again. Facts or legend. Always go for the latter. And everyone did.

The day of the funeral had dawned sunny, for November anyway, and three ministers had officiated at the service. Birds sang, cocks crowed and the organist played 'Blessed Are The Pure In Heart'. Subject Thomas's coffin was carried, not by any of the visiting dignitaries of which there were many – the 'big people' as I later heard them described – but by a cross-section of the local community including the local publican, gunsmith, milkman and taxi driver; and no prizes for guessing which particular one that might be. The wake in the nearby Brown's Hotel was everything that might have been expected to commemorate a life that may have burned briefly, as his aged mother apparently pointed out, but had burned brighter than most.

And then some.

'Well – well.'

A voice cut across my reverie as I stared down the main street. I'd carried our bags into the small bed and breakfast I'd stayed in the last time and I'd come out to take some air. I knew who it was before even turning round.

'Mr American.'

I smiled at the large, genial figure standing before me, ridiculously pleased to see him.

'Hey, Maddox – was hoping to see you again.'

Maddox glanced back up the hill towards the church. Even though the light was now failing fast there were still a couple of what looked suspiciously like disciples heading in through the gates.

'The funeral was months ago. Didn't anyone tell you?'

'Didn't think it was really my place.'

'Didn't stop anyone else.'

'You must have done a roaring trade.'

He just eyed me, amused. There was always that touch of amusement flecking his eyes no matter who he was with or who he was talking to. But maybe it was more pronounced when it came to visiting gumshoes.

'All that liquorice, eh Maddox? Those cakes, those burgers?'

'Now, now, Mr American.'

He shook his head, mock-sorrowfully.

'A clever man like you. Falling for a story like that.'

Then he eyed me again.

'Unless you're taking a rise out of me, of course.'

'Unless I'm what?'

'Isn't that what you people say?'

Then Maddox paused.

'Or maybe that's the Australians. We'd had quite a few of those here too this last year or so. And Austrians. And just about every other nationality you can think of. Some we'd never heard of. Strange times.'

Up by the church gates another gaggle of late afternoon visitors were streaming in through the gates. Followers on a pilgrimage. Paying homage to a simple white cross with plain black lettering.

'I thought I'd leave it a while. Let things settle.'

Maddox just smiled.

'Then pay our respects.'

Maddox looked behind me, picking up the inclusive reference immediately.

'Us, as in you and – ?'

I turned, followed Maddox's look. Beth had now appeared in the doorway of the small bed and breakfast. Maybe she needed some air as well.

'My wife.'

I waved over to her and Beth used her one free arm to wave back. The other was more than a little busy right now.

'The lady with the baby?'

I nodded, still – and ridiculously again – proud. Or maybe it wasn't so ridiculous. Maddox certainly didn't seem to think so from the smile that was now creeping across his face.

'Our son. Six months old.'

Maddox looked back at me and for once there was no touch of amusement flecking those eyes.

'Lucky man.'

It suddenly struck me I knew nothing about him. I didn't know how long he'd lived here, if he was married, if he had any family himself, what he'd done before he became a taxi-driver – or ran the generator – or the vehicle repair shop; anything at all in fact. On my previous visit other matters had rather more occupied me. And, if truth be known, it was that previous visit that was now occupying me too.

'The last time I was here.'

Maddox looked at me as I hesitated. For a moment I didn't know what to say. Or maybe I did, but didn't want to say it.

'I really tried to bury him, didn't I?'

And there it was, back again, that same fleck of amusement.

'From what we've all heard, he did a pretty good job of that himself.'

'I didn't help though.'

'Maybe.'

'No maybe about it, he's gone, hasn't he?'

I paused again.

'So that's that.'

He kept looking at me, and as he did I realized for the first time too that it wasn't just amusement in those eyes, there was something else there too. It was as if he'd been waiting for me to catch up in some way. As if he could see – and had always seen – the road I had to travel and was watching all the while as I journeyed the path ahead.

How far has he gone? How far has he to go? And do I do anything to help him along? Or do I just watch and see how many diversions he'll take along the way?

'Have you still got that book I gave you?'

'The one from the shack?'

'We still call it a garage.'

I had. It was in my pocket. I'd taken to carrying it around with me, not just on this trip, but when I was walking around at home, riding the subway, heading for some class or other. I still couldn't pretend to understand more than one word in every two but that was least an advance on that last Stateside flight when I'd called on a stewardess for assistance.

'Yeah. I've still got it.'

Like a magician producing a rabbit from a hat, Maddox leant forward, extracted the slim volume from the pocket of my coat as if he'd always known where to find it. Then he smoothed out the pages, tapped one in particular, and handed it back to me.

'That's the one you want.'

That evening I took Beth along that winding lane to Subject Thomas's shack. It was exactly as I'd last seen it and exactly as he'd left it before he set off on his last trip. According to Maddox it was probably always going to stay that way too and something told me he was right. Subject Thomas had commanded a fair amount of attention while he was alive, but it was increasing all the time now he was gone. Everything he'd left behind seemed destined to be preserved, as if in aspic.

Before we'd left for the UK I'd called into the White Horse. Already photographs of Subject Thomas and articles about him were starting to plaster the walls. While I was in there a burly Texan who must have stood six-foot-five, even without his cowboy boots, had walked in. He wore a long suede coat and carried a bunch of flowers. He asked one of the barmen where the poet guy used to drink, then sat at his table and proceeded to drink whiskey after whiskey. There was some story going round that Subject Thomas had drunk eighteen of them, one after the other on that last visit of his, although I never saw it. Then he put the flowers in a vase the barman had provided along with the shots of whiskey and left.

But he wasn't the first pilgrim to pay a similar homage and he wouldn't be the last. Look at Beth and myself. What were we doing, right here, right now? I guess, pretty much the same.

Beth looked in through the window at the table that served as a desk, at the pieces of paper discarded on the floor, the photographs torn from magazines tacked up on the walls. I looked down the lane towards his old home but we didn't approach. Local gossip had it that Subject Thomas, female, had left the village and was trying to build a new life for herself in Italy. There were too many memories there, good and bad, according to that same local gossip. Not to mention all those pilgrims paying homage to a ghost.

We turned back down the lane and went down into the town square which wasn't any sort of a square at all, settled ourselves on a bench overlooking the estuary in the shadow of the old castle walls and watched the sun set over his writing shack and his old home.

Tomorrow we'd head home ourselves, our own pilgrimage over. I'd finally enrolled in college. Beth had found a teaching course she could do part-time. Between us we'd worked out a system of day care which meant we didn't need to employ much more than the minimum help. Things were going to be tough for the next few years which was going to make a nice contrast to the previous few years when things, as had become all-too obvious to me now, had become impossible.

A few weeks before I'd dug out all my old papers. The log I'd never handed over to Con. The minute-by-minute record of all matters Subject Thomas. I hadn't looked at it all since the day he died and wasn't too sure why I'd hunted it out then. But I read through it all anyway and as I did I realized something.

Because everything I put down in that log happened. Everything I wrote was true. But, as Beth had once pointed out, that wasn't the same as the truth, was it? Because in the end what really mattered? What he did or what he was? What he said in some bar or in some flophouse – or what he wrote in that shack?

Beth had my book on her lap. It was open at the page Maddox had picked out. It was one of the poems I'd struggled with the most on a first reading but it was the one – and maybe he knew it – that I kept coming back to more and more.

Especially the last four lines of the first verse.

Though they go mad they shall be sane,

Typical Subject Thomas, right? Say one thing, then say the exact opposite straight afterwards.

Though they sink through the sea they shall rise again;

And through? You sink down, don't you?

Thou lovers be lost love shall not;

I paused as I always did at that line, reading it over and over, loving it more and more each time.

Almost as much as the final line.

And death shall have no dominion.

I closed the book and Beth took my hand. Then we headed back to the strange, crooked little house in that row of other crooked little houses and in the morning we went home.

Dylan Thomas:
Portrait of a Friend

"By far the best personal memoir of Dylan Thomas in the fifty years after his death."
—Paul Ferris

GWEN WATKINS

y Lolfa

£9.95

'Visceral, strongly visual and beautifully structured... powerful, quirky characters.'
Andrew Taylor, Winner, Crime Writers' Association Cartier Diamond Dagger

Gimme Shelter

———

ROB GITTINS

y|_olfa

£8.95
£17.95 (hardback)

The Poet and the Private Eye is just one of a
whole range of publications from Y Lolfa.
For a full list of books currently in print, send
now for your free copy of our new full-colour
catalogue. Or simply surf into our website

www.ylolfa.com

for secure on-line ordering.

TALYBONT CEREDIGION CYMRU SY24 5HE
e-mail ylolfa@ylolfa.com
website www.ylolfa.com
phone (01970) 832 304
fax 832 782

Dylan Thomas:
The Pubs

JEFF TOWNS

Illustrated by Wyn Thomas

y Lolfa

"A poetic happy hour
– a literary lock-in"
CERYS MATTHEWS

£12.95
£19.95 (hardback)